When Wolf Comes

John Pappas

Orca11 Books,
PO Box 17216
Seattle, Washington, USA
98127
orca11.com

Published in the United States of America and printed on acid-free paper.

First Trade Softbound Edition, Spring 2009

Cover and interior graphics compiled from original art, vintage photographs, stock photographs and photographs by the author.

Original art by:
Joe Wilson, islandart.com
Allison Acton, actoncreative.com
Kassidy Riker

The cover photograph of Cape Alava is used through the courtesy of Mike Baum of Vantage Point Photography.

ISBN 978-1-4276-3724-6
When Wolf Comes; novel, historical; Pappas, John
CRS#295627474

Dedicated to the wild country I love

And to the memory of Micki

Special thanks to Dennis Held for his editing expertise, and Steve Nevins and Tim Davern for their valuable input, and to Joe Wilson of Vancouver Island for the use of his fine art.

I also respectfully thank James G. Swan, who so long ago labored on behalf of the Makah people to write down his observations of their ways truly, and came to be trusted by them, and who's words appear in opportune places in this story.

Preface

When Wolf Comes is based on firsthand accounts and ship's logs, historical records, native legends and ways, and the writer's imagination. In some instances real names of places and people of the time are used and some actual events are included. However this book in the whole is a work of fiction and is not meant to depict actual people.

The Makah People occupy the Northwest corner of the contiguous United States, a beautiful and rugged coast that is part of the last undeveloped coastline in the country. To make it easier for the average reader the Makah words presented here are a simplified phonetic form from the original Wakashan root language of Vancouver Island; this is the only place in the U.S. where this language is spoken. The correct name for these people and their language is Qwiqwidicciat. To pronounce that correctly certain throat sounds must be used which are difficult for anyone outside their culture.

The site where the ancient village of Ozette once thrived, at Cape Alava, was abandoned in the early part of the twentieth century and is now part of a federal reserve that hopefully will remain in it's present pristine state forever. The archeological dig there, discovered in 1970, has produced most of the artifacts displayed in the Makah Museum in Neah Bay. Cape Alava is a popular camping area for nature lovers willing to walk the 3.1 miles from the ranger station at the north end of Lake Ozette.

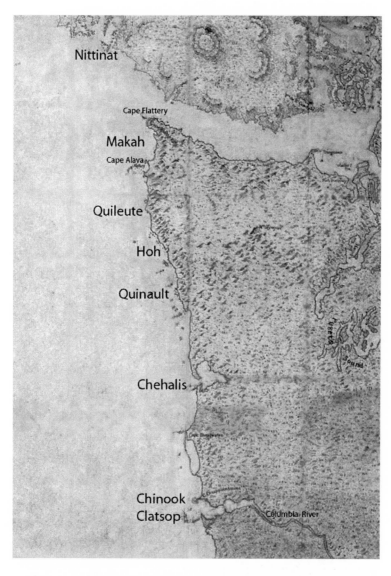

This reproduction of a mid-seventeen hundreds Spanish map of the Washington Coast, though grossly inaccurate by modern standards, was one of those used by seafarers during the last half of the eighteenth century. The locations of major coastal tribes are shown.

... a few men of the tribe may be found who measure six feet, but only three or four of that height were noticed. Their limbs are commonly well proportioned, with a good development of muscle. Some are symmetrically formed, and of unusual strength. Although to a superficial observer they present much similarity of appearance, yet a further acquaintance, and closer examination, show that there is in reality a marked diversity. Some have black hair; very dark brown eyes, almost black; high cheekbones, and dark copper-colored skin, others have reddish hair, and a few, particularly among the children, light flaxen locks, light brown eyes, and fair skin, many of them almost white a fact perhaps attributable to an admixture of white blood of Spanish and Russian stock.

James Swan, *The Indians Of Cape Flattery, circa 1868*

Chapter 1

NORTHWEST COAST 1801

The veiled sun grows weaker and the rain colder. A decision must be made soon. They are being patient with me, but the weather is no longer favorable for travel and more than my future is at stake. What I consider the responsible choice is unacceptable to the spirits, an irrefutable point. I still think of distant home, father, brother and sister, familiar sounds and warmth, but these images are no longer so clear. I keep remembering a closer time, a new day. It was early April last, of that I am sure, the Spanish are meticulous with dates.

Mist rose from the clay buildings of the *Mission Dolores de San Francisco* that sunny morning, the day it began at Spain's northern outpost of *Alta California*. Really the adventure began a year earlier in a Boston grog house, but then all stories begin before they occur.

What a pleasant, rare morning without the usual chilling fog covering the great harbor, spring's promise in the strength of the sun, new mint in the air, fine grasses pushing up among clumps of dark rocks. In recent weeks the landscape had changed dramatically after the rains. Tiny flowers burst forth, turning the hills into colorful quilts. Through half-closed eyes I watched a cruising hawk stalking ground squirrels that darted through vivid colors from one underground hotel to the next.

My peace was interrupted by the distant wails of stout Padre Urie hurrying up the hillside toward me. *"Pare! Pare!"* Stop. Stop. He was far below, clenching his nightclothes to keep them off the ground, the other arm swinging out as if to propel him upward.

"Come back! Come back, Chooly. I shall personally flay your sinful ass!" These were the general words in Spanish, which I had become familiar enough with in the past few months that I could communicate with the *missioneros*.

I saw Chooly then, running in a crouch, following the zigzag path toward the place I had been enjoying a comfortable view. He stopped abruptly when he came abreast of where I sat near the fork in the trail. He stared, naked as God had delivered him, a small, brown man with flat forehead and expression. Most of the Ohlones from the mission went without clothes. I nodded my head to the left and he went that way, moving quickly up the trail toward scrubby trees clustered atop the verdant hillside.

"I will send soldiers," Padre shouted, but not so loud now, his words strained through short breaths as he drew nearer.

I looked up beyond the trail at an area of sage and new grass in time to see James's shaggy head pop above the foliage. He had heard Chooly and perhaps imagined soldiers were coming for him. I motioned him down again.

Padre stood unsteadily at the fork in the trail, glaring expectantly. I nodded to the right. He looked in that direction, the most direct route to Chooly's village. With resignation he plopped his ample posterior on a round stone worn clean by weather and generations of native travelers. A sleeve of his nightshirt was used to mop sweat from red jowls.

"Why did you not stop him?" Padre demanded.

"Too quick for me, Father. Here, share my water." I rose and slipped the rope tied to the gourd from my shoulder and handed it to him.

"God has blessed us with a fine morning," I said, gazing over the harbor. The veil of fog around the entrance would soon be driven back by the sun. White gulls floated above strings of mist, dark rocks of Alcatraz and other small islands, and far beyond mountainous country no civilized man knew. Padre gulped from the gourd while water dribbled from his cleft chin.

"Why are you not in the garden doing your work?"

"The sun woke me early, Father, and I came up here to pray."

Padre Urie considered me suspiciously. He looked up the trail. With a sigh he rose and handed back the gourd. "I will send Sergeant Joaquin and some boys to fetch him back. Saving thankless souls is a weary task."

"God has given you a difficult mission."

Padre gave me a severe look. I watched him lumber down the trail, back to his mission and native captives. Of course the attending men of God at the Mission Delores did not think of them as captives but as souls to be shown the True Faith, the Spanish gift to the heathen, those who had survived the round of measles gifted them during the winter. These natives comprised the mission's and Presidio's dwindling labor force and they could ill afford to lose any more.

James raised his head again and I motioned all was clear. Since our escape from the *Lucky Wind* James had made the most of our servitude at the mission and everyone was taken with his excitable charm. He and the girl, Non, came and sat near me. A short grass skirt was her only clothing. Her sparse necklace carried a few beads and tiny carvings partly covered by woven dark hair that hung in dirty ropes. She began picking at scabs around her nose, the flakes falling between small breasts. Her husband had died soon after James and my arrival and she was now in a kind of limbo, able to move about freely instead of being confined with other unattached women in their compound behind the church. She seldom had specific duties, as if the padres expected her to soon join her husband.

James indicated she should go and she moved off in the sluggish amble common to these Ohlones, angling downhill through the grass where another trail lead to a low damp place full of vegetation. She would probably dig a few roots, take a nap, and return to the mission as if she had been out gathering all morning.

"You really should give her a try," James said, stretching. "She's not so bad, and she seems to enjoy it."

"You'll both be flogged if you're caught." I took a mouthful of cool water from the gourd. "Don't think I could get past the flies that follow her around."

"Hell, mate, they're the same flies we sleep with."

Something there. In billowy fog around the entrance to the harbor. I squinted past the Presidio, partly visible from where we were on the hillside. There it was again, a shadow, dreamy apparition, then only whiteness.

"What'n hell you looking at?" James asked.

I tensed and stood. A ship appeared from the fog with tops'l filling and her lead jibs white in the sun. "Now I do feel like I've been praying this morning."

James sprang to his feet. "God help us, is she American do you think? Or just another Spanish packet boat?"

"Can't be sure." Two puffs of smoke to her port side, then the roll of cannon in salute as she entered the harbor.

"Sounds like American armory to me," James said.

"Cannon is cannon." I squinted to make out some detail. "But her rigging doesn't look Spanish. Whoever she may be, she's got either a very smart cap'n or a dumb one, making the harbor through that curtain. Ample sheet, no holding back."

The Presidio replied to the ship, a pathetic little boom compared to the ship's cannon. Two musket rounds followed the small cannon's report, mere pops. James and I looked at each other and laughed.

"A real Spanish salute and show of force," he said, blue eyes flashing. "She's American, Aidan, I know it. I see red and white on her flag. Let's go give them a welcome."

The ship was a considerable distance from us, but it did appear James was correct. "Let's see where they drop the hook," I said.

The ship sailed past the Presidio, above and barely visible from the water. They seemed to be following the current line and headed between the land and Alcatraz Island. From our vantage on the hillside we watched as she began pulling sheet and coming to, positioning to anchor in Yerba Buena Cove right off the village below the mission. A good place out of strong tidal currents, but it had its disadvantages.

"He's picked a fine place to put in," James said. "And a convenience for us too."

"I'd bet he has Vancouver's maps," I said.

We started down the hillside with some casualness, but soon cut from the switchback trail and began running straight down through startled sheep and dodging squat cattle grazing on new grass. I had the longer gait though James was not to be outdone – sliding in a cow pie barely slowed him. We passed groups of natives tending stock and tilling the gardens for new plantings, ran through the mission courtyard as bells atop the church began clanging, rushed between rows of conical huts in *los Rancherios* causing dogs to bark, children's excited squeals, crying babies, natives flowing into our wake like backwash.

We reached the shore breathless, waving our arms even as crew were playing out anchor line. Up the beach natives slid several small craft into the water, odd little boats made of twisted grass and rushes lashed together. The natives waved a few furs and baskets, eager to trade.

We paced as a small boat was lowered and four oarsmen and two others headed for shore. With shouts and waves we guided them away from the mud bank and over to solid footing. James began yelling greetings when they were still well out. Some padres arrived, but we ignored their orders to stand back.

"Where be you out of?" James yelled.

"We're the *New World* out of New York."

James grabbed my arm and began shaking it. "You hear, Aidan? New York, it's New York boys come to get us out of this Spanish slave camp. You hear? They'll take us, I know they will, be needin' some able seamen. We're done'a this place, finished our penance, God is merciful in the end."

"Shut it," I said, "or He'll be laughing at you."

"James Gregory O'Connell, at your service, sir," James declared. "And this be Aidan Ephraim Martin. Our pleasure to board your fine ship. We been waiting for a righteous ship like this to come so we could offer our services." James kept talking while the captain studied me, seeming to ignore James's praising speech.

"*Lucky Wind,* you say? Where's she out of?" Captain directed this question to me.

"Don't know her origin, sir. She flew Portuguese or American colors, depending on location. We were never told where she rightly hailed from. When you get bonked and thrown into slaves quarters they don't show the log." I held the captain's gaze, a man solid and craggy as an old tree, gray streaks through his beard, firm mouth and brows you could gain shade under, eyes of burnt iron. He was the sort of hard man to inspire confidence enough for an owner to give him a ship to sail into hostile waters, and a fine ship she appeared to be; only two main masts, but stout and high enough for frigate class, three ample square rigs on each. The crew looked a cut above, and acted like civilized men.

"I'm a New York lad myself," James said, fidgeting. He was not one to sit still even when the atmosphere was calm, and in this situation it gave the impression he was fearful. "A bit north of that fine city. Came to town for supplies and got waylaid." To James's right a sea-man sat rigidly, thick arms crossed. James glanced several times at the man who simply stared at him.

Captain Stark shifted his gaze to James. "Got waylaid where? In a grog house no doubt. And what's your seaman experience?"

"Sir, I'd never sailed out'a the harbor before, but we been nine months at sea on the *Wind*, and we learned plenty. Eleven days off Cape Horn. Eleven days and nights working frozen lines and slammed from post to bunk. Lost a man there, we did, turned around and he was gone. *Lucky Wind* she was called, but barely seaworthy compared to this vessel. We had plenty'a hard times. And Aidan, he's a fisherman up in Boston, and a fine navigator too. We'd be a credit to your mission, sir, whatever that might be."

Captain leaned back and appraised us from a little more distance. "Jumped ship did you?"

"Yes, sir," James replied. "Cap and his main ones was drunk and we made off with a skiff. Only pay we received, to be sure. Gave our little freedom boat up to the Mission for board. 'Course, they put us to husbandry chores too."

7

Captain looked at me. "You don't talk so much. Fisherman, eh, and a slim one at that, though tall enough. Shallow water don't teach you much about navigation in the real sea."

"Teaches you shoals and currents, where food's likely to be," I said evenly. "Teaches you depth by color without dropping a line. 'Course, seeing you come into the harbor through fog and riding the currents, choosing your anchorage, guess you've already got a good harbor man."

"That I do, and you see him before you. So how would you have stood in?"

I noted the captain's large hand extended on the table, fingers hard as the miles of rope that had passed through them. This man was not highborn. "Well, sir, the current favorable and the fog not being too thick, I'd have a man forward at the sprit, and put up enough sheet for good steerage, as you did. And having knowledge of the entrance, I'd come along the south side, as you did, and I'd be listening close to surf on the rocks to maintain proper distance."

Captain's mouth twitched as he studied the table next to his hand.

"Then again," I continued, "seeing as how I have some knowledge of this harbor, I'd a chosen other than where there's a big mud bank showing at low tide. Not so convenient for those assigned to bring supplies aboard."

"Yes," Captain said, "I do recall that now. Haven't been here since ninety-two. Where would you have dropped hooks?"

"The anchorage off the Presidio has the better shoreline. Mind, there's some current, but you wouldn't be so bothered with natives trying to trade their ragged skins. The soldiers and padres grab up the best ones as they acquire them. Decent fur's in short supply here." Captain's cabin was nicely laid out with what appeared to be the latest navigation instruments, and Captain himself was well dressed in tailored woolens and fine boots, a stylish leather hat trimmed with dark velvet. His garments were soiled, but of a high style, which made me aware of my poor clothes. Can't say I liked him at that moment, but I thought he must be competent, and perhaps fair.

Captain laughed, gave the table a heavy slap. "All right, boys, I do need some hands. Lost three men, God bless." He produced a crock from under the table and addressed the man in the chair, Mr. Kirn, who turned out to be his first mate. The mate brought cups, sat down and poured the rum. Mr. Kirn shook our hands. We drank.

"Listen, lads, you better know what you're in for," Captain Stark said. "We're headed north to the big channel, de Fuca's Strait of Anian to the Great Lakes, which don't exist as any sensible man knows and this is no fool's mission. We're going into Puget's Sound, Whulge the natives call the harbor, to find a good place for a post, a settlement. Something permanent. We'll be mixing pretty close with the natives in that area. There's conflicting reports about them and we'll be needing to find a place where the local people are well disposed to our intentions."

"Would that be fur?" I asked.

"A bold question," Captain said sharply. "Fur's only part of it. There's a number of things I must ascertain. The men who commissioned me have eyes on the future. They have resources to proceed in any way that shows promise."

"Sir," I said, "can you tell me how long before you make home port?"

"We plan to winter in Puget's Sound. We hope to make New York sixteen months from now. Could be a bit longer."

Another sixteen months. James and I looked at each other. Yet what other choice was there? More months of drudgery and disease at the mission? Wait for the chance of a ship stopping off here that was headed for home sooner? This was a solid ship, well equipped and armed. The crew looked fed and healthy.

"May I ask, sir," I said. "How did you lose three men?"

"Fair enough." Captain motioned Mr. Kirn to replenish our cups and then tested his well. "Two got the fever in the lower continent. I sent them ashore to bargain for fresh fruit for our stores – I apply Captain Cook's recipe for my men. Anyway, some jungle creature may have given them a bite, or they got too close to one of those festering natives. And the other fool, Jacob, good hand he was, took some men in to fetch fresh water at the first port after the Horn. We had already established relations, but Jacob couldn't leave the native women alone. One of the chief's men cut his cock off with one of those big knives they use to remove your head if you're not careful. Bled out before we could get to him. 'Course we shot a few, including the chief, one extreme deserves another. We brought poor Jacob aboard and gave him a decent sea burial. So there it was."

Captain showed us a map of Puget's Sound depicting a huge inland harbor and waterway, larger even than the Port de San Francisco. He had copies of all of Vancouver's maps and several Spanish maps. It seemed he had every scrap of information anyone had ever recorded about the remote Northwest Coast. Then he told us he'd been with Captain Gray in ninety-two when the famous Boston trader had discovered the great river to the north and named it after his ship, the *Colombia*. Now he was back as master of this fine ship, and why not? His employers had chosen someone who had sailed with the best trader we had, the first American to sail around the entire world. They wanted to build a real post, perhaps a series of post forts. After a bit more rum Captain Stark told us there was a geologist on board, a man expert in assessing minerals. They were looking for any way to exploit this wild land, no stone left unturned – might be something precious under it.

Another year and a half. James and I were surviving here, rooting in the dirt for a few vegetables and a little meat, praying morning, noon and night, mainly that we wouldn't catch one of the ever-present diseases. They'd quartered us in a lower mission building twenty steps from the nearest native dwellings, the *los rancherios* of Yerba Buena, laid out in rows toward the water. We were in the path of the prevailing breezes rising from their filthy huts.

So there it was.

Captain said he must prepare to go ashore to take a repast in the Presidio at the home of the temporary commandante, Alfe'rez Don Luis Antonio, the son of the commandante permanente, Don Jose Dario Arquello, who I had heard was in Monterey on some business with the commandante of that port.

On leaving, I volunteered James and my services the next day for whatever duties he wished to assign us.

"I will send a boat," Captain said. He shook our hands, James pumping Captain's vigorously. Much as I wanted to leave this place, I could not match his enthusiasm. Yet signing on this fine ship seemed an answer to our prayers.

Chapter 2

James and I took our usual evening meal with the padres and three soldiers, and at the end of the long plank table the two Russians who understood little beyond their own language and were conducted by the padres with sign. It was my understanding they had been left behind over a year ago due to some illness their captain deemed too contagious to further expose to the rest of the crew. They surprised everyone by not dying. The mission women, those who cooked and served, took their food at separate tables in the rear of the large mess. We were given a watery stew of tired vegetables and potatoes from the sand barrels where they had been stored last fall. There was also a little greasy mutton and some dried figs that had been boiled to wet-leaf consistency.

I was aware of Father Urie staring at me from the head of the table and finally met his eyes. He always seemed to single me out, though everyone knew James was the more delinquent.

"You went aboard that ship," the padre accused, speaking English for an added sense of sternness. "It is not your place to impose yourself on a ship's captain before he can be greeted by the commandante and myself."

"He hailed us, Father," I lied. "He lost some men in the southern continent."

"And why would he think you two would be adequate replacements?"

He wore the sacred robes and I had grappled with my feelings about this man of God, and now, with full intent, let them out in the tone of my answer. "He wanted Americans."

Father Urie's meaty face flushed. I knew he could order me beaten even in the face of my imminent departure. He abruptly turned and spoke sharply.

"*Tráigame vino.*" One of the women came with a wine pitcher.

That night I sat on a stool outside the milling house across from the church. Dark shapes moved in and out of the lamplight inside. A scalloped wall of stone enclosed a small front courtyard in front of the church where the padres, weather permitting, conducted lessons to native children. At the end of the lesson the children would receive a treat of bread and honey, perhaps dates from the church orchard, an enticement to other potential recruits who were watching. The church itself was two high stories and finely built, a contrast in workmanship to the other mission and Presidio buildings. The windows were smoothly contoured and complimented the corniced roof gable. Outside the courtyard stood a cross atop a shaft tall as the peak of the church roof. The three points of the cross were carved in the shape of lance tips.

A familiar sound caused me to look above the cross. There in the light from the moon were reflected moving wings and I could hear the geese talking on their northern journey. For two weeks I'd heard them and soon would be headed in the same direction, away from home. But, I thought brightly, this adventure would give me even more stories to tell back in Boston. My brother and sister would be amused to know I was living in a Catholic church. Father would probably say it might teach me to drink at home.

Another year and a half. Well, I was newly twenty-one so I might still be twenty-two, not too old to establish myself and perhaps get married. Unlikely it would be Gretchen, surely she'd given me up for dead by now and married someone else. Perhaps everyone thought I was dead.

Repairs began on the *New World*: rigging, sails and the like, and as soon as Captain Stark gave us the come ahead James and I moved aboard. Now the smell of a ship's quarters are not always pleasant, but I must say the *New World's* below decks was a like a breath of fresh air compared to James and my quarters on the downhill side of the mission. That first night Captain called us into his cabin to join him in our rum ration. He addressed us as Mr. O'Connell and Mr. Martin. Certainly we had been called worse. Mate Kirn introduced James and me to some of the crew: Jeremiah the armourer, Karl the shipwright, Josh and Catman who worked the high arms where the roll of the ship could swing you one hundred feet and make you think you'd surely get a dunking. We sat nearest Thomas and Jonathon, shipmates we would be working closely with on the lower rigging.

"Let me say," Captain Stark said, looking between James and me, "the commandant's son is a gentleman, and the senora and rest of his family are a handsome and gracious bunch. But are there other soldiers stationed somewhere? I counted no more than ten inside the Presidio, a few more at the mission. Where are the rest?"

"There's no more than twenty total, sir," James said. "That's all the soldiers between here and Monterey, unless you count Mission Santa Clara de Asis, there are a few there. Did you see their armory?"

"I saw only two rusty three-pounders, one mounted on a log. Do they have the big guns stationed higher?"

"They have no other cannon, sir."

Captain Stark's metal eyes glowed from the shadow of his brows. "You're sure about this? They have no permanent launch to traverse the inner harbor? They have little more than the men I saw inside the Presideo and those two pathetic cannon? That's less than was here in ninety-two."

James brushed back brown curls and set down his rum. "That's about the lot of it, sir. They use the natives for rebuilding the Presidio walls, keeping up the mission, tending the stock and fields. The women do the cleaning and milling while their children are being schooled. Aidan and me figure there must be nearly a thousand natives living in the proximity, counting the little ones. Heard there used to be more, but they die off about as fast as they bring them into the faith."

"This morning I observed a mounted soldier with a lance driving a group of thirty to the field." Captain frowned, as if doubting his own observation. "There are so few soldiers, do the natives never rebel?"

"They run off," James said. "The padres take a soldier or two and bring them back. Once they're baptized they are church property. The padres pound that into them like a smithy pounds iron. They aren't who they were. It isn't like they give up all their ways, but they don't think on their own anymore."

On the third morning aboard the captain asked me if there were any edible fish about. The natives had offered mostly dried cod and it was too early in the year for salmon. Trying not to sound eager, I told him if he would allow me a skiff or the longboat and could spare another rower I'd certainly get him some fresh fish for the evening meal and perhaps extra to salt away. He gave me some good English line and several iron hooks, and said to take James along as the second rower. He assigned me the longboat, the larger choice, and by this I knew he meant to challenge my bold claim for a good catch.

We pulled hard on the oars, angling across the ebbing tide to the lee behind *Ysla de los Angeles*, Angel Island. I directed us onto a nice sandy spot and left James with the boat. Scrambling over rocks and debris I soon found a place where there were clams spitting and dug up several with a stick. I thought we might have another hour or two of ebb and told James we'd take her out in the current, drift out to the harbor entrance, holding to the drop into ten fathoms or so, and when the current reversed we'd drift back. I had not fished here, but I knew the areas the natives preferred. They didn't like to get too close to the harbor entrance with their little grass boats, but our longboat was much sturdier and the wind mild. If we could try the churning currents near the entrance I figured we might have good luck.

With an iron clevis for a weight I lowered my line baited with clam meat. I didn't drop the offering far before there was a take and I hauled in a golden-brown cod. I cut the flesh into strips and made two dozen baits. The next time I felt the weight hit bottom, then a hard take. This was a different sort of cod, a big head and mouth full of sharp teeth, similar to some I'd caught near Boston, though the coloring was different. We used a club to subdue him. James wanted to fish too, so I gave him the spare line. A few gulls had spotted our activity and were on us, drifting overhead and paddling alongside screaming for their share.

The fishing was good in spurts until we got into fierce currents where it shoaled up near Southeast Point. We had to pull with all we had to gain deeper water. Finally we couldn't row against the current that moved us seaward. We weighed oars and drifted out into the swell. It got pretty rough for a ways, then we pulled for a flat area behind the rocks around *Punta de Cantil Blanco*, let the current turn us this way and that while we worked our lines. We got into a patch of fish that kept us so busy we barely realized where we were in time to man the oars and pull out away from the rocks.

At flat water we took up the oars and rowed for the harbor entrance, knowing the current would soon stand the sea up again and turn the narrowest part into white caps. Once we felt the current under us we laughed and put out our lines. We bounced along and were soon back in the harbor, and in the calmer water kept fishing another two hours. The deck was so slimy from fish we had a hard time keeping our footing. In late afternoon we stood in at the *New World*, and the crew that greeted us was indeed happy with our catch. There was more than enough for everyone.

Repairs on the ship continued and I grew impressed with the thoroughness with which Captain Stark checked every detail. He was indeed a proud man but his was pride come of respect for his ship and the crew that delivered her function. He had no patience with shoddiness, yet you could gain his good will with diligence.

In the evenings a number of us took our modest rum ration in Captain Stark's cabin. When the work of the day was done he became one of us, and he wanted to hear our concerns, mind they should not be trivial. I began to understand his mission and mindset, which he had said straight out but it was a new thing to comprehend, that we were not simply traders out to seize anything of value. We were explorers. True there was an underlying profit motive – this ship had arrived on the other side of the continent at great expense and risk – but it seemed less mercenary because of the range behind the motive. To make a permanent post and incorporate the local natives into your plan, even give them the opportunity to come be part of the enterprise. This approach had worked to some degree in my home area. Another fisherman with a larger boat than mine had hired a native to guide him to the best lobster ranges, and paid his wife and boy to dig clams. It had been shown that if the indigenous people shared in your take from their territory the enterprise had a better chance of success. I often delivered some of my catch to the same native family for his help in guiding me to the best places to fish.

A few days later Captain was taken ashore in the longboat for a farewell supper at the Presidio. The usual contingent of natives appeared from their huts and came down to the beach to beg trading. The able men were still working, so these were mostly women with baskets and mats. Looking at the conical willow and grass huts in rows down nearly to the water, I wondered how many of these quiet people would fail to see another spring. In the few months James and I had quartered in a mission house we calculated at least thirty had died. The true number may have been higher. The *missioneros* minimized the count by taking the bodies out in the night and burning them beyond the hill to the east, at the Altar of Transformation.

James slapped a hand on my shoulder. "Tomorrow we make ready, the day after we catch the ebb at daylight," he said. "Are you sad to take leave of this place?"

"It will be good to feel a deck under us. But we head north, on the trail of the wind. We know no more about our fate than we did three months ago."

"If we're yet to die on this adventure," James said, "at least we'll be facing our maker as free men."

On the second morning we helped the anchor crew and joined in their chant until we heard iron clank against the chock.

"Make Sail!" came Mate Kirn's order, and James and I pulled hard on our lines, as others were doing, dropping sheet, yelling encouragement to each other. Kirn continued to shout orders and all hands were busy, excited, as a seaman is beginning a new adventure. I saw why the tall, dark man was called Catman as he danced across yard-arms and worked with one hand while swinging from a rope. The southwest breeze filled our sails like billowing clouds and we were underway. A longboat with four strong rowers pulled us toward the middle of the channel, but it was soon unnecessary. The boat came alongside and men scrambled up rope ladders. "Square away!" Kirn said, and the longboat was pulled up on creaking lines and swung aboard. The men began singing a seaman's song as we adjusted the angle of yards. We secured rigging, putting our backs into it, and James and I joined in, our voices mixing with shipmate's and screaming gulls.

Out we headed between dark cliffs of the north and south points. A distant pop from the Presidio was their parting salute, an answering roar from two of *New World's* cannon. This struck all of us as high humor and a few crewmen climbed rigging to wave. We passed close to the surf-beaten rocks off *Punta de Cantil Blanco* and I saluted the place of our best fishing.

Punta de Reyes passed to starboard and the ship made a slow adjustment to northwest. This course continued until the land was an uneven purple line to the east. Kirn shouted an order for the spanker to be raised and full sheet to all positions. The ship took a new heading closer to due north, running ahead with the southwest wind. She trimmed to our course and we were making good speed, fleet as I'd figured her. I looked up to see a school of dolphins cutting our path, always a free and uplifting sight. They had a destination in mind and did not stop to play in our bow waves.

That night Kirn again invited us to Captain's table to partake our rum ration. Besides two mates and the scientific fellow, Mr. Funter, there were eighteen of us crew, including Big Chink the cook, and half our number crowded into Captain's cabin that evening. Captain told us what we might expect in the short term during the journey ahead. This was such a departure from our treatment on the *Wind* James and I kept looking at each other, as if to confirm what we were hearing.

The rum and friendly atmosphere relaxed me so my thoughts turned to home and family. "Captain, might I ask," I said, "is Mr. Jefferson our president now?"

Captain seemed surprised. "Well now, can't be sure since we left before the vote was in, but most thought he would get the post away from Adams. Virginia wanted Jefferson, so I'd guess that's what we got. Of course there was some trash about Adams in the papers by that Callender fellow, but no one with good sense gave it much mind. Still, there it was. Since General Washington's passing I don't take much interest in politics." He cocked a shaggy eyebrow. "As a Boston lad I'd think you'd favor Adams."

"Yes sir, my father favored John Adams," I said. "Although he said Mr. Jefferson might be all right if the Boston boys kept an eye on him. He didn't like the way Mr. Jefferson changed his stand on slavery."

Captain Stark became thoughtful, finished his rum and turned his cup upside down on the table. The rest of us followed his example. The captain spoke quietly. "You named the pig in the parlor, lad, and everyone knows he's there. General Washington was the first grower with the stomach to stand up years ago and say what had to be said about slavery. Goes against everything the boys had in mind clear back to The Declaration, and many of those fine men suffered for it as we all know. But Jefferson's with the rest of the growers, and the power is in Virginia. They say we'd likely lose the union if open discourse were allowed on the subject. May God help us, we can't lose the union, though by heaven the North will keep taking those poor devils as fast as they can escape their slaveholders."

After a moment of silence Kirn held up the crock. Captain nodded. "A salute to the gentlemen I just spoke of. To all the brave men that signed The Declaration."

"Aye, aye," echoed through the cabin.

That night in our bunks James questioned my judgment about stating my preference for John Adams. "He could have been a Jefferson man," James declared. "And then where would we be? Swabbing below deck or doing the high swing, that's where."

"Doesn't matter." From my top bunk my eyes followed the grain in oak planks less than an arm's length above. I did feel some contentment, the good ride of this solid ship under me and looking forward to seeing things I'd never seen, this being the best day I'd had aboard ship since being bludgeoned that night in Boston.

"Doesn't matter to you, 'cause you're a bit mad," James continued. "This cap seems a reasonable sort and I prefer him that way. We're getting our rations and pay too, and Big Chink puts out a good table."

"Doesn't matter because Washington wanted Adams," I said, "and Cap served with General Washington."

"How the hell you know that?"

"'Cause of the way he said it. My father served with General Washington. Those that were with him always will be. Now shut up and go to sleep. They'll be calling me for early watch."

I turned and stared into the blackness against the protective three-inch wall of timbers, the sea right on the other side beating on those timbers, trying to get in and end thinking about the future. But that night I kept telling myself the worst was surely over, this was simply the next step in finding our way back home.

Sometime in the darkness I awoke covered with sweat and terrifying sounds ringing in my ears. Gradually I recognized the sounds of men snoring, grumbling sleep talk. The creak of cordage and straining yards was not screaming. Still, my cowardly imagination would not let sleep return until shortly before seaman Fargus bumped my leg for my turn topside.

Makahs, in common with all the coast tribes, hold slaves; they are for the most part well treated, and, but for the fact they can be bought and sold, appear to be on terms of equality with their owners . . .

Chapter 3

Through a white veil uneven dark shapes of land appeared, and we saw what might be the entrance to the great river Captain had spoken of with such reverence.

Our captain had been mate in command of the pinnace nine years before when Captain Gray claimed discovery of this river. The previous night he'd got us thinking with his talk of the adventure.

"Truth is," Captain Stark confided in a moment of pride, "I entered that river before Gray, and a rough ride she was in the long boat. Though there's been other ships since then, on the morrow you lads will still be among the first civilized men to see her. Hundreds of natives inhabit the shores, and they'll be glad to see us, you can count on that. But don't be thinking these are the likes of those poor devils in Yerba Buena. Keep a sharp eye, and don't be making sport around their squaws till Mr. Kirn or myself gives the go-ahead. Not that these women won't be offering their charms – while trading you out of your breeches!"

The longboat was put down and a party of six chosen to lead us into the river – standard procedure to minimize risk to the ship. We had the flood tide running for us, but a swirling easterly blew off the land. The fog persisted, as if being manufactured in vortexes of this errant wind, and the waves across the entrance to the river stood up like rocky atolls against the current.

Mate Kirn bellowed from the bow, the wind whipping his words back to us manning lines to adjust sheet the moment a command came. "Stand hard port, Mr. Tuplin!" he directed the longboat mate. *"Get your backs into it."*

As the bow rode over a steep swell I lost sight of the longboat, then the ship slammed down the side of the wave and I saw them ahead, straining into the oars as the small craft was tossed about, momentarily lost to view again in steep froth – next moment a log struck the longboat putting her sideways. Immediately she was foundering, Kirn yelling and behind me Captain bellowing orders to pull lines to reduce sheet.

Men were in the water and everyone on board was in a frantic scramble. The distance closed as current and wind brought the small boat toward us. Second mate Tuplin managed to hurl a line secured to the bow – Kirn caught it and made fast. The boat swept past and was pulled high as the line tightened. Three men were in the boat and two hung on as the longboat's bow cleared the waves – the water in her sloshed a seaman out the stern. Tuplin and the other man grabbed the rope ladder and were pulled aboard.

The third man had caught a line and was dragged up over the rail.

"Hard starboard, Mr. Leard!" Captain's words whipped by the swirling wind. "Drop that port main'sl, Mr. Jenkins!"

As the ship made a sharp, wallowing turn all hands that weren't gripping rigging lines were braced at the railings with coils of cordage to toss at the sight of a shipmate. We searched the rest of the morning, but found only one man.

Big Chink brought us some hardtack and salt pork and we wolfed down the nourishment while manning our stations. The wind eased and as evening descended we stood off just south of the river mouth. Captain Stark addressed the lot of us from the aft deck, his voice grave.

"Gentlemen, as you well know we have two men unaccounted. Tonight we'll stand double watch, two men to each railing, and Mr. Leard has volunteered to man wheel the whole night. I will insist he be relieved at two bells. We will continue the search and not anchor. It is possible that one or both of your shipmates could be riding drift like the log that struck our longboat. If so, with God's help, we'll find them." Captain turned to go, paused to look back at the faces before him. "There will be no gathering in my cabin tonight. Mr. Kirn will distribute half rum rations. Except to those attending first watch. May the rest of you find sleep to be alert for your watch. Gentlemen." With that he disappeared through the hatch that lead to his quarters.

"Could easy enough been us in that longboat," James said, as we sipped rum under the shelter of a skiff lashed over a yard. "Hell's own bar where this river meets the sea, waves every which way. Could'a waited till the morrow. Wind's down now and maybe be a fine morning. Could'a tacked into her tonight, little sheet . . ."

"Shut that crap talk." I thought about the two men out there. Maybe Cap was right, there was plenty of drift about. There was a chance for them. But the water was damned cold. Cold and steep like the Horn.

"Think Cap'l try for the river again tomorrow?"

"How would I know such a thing?" My voice sounded odd, as if someone else was speaking. Rain had begun soon after Captain retired and steadily increased. Wet darkness settled over us.

"He's already lost five men and not even to the place he's bound for yet," James said.

"They're not lost so long as we're looking."

"Right you are." James turned away, stared out into darkness. We were too low to see the water except when she took a good roll.

24

"You rather be back on the *Wind*?"

"Hell, no," James said. "Just seems unlucky, that's all I'm saying. Gray stood in with Cap leading the way. Here we are slogging around looking after men in the water."

"Spring runoff all rivers have drift," I said. "Who can say what's over the next wave?"

James raised his cup.

The next morning Big Chink issued everyone an orange first thing. We had been getting fruit every other day or so to guard against scurvy, and none aboard showed any signs of it. Captain also insisted we eat some greens or tubers regularly, which some of the men complained about but I enjoyed, being used to this diet. We were two weeks shut of the mission and dangers be damned, it was a better life we had now.

The rain had stopped and fog hung like a death curtain. Captain was a dark figure on the poop, staring into fog, staying to himself. Mr. Kirn issued orders in a subdued tone this dreary morning and we performed them in kind. Captain seemed to be genuinely grieving. He'd been a seaman like the rest of us and had earned this position. Now he seemed weighed down with such responsibility.

The fog became mist and we felt damp sun. We drew abreast of the river mouth once again and I kept glancing up at Captain, as others did, wondering what he'd decided. Kirn issued an order to the man at the wheel and we corrected slightly to north-northwest, away from the land. Captain had made his decision. Our search for shipmates was done, had been done, and we all knew it.

The next morning we were about five miles from land. Patches of blue sky and watery trails shown through mist. Captain was looking through his spyglass at what appeared to be the entrance to a harbor. We tacked nearer until it was clear the frothy waves across the entrance indicated a bar similar to the Columbia's. Captain conferred with mate Kirn, and soon we were headed seaward once more.

"That be the harbor Cap showed us on the map four nights ago," James said. "Wouldn't you say?"

"Maybe." I recalled Captain had spread the large map on his desk showing the harbor he had entered with Captain Gray. Inside the harbor they'd been the first white men the natives had seen, of this he was certain. Trading had been good that first day, but in the night canoes approached. They could not determine if the natives meant harm, and fired muskets over their heads, warning them off, but one very large canoe of twenty natives had persisted. I tried to imagine such a canoe as Captain described these men: muscular, painted vivid colors and very animated, ornaments dangling from nose and ears. Unable to discourage them from approaching further and fearing attack they had opened fire with cannon, surely killing all in the canoe. If this was the harbor, Captain may not want to risk approaching the same tribe who could well be hostile toward anyone on a cloud ship.

"We need to fill the water casks," James said.

"Tis' common knowledge among the lot of us, even you." I felt stupid taking my uneasiness out on James, yet he said what many of us were thinking. Captain had only replenished four casks at the Port de San Francisco because he thought the water procured from the shallow wells tainted, also water from the small lake near the Presidio. "I'm sure he has a place in mind," I said. "There looks to be plenty of water in this country."

"He's spooked, isn't he?" James moved closer. "He lost more men and now he's lost his nerve. We're in the middle of goddamn nowhere with a cap scared to make harbor."

"Shut yer hole. He's the one been here before – not you. The main destination is that Puget's Sound. Would you rather he be careless?"

The next morning I arrived on deck to the clear sight of land, fine green hills and slashes of white beach between stacks of log drift. We were only a few miles out and easing into the lee of a ridged point of land. Inside the point columns of smoke between fir trees indicated a village. A sand bar marked the mouth of a river and we angled toward it. Captain was watching through his spyglass. He lowered it and uttered an order that Kirn repeated. The anchor crew rushed forward to prepare a drop. We came slowly toward the point and Kirn gave the order to pull sheet. The anchor chain clattered out and already canoes were approaching. Four cannon were readied and muskets stood in chocks around the main masts for ready access.

These natives approached in beautiful canoes made from giant trees. I then understood how one canoe might accommodate twenty people. They held up prime skins of otter and lesser animals. These were as Captain had described, quite unlike the natives to the south, bearing a fierce demeanor with red and black paint on their faces and chests. But they seemed eager to trade. Mind they were no fools, a prime otter pelt brought a good wool blanket or a few spikes and handful of beads; they were aware of their fur's value.

Captain Stark invited the occupants of one canoe aboard and several came, one in elaborate attire, obviously a chief and sporting a Spanish officer's hat. They did not come shyly, rather they looked around with an unsettling arrogance. Captain offered them bread from our oven and salt pork, which they nibbled at with discretion.

When the fur was nearly all traded the natives became more difficult and haggled for more blankets, beads, copper and iron. Iron and copper were most desirable, but Captain was reluctant to trade much, saving it for his foray into Puget's Sound perhaps. The chief became agitated over his desire for more iron and copper, but Captain made him a gift of a knife and this seemed to calm him. The canoes departed with everyone in good spirits.

Water casks were brought on deck. Captain continued to watch the village through his spyglass. Finally he gave the order and Mr. Tuplin had the longboat lowered, then the casks. At first four hands were ordered to go, but at the last moment James was held back to make room for the casts. We could see natives moving about on the beach. The longboat made the river mouth and a group of natives gathered along the bar and trees, watching. Soon enough the longboat was returning.

"Sure brought the crowd out, didn't it?" James said.

We hoisted the water casks aboard, lowered two empties. The longboat headed back to the river.

I approached the first mate. "Mr. Kirn, who are these people?"

"Call themselves Quinout, Quinaut, something of the like. They've traded before, as you can see. Not much known about 'em."

The longboat entered the river. The tide had ebbed further, increasing the height of the sandbar at the mouth, so we lost sight of the longboat.

A distressed yell shot across the water. I looked to the Captain at his higher vantage point on the poop, but before he could say anything the man up in the nest was shouting they'd attacked.

"Block those cannon!" Kirn commanded, and the front wheels of four cannon were blocked up for maximum range. People were yelling at each other and moving around, but there was nothing immediately to be done. "*Fire*," Captain ordered. The first cannon bellowed, then the other three.

Three rounds fell short of the beach and Kirn ordered the guns blocked higher while the rest of us stood there, muskets in hand, helpless as yelling and the sound of shots came from the river. We heard three pops, then nothing. They had not had time to reload. The cannon blew the hell out of the beach but could not reach the village. A man yelled as his hand was smashed against the port by the recoil of a high-blocked gun.

"*Weigh hooks!*" Captain yelled, not waiting for Kirn to give the command. "Ready all cannon! Drop the top'sl! By God we'll give the heathen a taste of cannon ball. Ready two skiffs for rescue!"

Of course it was not possible to do all these things at once. Captain wanted to go in and broadside the village, but Kirn insisted we did not know the depths, the ship would be at risk, we must accept the three men were already lost.

Catman, who had been in the high nest with a spyglass, said even as they were clubbing our shipmates others were smashing the longboat and ripping off her iron hoop stays. Our shipmates were drug ashore to be stripped of clothes and weapons.

We stood out to sea and those of us not on immediate duty were issued an extra ration of rum. Captain Stark was one of us for sure then; through our anger and fear we felt sympathy for him. Even James accepted this was bad luck but it could change, and surely it would since we'd used up our share of bad. Seamen's superstition perhaps, but we all believed it, for it came from the desperation of hope, the universal religion a seaman felt in his gut as his ship took the next swell.

That evening the wind came to a breeze and we slid behind a small rock island and the hooks went out and caught in fifteen fathoms. The little island broke the swell and we lay calmly. We had barely come to rest when a school of porpoise came by with amiable slowness, little cousins to dolphin, perfect quarter-moon dorsals slicing the surface and sliding down. Captain was a silhouette on the poop, spyglass stuck to his eye. There was a faint smell of wood smoke and I thought it must be our oven and hoped Big Chink was making some of the good bread with rice and fruit in it.

"Another village in there," James said as we stood at the railing, looking toward the blackness of the land. "More heathen thirsty for our blood."

Men were loading our starboard cannon. "I have first watch," I said. "There will be four of us on deck the rest of the night. All the natives can't be that treacherous, Gray's been trading along this coast for years."

"That's Captain Gray," James replied.

Kirn called a meeting on deck. Captain Stark addressed us in darkness:

"There will be no lanterns this night. Those standing watch will not smoke." Captain paused, continued in a lowered voice. "A native village stands about a league away, and a good river. Most of the information I have is that these natives are eager to trade. I must ascertain this, and perhaps fill our casks. We will be ever cautious. Tomorrow they will come and we will be on alert. Before then we meet in the morn to determine reassignments. We are short-handed and everyone must accept additional duties. Mr. Kirn will distribute preliminary reassignments until then. Thank you, gentlemen."

Captain disappeared through the hatch to his quarters.

I was told to be a regular part of the anchor crew and also assist at cannon three. James would be working below Catman on mains'l rigging. "I'd prefer something a bit closer to the deck," James muttered.

"That's what you get for climbing around like a monkey."

"Just because a man wants to take a look now and then."

Clouds blocked any light from the night sky. Second mate Tuplin and I stood first watch. We paced and peered across black swells. "In this quiet there'll be no surprising us," Tuplin said in a low voice.

"S'pect it's the calm before," I replied.

"Yep, weather feels due," he agreed. At sea the weather was always an important subject and a convenient haven from talking about something no one wanted to speak of.

In the morning I saw canoes just clear of the river. "They'll be coming, lads," Kirn announced. "Carry on till I give the order to take positions."

Eight canoes approached, similar to the near natives to the south, two of the craft quite large. Captain had told us these people called themselves Hoha or Hoh. As they drew near I could see they had similar colors painted on their faces and chests, and if anything looked even more ferocious. Yet as they drew near they held up beautiful otter and other pelts and seemed of friendly bent.

Kirn and Tuplin offered a greeting and commenced negotiating while the rest of us tried to look friendly. No one was allowed to board, nor did they seem to want to. Trade goods were passed back and forth, then bread and fruit was given those in the nearest canoes and they passed several large, flat fish up to us. Everything was quite congenial. The canoes in back waited their turn to come alongside. There were a few misunderstandings about the price of something, and in one instance Captain Stark intervened on behalf of the native. Captain was more than fair in these negotiations, while at the same time wearing his sword and two pistols in his waistband.

Before the canoes left Kirn had a sign language parley with a native sporting an elegant fur vest who appeared to be high-ranking. Kirn indicated we wanted water from their river, and with hand motions the native gave a friendly invitation to come ahead.

After they left Captain came down on deck and spoke quietly to Kirn, who was near me. "What is your view, Mr. Kirn?"

Kirn's square jaw took a set. "They're a tough-looking bunch, sir."

"Yes. The water?"

"My feeling, sir, is to pull hooks by first light and look to the next source."

Captain Stark gazed out at the receding canoes. "All right. Inform the crew and make ready." He added dryly, "Hopefully God will provide the method."

"I think the wind is on its way, sir."

After nine bells the deck was kept dark again. I stood second watch and soon after midnight felt a few puffs of wind, the smell of rain. Soon a steady breeze brought curtains of mist and moved our anchor position a little. Tuplin whispered orders to ready two portside cannon for proper coverage. I heard a sound out there in the flowing white and listened carefully, but it did not come again.

My watch ended and I went below to rouse James for third watch. He was twitching away and whimpering like a lost puppy and I tried to be gentle bringing him out of fitful sleep. There wasn't as much snoring as usual in the foc'sl and I guessed most were having similar thoughts. We all respected Kirn's judgment and if he said it was time to go we were ready to leave right then.

I'd just settled in when a sound caused me to prop up on an elbow. A scream pierced the night, cut short, then a bellowed command –

"To arms! To arms!"

Men banged into each other in the dark, yelling, running, musket blasts above, all of us trying to get up the steps with our knives, muskets, short swords, falling and cursing. Screaming and worse sounds above as we piled out on the dark deck to unrecognizable bodies fighting each other, native war screams, men yelling for help, hollow sounds of clubs striking skulls, knives thudding into flesh. A sharp pain as I fired my musket into a red chest – weight to the back of my head . . .

Chapter 4

Consciousness foamed through turbulent scuppers and I tried to stay upright. We were moving, underway, but the rhythm was wrong. Something wrong with the ship? Why was I left lying on deck confined with water sloshing around? What godawful thing were they singing?

My head lolled against something. Salty stench penetrating my senses beyond blood and burnt powder. I forced crusty eyes open. Hideous painted face panting over me.

My God. They'd won.

Why then was I alive? Mist swirled, water splashed my face, my feet tilted toward night sky, down at wet blackness. Numbness, though in a strange, detached way my head ached beyond anything I'd experienced. I felt along my body to see what might be missing. A place on my right side ached, remotely warmer, sticky. My hand went farther and found the empty knife sheath.

Ahead a wet back tensed and shimmered, thick arms pulling a paddle back. Voices chanting, *"Ut a, Haa ... Ut cu, Hey ..."*

I moved slightly and a foot pressed my shoulder, a warning. My captor was sitting up on a thwart, leaning into the task, so his dark face came into view with each pull of his paddle.

A sudden jar caused my back to scrape the bottom of the narrow craft. I was hoisted by the arms, dragged through shallow water onto sand and dropped.

The chanting was much louder now, many voices. I was roughly lifted to my feet and stood unsteadily in flickering firelight. Faces crowding in, hideous mad painted faces laughing wildly and yelling in their strange tongue. Another was stood up next to me, first mate Kirn, bloody face barely recognizable. Big Chink joined us, also showing wounds, chattering desperately in different languages, trying to communicate with our captors. Spears and clubs prodded, containing us in a fierce circle of shadows and light.

A powerful native wearing copper armbands came forward, black and red face shiny in the firelight. His eye whites glowed as he showed us an iron knife, holding it below the pointed bone protruding out each side of his nose septum. "Slave!" he declared in guttural English. A roar from the crowd. *"Slave,"* he repeated. "No fight, no run." He made a chopping motion with his arm. "Die!"

The three of us were hauled away from the jeering crowd and taken in different directions. I was pushed through a doorway into smoky gloom and motioned to sit on a mat. Two low fires provided little light. One of the men who had brought me ripped the front of my shirt and peeled it off. He muttered something that did not sound complimentary and took a seat on a mat a few feet away. The other man left.

I looked down at blood smeared across my chest, caked on my side. My fingers explored the throbbing knot on the back of my head where I'd been struck. It was hard to keep sitting up when all I wanted was to lie down and sleep, perhaps forever. Blearily I took in my surroundings.

A large wood house, low fires, things hanging overhead, two staring children on a bunk along the far wall. The little girl pulled a mat up to just below her black button eyes.

A woman hurried through the entrance carrying two wooden bowls, placed one at her side and kneeled before me. The man said something and she answered sharply without looking at him. Her weathered face looked like my leather belt pouch, black hair tied back, stoutly made.

She dipped a cloth into a bowl and began to clean my side. The solution stung. I recognized the smell; urine. Ear ornaments made small clicks as she worked, mouth set, dark eyes revealing nothing. When she finished my side she moved on to shoulders and chest, neck and head, strong fingers without gentleness. She placed the second bowl between us, dipped a different cloth and began going over the same areas – warm water!

The man behind her spoke gruffly, drew his knife and came around behind me. I anticipated the knife plunging into my back or slashing my throat. He began sawing off my long hair. He tossed the wad of hair into the nearest fire. "Slave, *ha*," he uttered and sat down again. The woman threw harsh words over a shoulder at him. He rose, glared at me a moment, went out.

Alone with a woman and two children in a long plank building. I wondered if there might be another entrance. As if reading my thoughts, the woman leaned back and put a thick hand around the handle of a knife in her waistband. She shook her head. We stared at each other a few moments until I sighed and nodded. To attempt resistance now would be foolish.

She applied a blackish paste to my side wound, bound it roughly with a bandage tied off around my upper waist and indicated I should lie on a bunk along the wall, which I was thankful to do. I lay gingerly on the mat covering the bunk and she put another mat over me. She put a bowl down and indicated I should use this to pee in; beside it she placed some dried fish, a yellowish root and bowl of water. She left, flopping the mat over the doorway. Propped on an elbow I managed to drink all the water, lay back down. A feeling like sharp icicles shuddered up my spine and I gathered the thin mat snugly around me. Cold wind from cracks in the plank wall seeped into my bones. Hazily I saw the children still across the room, staring fearfully.

The woman who had cleaned me came back with a younger woman who went to the children. The older one tended the fire and began propping up slabs of fish impaled on sticks to take the heat.

Chanting continued outside – murdering heathen celebrating their victory. Were there just the three of us left? James gone, Captain, everyone else dead? Why was I still alive? But I was too weak to think beyond the moment and welcomed blackness flowing in over the pain.

Howls and hooting brought me awake. The pain in my side and head was more intense and I cursed the swine for waking me. The merriment outside became louder. I poked out sod plugging a knothole in the plank wall and peered out. Fire licked against night sky.

She was burning, flames licking high, bound sails falling in burning strings. If just the three of us were left there were sixteen murdered shipmates in those flames, including the scientific fellow. We'd meant these people no harm and to their lot it meant nothing. Perhaps we last three would soon die anyway; certainly I was of marginal value at the moment. Maybe it was a bit of torture they sought to cap their treachery.

Thunderous boom and light pouring like sunlight through the knothole. Fire shooting into the sky, ballooning into a red-black cloud that sealed her fate. The fire had found the powder stashed beneath the foc'sl quarters. After an awed silence whoops and yells erupted, a musket discharged. I eased back on my mat and let dizziness take me back to darkness.

Voices and clumsy human sounds as savages spilled into the lodge, bumbling drunk from our rum stores or simply the blood on their hands, loud and careless. Gray bands of light penetrated from roof slots through smoky gloom. I eased the mat over my head and slid back into sleep over the clamor.

I awoke to more light in the lodge and the smell of food brought hunger. But when I tried to sit up the pain knocked me down again. Yet I knew I must rise or they might simply kill me now as too much of a nuisance, so I tried a different leverage and finally managed a sitting position. The woman who had cleaned me brought a bowl of putrid fish with something else mixed in it. She spooned some into my mouth and with effort I swallowed. I managed to get half the bowl down before refusing any more.

It was a day of fading in and out, welcoming sleep when it came, sounds of grievous singing always there when I awoke. For their dead, I realized, the murdering heathen we managed to kill on the ship. Too few was my thought.

I ate a little food when the stout woman shoved it into my mouth. I was just one of her chores and she ministered me with the same deliberate motions she tended the fires or processed clams, which she had steamed in the shell somewhere outside and brought into the lodge. She quickly shucked meat from the opened shells and laid the edibles on planks. From my prone state I watched her place large leaves over each clam and carefully step on it, putting her full weight on the meat to smash it down. She began stringing them on gut line.

When I woke again the clam meats were hung up like necklaces with other flesh from the sea over the fires to smoke cure. She had squashed them to break down the flesh to tender them. Back home dried clams were put in boiling saltwater because they were too tough to chew otherwise.

Whatever bilge I was being fed, they must have thought it would improve my condition or they wouldn't bother. I tried to keep it down and appear to be getting better, yet I knew this could be the end. If it were, and if Kirn and Big Chink didn't make it back to a civilized port, no one would ever know what had befallen us. James, Captain Stark and everyone on the *New World* would have simply disappeared, swallowed up by the wilderness as others had been. James had told me a little about his family, their approximate location. If I were to ever make it home I would go to the New York Colony and let them know what happened.

They left me alone except for the ministrations of the woman, who changed the dressing on my side, ripping off scabs, applying more murk and leaves. She dabbed some of the stuff on my head wound and left. A mat was hung in front of my bunk, offering a little privacy; for their benefit I was certain, so they wouldn't have to look at me. I took the opportunity to squat over the bucket, the effort causing pain and a chilling sweat. There were several wood fiber mats hanging on a low partition at the foot of my bunk, and a good wool blanket. I didn't dare take the blanket, but slid a mat off the pile, a ragged one, so I had two covering me and was soon warmer. Under me were two mats laced together with feathers between, quite as comfortable as my bunk at the mission.

Soon the woman came and took the bucket, returned it empty and left me a bowl of meat, some water. The meat I recognized as seal and was better than the rations I'd been getting. I always drank the water I was given and wanted more, but didn't know how to ask for it, or if I should.

Days and nights passed, more than a week by my reckoning. I slept for longer stretches and was able to stand and move around a little without becoming dizzy. A storm blew for three days, maybe four. Rain and wind puffed through the knothole and I stuffed a mat fragment into it. Natives climbed up to put boards over roof slots, leaving a smaller hole for smoke to escape, and much of it didn't. The lodge was crowded during the bad weather and the scent of these humans packed together was indeed rank. Yet a few seemed quite clean, even if their clothes were soiled. The mat in front of me, and some low partitions separating family spaces, kept me partly secluded, but I could see slices of activity. Women wove baskets, others made mats on rectangular looms. Men worked on weapons or fishing gear, sometimes just sitting in circular groups and talking, gesticulating to emphasize words I did not understand.

One evening the big native who had declared the three of us slaves abruptly arrived at my bunk and demanded with sign language that I should stand and move about. I obeyed as he and two armed natives with him watched. He indicated I should pick up the piss bucket and raise and lower it, which I accomplished with some effort. He grunted something and left with his henchmen.

The following morning I was awakened with a start by the blast of a musket. My God, had they sunk another ship? I pulled the matting out of the knothole and blinked at the sudden sunshine. Brilliant points of light danced along easy swells bringing canoes full of savages. Several well-painted natives ran up and down the beach between two large fires, jumping, yelling, waving poles with feathers and other trailings. Drumming on wood came from several directions. People milled on the beach, women, children, baskets of food being held up – snacks for the weary travelers? It had all the makings of a party.

Two separate groups were arriving almost at the same time, from north and south. The canoes coming from the north were very fine, black hulled, high riding and trim of line, gliding across the water. Three canoes about thirty feet in length and one larger with a dozen rowers. When they beached their craft and came ashore I noticed many wore conical hats that looked similar to those used by China people, a type the natives in this village wore when they had come so peacefully to trade.

I was led out and joined my shipmates near a fire. We guardedly acknowledged each other. One of Kirn's arms hung limply and he looked to be in no better shape than me. Big Chink, though bug-eyed, seemed little the worse for wear. Some shipmates had told him the natives along this coast liked the taste of China people. At the time it seemed a joke, but maybe there was some truth to it, and they might roast the lot of us for all I knew. Since being forced to crew the *Lucky Wind* I'd lost weight and had not gained it back on the sparse fare at the mission, which perhaps would put me in position to better serve as slave than supper.

The big native with copper armbands appeared briefly, acting quite imperial, and motioned we should move apart. Several hundred natives occupied the pebbly beach near the delta of a large river, this mob extending to a snarl of drifted logs a ways down the beach and into the trees in the other direction, copper decorations much in evidence. There were six rectangular lodges, another mostly hidden by trees. In front of one lodge stood a wooden carving of a naked man with one arm across his midsection. The village area was quite untidy, not much different than the los rancherios at Yerba Buena.

Various natives poked and prodded us. Twice my mouth was

jerked open so my teeth could be examined. I kept reminding myself that we had, in fact, been declared slaves, and at this moment were apparently up for sale. Few of the prospective buyers seemed impressed with us; quite the contrary, they kept directing covetous looks at the metal items laid out on a string of mats a short distance away, our good wool blankets stacked along the edge of the mats and more swag from our doomed ship. Big Chink shrieked when one of the prospective buyers grabbed his balls, which set them to laughing and brought the big fellow who warned the visitors. He was dressed more formally in sleeveless leather vest, fir boughs and wispy bird down in his hair.

Two of the north people approached; one squat, broad shouldered individual stood very close and stared at me the way one might examine a donkey for possible service, the sea's contours etched in his oiled mahogany face.

The other native was different. Taller than me and very well made with lighter skin, though where the sun had good access he was nearly as dark as the others. What captured my attention was his expression: serene, yet at the same time intensely confident, as if his order was so elevated the fierce appearance of the men around him meant nothing. His gaze moved between us and came to rest looking into mine. I cast my eyes down. He moved his hand slowly to push aside the mat I had wrapped around me against the chill. He began to peel back the bandage over my side wound and I grimaced, began to bend over, and he stopped. He took some of my cropped hair in his fist, not roughly, and raised my head until our faces were close. His eyes were a startling dark hazel. He stared with a gaze so steady I was mesmerized.

"Talk English words?"

"Yes," I said.

He released me and stepped back, nodded slightly, then blended back into the crowd. Very soon a woman came with water and some fish. I wondered if the tall native had ordered it brought, though I had no reason to think such a thing. I welcomed my share of the water, as did my shipmates. As we huddled together to distribute the rations, I whispered to Kirn. "Your arm?"

"Shoulder may be broke. Clubbed me when I wouldn't bow to the heathen chief. Two back wounds from the ship. Swine couldn't take me from the front."

"Survive now," I said. "Our chance will come."

"Eat us," Big Chink said.

"Don't think they eat people." I didn't really know, but he looked so terrified I hoped to say something to calm him so he wouldn't go nutty and have no value as a slave. We took turns gulping water. Hands trembling, Chink raised the gourd and shook the last drops into his mouth.

After considerable examinations of all the merchandise, potential buyers squatted with glint-eyed sellers. Quiet bargaining, an occasional shouted exchange, groups coming together and dispersing. Women clad in wood fibers, skins and bright pieces of cloth brought food while sea birds floated overhead, watchful for any scraps to filch. We three stood there, not really part of anything, just items on the block. Little was said between us. We all understood the situation well enough, as we knew escape this day was impossible. It did not seem advisable to sit, but I felt weak and things began to look blurry. The sun was high enough to give some warmth, yet I shivered from exertion. I sank down on a knee.

Beach fires were banked and children ran playing their games, laughing and squealing through the groups of traders. A few women were already stringing colored beads. Much handling of short swords, knives, pots and pans, cordage, barrel staves, hammers – tasting from barrels of salted meat and fruit from our stores. On to muskets and bags of musket balls, iron bars used to lever rigging, sail cloth, sheet copper and a few copper rods, many common iron odds and ends on a ship you don't think about while doing daily duties. They had several buckets of our iron spikes, and I recalled Captain saying even with otter more scarce now you might still buy a prime pelt for ten spikes or a small sheet of copper. Mind it was worthwhile to give thirty spikes because that fur would bring many times the value in the finest silk at Canton.

The big fellow with armbands came toward us, burly friends in tow, and behind them were the two natives from the north that had examined me. He pointed at me. "You. Go him."

I shrugged, and the big fellow took this as insubordination. He grabbed the back of my neck and shoved my face into the gravel.

"*Slave,*" he spat.

Another voice spoke sharply. The tall native put a hand under my shoulder and helped me to my feet. I followed him down to the beach where their canoes were lined up. By his direction I sat on a canoe thwart forward of the stern. He removed the stop from a skin container and handed it to me and I drank hungrily. I followed his gaze to see blood seeping down my leg. In the stern of the canoe he found a woven cloth and placed it in my hand, lifted my shirt and pressed my hand holding the cloth over the side wound. He gave me some smoked meat on a stick and left.

The tall native came back with two men and a woman, all carrying trade items. They spread iron and copper pieces in the bottom of the canoe, a few wool blankets in front of me wrapped in protective mats. Other natives were filling canoes all along the beach. Kirn and Big Chink were getting into a very large canoe that belonged to the people from the south. Chink was clumsily trying to step in when a native gave him a whack across his big butt with a length of flat iron. The others laughed as he went sprawling.

I thought of Big Chink's round, cheerful face at mess every morning and evening, the food he served us with a cook's pride, and I felt a surge of hate. A sudden need to survive burned in me sharper than the pain of my wounds and I made a tacit promise the time would come when I would avenge this treachery. Until then I would study my enemy, and learn how to live as a slave.

There seemed to be a change of plan. I followed the tall native and others along a muddy path up the river through fragrant evergreen trees. We soon came to an open campsite next to a small, clear stream that emptied into the river. A makeshift camp was assembled and the three women began a fire while the men restored the boards on the roofs of several small lean-tos. That evening women from the village brought freshly cooked fish and greens that had been boiled or steamed, as well as flat bread with a nutty taste.

Morning came and we ate some leftovers from the night before, and soon boarded the canoes. I took my place and kneeled on the mat in front of the tall native's station. Behind me were many jovial farewells, but I only looked ahead now, measuring the wind and our path across water.

Chapter 5

We cleared the point and angled into the northwest swell. Thin offshore fog filtered the sunshine and I pulled two mats tight around me against the chill. I tried to hold them in place while steadying with one hand on the gunnel. Forward a short mast pole was set into slots and a rectangular sail of woven material raised. The stubby arm was set and secured and the craft yawed as the small sail filled. Though we angled into the breeze the sail steadied and helped propel the craft, similar to the even smaller sail I used on my little boat at home.

The mostly naked natives had oiled their bodies and wore those conical China hats that shed water and deflected spray from the eyes. They began singing with a lot of guttural tones, some aborigine chant I'd never heard the like. We were about a mile from the rocky shore where the tops of waves shattered against jagged dark teeth in recurring jaw lines. Between these rocks were smooth beaches and piles of drifted logs in cluttered jams. Up over the hills dark green trees stood thick and tall, higher and thicker as we made our way north, and further inland I glimpsed mountains between clouds of mist, white-topped mountains that rose to the real clouds.

Cold spray hit us as we crested every swell and the paddler's bodies glistened with the grease they'd applied before departing. I spit out salt and felt wet cold penetrating the mats and my tattered clothes, my teeth clenched to keep from chattering. If I was allowed a paddle I might be able to hold back the cold, but none was offered. The tall native passed me a conical hat that I pulled down tight over my ears.

The wind built momentum, growing the swell high and dark. The carved bowsprit buried in the trough of every wave, their chant would hit a loud chord as water sloshed over gunnels and we would be heaved up again to see the hostile world surrounding us as the little bailer in front of me worked quickly to get rid of water sloshing about our knees. This was hardly a craft to be taking such a sea in routine fashion, yet none of this bunch showed the slightest concern, croaking away like a phlegm-throated choir and leaning to correct the pitch of the canoe. We were as close as a man could get to the sea without being consumed by her, and I thought if we swamped I would certainly hold onto one of these madmen on my way to the bottom.

I wondered where we might be headed. These natives had arrived early so they must have camped close by the night before. Unless they had traveled this great water by night, which I was sure they were capable. An oarsman would pause to pee into a spare bailing bowl or eat a quick snack, then resume his paddling while another oarsman tended some personal need. I did look away when a forward oarsman squatted over a bailing bowl, and wondered a little desperately how long our voyage might last.

Hunched with head bowed, I let my hat take the spray, and in spite of my general discomfort began to lull into a light sleep.

The near boom of a whale blowing brought my head up. Several whales close by, a relatively small type I recognized, called killer by some seamen, blackfish by others. It was said these ate larger whales, could swallow a man whole, catch a porpoise in mid air, cut a shark in half with one bite. They came straight for us and the natives were yelling and waving their paddles as in greeting. Shouts astern and I looked back to see the others waving too. The lead whale had a rounded dorsal nearly the height of a man, an amazing thing tapering to a whip-like floppy top. The creature's ebony body gleamed, but when it blew, brilliant white markings could be seen around the eyes and lower jaw and this pattern extended back on the sides. When the leader was nearly on top of us he went down and the others followed. I braced for the jolt of one coming up under our canoe.

Everyone seemed quite jovial and I glanced back to see the tall native smiling.

Sleek black backs appeared to starboard and three whales blew in the same second, as if to say s'long mate. Their breath spray drifted over us as they disappeared.

I settled into my bowed head position again and relaxed into the rhythm of endless swells. The wind's force diminished. I was jolted out of near-sleep by the man in front of me yelling some new chant, and saw him pointing his paddle at a group of seals two hundred feet off our bow. The others took up the chant, as if calling to them.

We continued on as I drifted in and out of an approximation of sleep, weary and weak, sometimes catching myself leaning too far one way or the other. Clouds shut out the sun and I drew the mats tightly about me.

Finally I was brought awake by a change in rhythm; the singing had also changed, and we were angling in toward land. An island nearby, perhaps a half-mile long, and on the mainland columns of smoke against the treed hillside. We drew nearer, passing near treacherous wash rocks and huge beds of kelp rising and falling with the swell. And there in the kelp were heads, heads too small for seals, and I realized these were the most valuable prize any trader could obtain – sea otter. Five I counted before we came close enough to cause them to dive out of sight.

Our chain of canoes slid past the south end of the island between great rock seastacks and into the lee, behind the island, where the swell lessoned to the lull of a porch swing. I was surprised by the abrupt barking of dogs. On the island white dogs ran along the beach!

Rocks everywhere, protruding or just under the surface in a maze of risky fingers. We skirted rocks and floating beds of kelp. Ahead I counted ten rectangular buildings big enough to house more than one family, and several smaller shelters. As we drew closer I could see the bow of a large canoe sticking out the end of one of the smaller buildings. Natives were occupied with various tasks, children running about on the beach, women dragging baskets while wading. We were in a shallow, rocky protected area – not an actual bay – at low tide. People stopped what they were doing and watched our approach.

The keel of our loaded canoe dug into sand. A solemn group led by what appeared to be a couple of chiefs stopped at the water's edge. I was ordered out and the paddlers picked up our craft and began carrying it, straining under the canoe loaded with swag as young men ran through the shallow water to help. Through signs I was ordered to help unload and we laid everything out on mats above the water line. I was trembling from cold and the side wound had stiffened, causing me to walk bent. I sat near some muskets and iron and extended cramped legs. Several naked children gathered a short distance away and stared curiously. My muttered greeting caused them to step back and look to each other for reassurance.

The tall native and the two stout, barefoot chiefs approached and looked down at my wretched state. After a short exchange the chiefs left. The tall native put a hand on my shoulder and when I looked up he cocked a thumb at his chest.

"Squintanasis." He cocked the thumb at me.

"Aidan."

"Ai-dan," he repeated.

"Squin-tan-a-sis," I said. "Quite the handle."

"Han-dle?" He helped me to my feet.

"Name," I said shakily, taking in my surroundings. "Handle same as name." A large iron pot hung over an inviting fire not far away, a woman tending it. The children had moved a little closer, pointing and chattering regarding my strange presence. A hulking bear of a man approached, causing the children to move back. He snarled some phrase, repeated it. He was close to my right side and I caught his stink, but wouldn't look directly at him for fear this might be construed as a challenge. He cuffed my shoulder a glancing blow, putting me down on a knee.

Squintanasis moved past me and kicked suddenly, causing the big fellow to utter a surprised grunt. A shove and sharp word from Squintanasis sent the big savage huffing away.

Again he offered a hand and helped me up. He pointed toward the fire and I readily moved toward it. The woman at the fire skirted to the other side as I put numb hands in close, rubbing them and feeling the warmth as a gaudily dressed shaman approached waving rattle and stick. Trailing feathers danced from his props and I recalled a blurry memory of a similar sight at the Hoh enclave. This shaman had angular features painted in black, red, a few streaks of blue and yellow. His spit hit my face, agitated trailings from carved figure and rattle flicked across my head and shoulders. I pretended to ignore all of this. After a time Squintanasis ordered him away with a wave. Shaman went reluctantly, backing with a parting curse.

Apparently I was under the charge of this pale native, the friendliest I'd met so far. The rest of these folks seemed no more cordial than the previous bunch and I wondered what I might be in for. Certainly I was of little use to them as a slave in my present condition.

"Handle," Squintanasis said. "Big?"

"Well, yes. Squintanasis big name." I spread my hands apart. "Me Aidan." I moved my hands close together. "Small name."

"Ai-dan." He nodded. "Small. Kwaowechuk."

"Small. Kwa-ow-e-chuk," I repeated, causing him to look at me with new interest.

"Slave here," he said, sweeping a hand at the row of buildings. "Ozette. Home Makah. Ozette Ai-dan home."

Squintanasis was studying me top to bottom. The heat caused steam to rise from my ragged clothes and I fluffed my shirt. "You part white?" I asked, opening my shirt.

His expression clouded. In a harsh whisper he uttered, "Poison," and started off, looked back. "Come," he commanded.

As we walked I noticed a carved figure of a naked man similar to the one at the Hoh village, though this one had his arms extended in welcome and his genitals carved with considerable detail. Two women tended a smoldering, steamy area of ground and were peeling back a covering of broad leaves and kelp, exposing many clams and mussels. We entered a large lodge and I was directed to a bench along the wall. Sleeping benches of one and two levels – not unlike a ship's bunks – along with storage boxes ran around the perimeter of the lodge. This great room was divided into family areas by chest-high partitions. At the far end, in the largest area, rose a commanding bench of dark wood inlaid with bright stones and shells and a broad backrest in the shape of a dorsal fin.

No sawn boards were to be seen, yet I was reminded of my home near Boston. Wall posts thick as a man and cleaned of bark were set into the ground around the perimeter. Down the middle, posts with strange figures carved into them served as center supports and all the vertical posts had saddles cut in the top to receive horizontal logs nearly as large. Smaller logs ran laterally across the width, the whole business tied together with lines locked into notches in the posts and more lines in the middle to fasten the smaller framework. Walls were split cedar planks lashed to horizontal poles and slanted roof boards lapped over each other with a smoke vent here and there.

I lay on a stuffed mat and stared up through the maze of poles and lines supporting several kinds of drying flesh that took smoke from the fires before exiting out the vents. Up on the walls, out of the main columns of smoke, hung strings of tubers and loose-woven baskets of other foods, and along the partitions that separated family spaces were stacked bundles of rushes and weaving materials.

Artistic designs and animals were carved into wide boards hanging around the lodge, some brightly painted; tanned animal skins, beautifully made baskets with colorful, intricate weaves, a copper ladle as decoration, yet the resilient strength of the lodge itself impressed me most.

The few people around paid me little mind, busy with their own matters. Squintanasis was speaking with a woman making a basket. She put down her project and came toward me; tall, slim, a waistband of yellow cloth, blue cotton shirt. I wondered about the shirt, then realized she was quite handsome. A quick hand motion and I stood so she could appraise me with critical amber eyes. She signed for me to remove my clothes. While I was doing this she put her fingers on the bandage and brought them to her nose, whiffed, uttered something that sounded uncomplimentary.

The woman left momentarily and returned with a skirt and sleeveless shirt made of wood fibers, which I quickly put on against the chill. She gave me two dry mats and abruptly left.

Soon two young women approached with warm water in a wooden box. They had me remove the mats I'd just wrapped around myself, as well as the clothing, and began washing me with a soap that had a woody-pitch smell. One of the girls had reddish-black short hair, though not as short as most slaves. I felt quite self-conscious, which seemed silly given my situation. A short distance away a sand flea jumped into a cooking fire. I closed my eyes and imagined home; Gretchen was washing me after a hard day at sea. Of course she would never do such a thing when we weren't married – and likely never would be, since her father considered our family inferior, not to mention the harsh words that had passed between him and my father.

The tall woman brought a small bowl of a dark, smelly substance and gave brief instructions to the girls. The washing completed, the stout girl removed my side bandage and applied the substance from the bowl, then placed two broad leaves and some soft bark over my wound and bound it with strands of bark around my lower ribs. The substance stung sharply, but soon the wound began to numb. The girls departed without a word and I lay down again. As sleep overtook me I felt a crawling sensation under the bandage.

That evening I was aroused with about thirty people in the lodge to partake of a meal. The chief and Squintanasis arrived together, moving through shafts of light from the roof vents. Two oblong circles formed and people sat on mats and boxes with a wide board between them. Squintanasis sat near the chief. He looked around and indicated I should take a place next to him. Most of the slaves sat on sleeping benches or the floor separate from their owners, and I wasn't sure I'd understood Squintanasis's meaning. Women began bringing food in from outside, also from steaming boxes near the inside fires. The food was put in oblong, shallow-bowl containers and placed on the mat over the board. Squintanasis looked back and with some impatience motioned me to sit next to him, which I did without further delay.

A bowl of warm water came around for us to rinse our hands in, behind it a towel of shredded bark, quite soft and absorbent. Several trays of steamed clams in the open shell, seal meat, which we occasionally ate aboard ship, some sort of fowl, and a little coarser meat I wasn't sure about. There were also greens and bumpy tubers that looked like narrow potatoes, and some flat bread similar to what I'd had in the Hoh village.

No one made a move to take any food yet. With eyes downcast, following most others in our circle, I noticed some of the women, having served the food, forming their own circle on the other side of the main fire pit where there were also children. Two women took places in our circle.

At the far end of the lodge a family sat around their own fire, away from the main groups. A pregnant woman came forward with a platter of cooked greens and passed it to the tall woman. She accepted a pot of food in return and returned to her group at the end of the lodge.

The chief spoke quietly while everyone kept eyes down. I heard "Tooplah" more than once, and then the chief said something that caused people to raise their heads. People began to take food and put it in wooden bowls held in their laps. I was struck by how quiet it was as everyone began the meal. The ritual atmosphere, and the way the chief had uttered what sounded very much like a blessing for this food, seemed almost as if I were back at the mission. I also did not understand why I was sitting next to an apparently high-ranking member of the tribe, within the circle of a chief, while fellow slaves were left in the background to eat together and perhaps with less variety.

With a few greens and a tuber in my bowl, I decided to try the slimy looking fowl; I picked a small piece from the pile and took a bite. It was the worst bird I'd ever sunk my teeth into. Squintanasis motioned for me to dip it into a bowl of oil the others were garnishing with, and I complied. The oil was strangely sweet, slightly rancid and made little improvement. The bird was no doubt one of the diving ducks that feed along current lines and scavenge the beach.

"Klooklo," Squintanasis said, encouraging me to eat more, but I put down the fowl and took a piece of the course meat, which none of the others seemed to want. Though chewy, it was surprisingly tasty. "Good," I said, and took another bite.

"Ai-dan eat art-leit-kwitl," Squintanasis said, and several men grinned. This got the chief's attention and Squintanasis repeated what he'd said. At my questioning look he pointed up at a bearskin on the wall of the lodge.

"Ko-thlo Ai-dan hah-ouk artleitkwitl!" someone said loudly, and murmurs passed through our circle and spread to the next one.

"Kothlo dah-shook artleitkwitl!" the chief added, and this elicited several approving grunts and a *Ha*! or two. I looked sideways to see Squintanasis smiling and the chief looking amused, and thought if they were happy at my expense it might be a good thing, so I bit deep into my piece of artleitkwitl and smiled, nodding approval while chewing away.

There was not much conversation during our meal, everyone acting quite mannerly. Near the end when a woman placed the washbowl near the chief, who they called Tomhak, conversation began to build. Though I continued to sit with head and eyes down, eating slowly with mouth closed as most of these men were doing, I remained alert. The situation had changed and I felt a need to pay strict attention to my manners and any direction I might be given.

Berry cakes were served and most of the men took a small amount, as did I. The taste was sweet and fishy, and I was sure they had been dried with fish oil, a common preservative. The natives at home used this method, but the ingredients here gave the berries a sweeter flavor.

The washbowl and towel went around again, women cleared dishes, and the men began to talk among themselves. A harpoon tip was brought out and examined. A man from the family at the far end of the lodge, having also finished his meal, brought a tool that looked like an adze to the circle. I had never heard of a native using this shipwright tool. Squintanasis motioned and I followed him outside. We sat on a bleached log next to a low fire and I pulled a mat around myself against the evening breeze. Smooth swells curled lazily toward us and expended sighs on the kelp-strewn beach.

"Talk English words," Squintanasis said. "Teach."

"Teach? You wish me to teach you English words?"

"Klooklo." He looked over and I realized I was frowning. "Klooklo," he repeated. "Tomanawos say, Boston Man come. Teach."

"Teach you English words now?"

"Klooklo."

"But you already say English words. I did teach English back home. To children. On Wednesday and Sunday afternoons. Do you understand what I just said?" By his expression I knew he did not.

"All right." I nodded, sensing a better role than most slaves can expect. "I can teach you. Aidan teach Squintanasis English words."

"Teach," he said.

From a pile nearby Squintanasis chose a single log, placed the end just so over the glowing coals. He wore a sleeveless shirt made of tough leather and a skin skirt, probably seal. I had to keep reminding myself that this man was indeed a native, a member of a savage tribe who had perhaps killed traders as the Hoh were inclined to do. Yet he was different, tall and muscular with long legs, a thin, light beard along his jaw and over his chin that appeared as though it had never been shaved. Yet these attributes alone were not what made him stand out, other natives here had facial hair in varied quantity. Nor was it simply his quiet confidence. There was just something about him that exceeded the bounds of this village and went beyond our master-slave situation.

Two natives came to sit on the opposite side of the fire, but Squintanasis spoke to them and they paused. One grunted something and they moved away.

I began with the names of things I thought Squintanasis most needed to know. Using sign and the English words he knew he asked questions, most of which I was able to understand, and as we went along he had me repeat Makah words. We soon developed a pattern for simple meanings. His grasp of English words was much better than my pace with Makah, yet I made a little progress. I could not make the guttural sounds of his language, but my pronunciations began to satisfy him.

The moon slid over the hill behind the village and the log end he had placed over the fire was reduced to a few glowing coals. Squintanasis called a halt because it was ut-haie (night). My head ached and my side was stiff around the wound from sitting so long, yet I felt refreshed; using my brain for something constructive had produced a sense of well-being, though by the time I entered the lodge I'd discounted this as reckless thinking.

Most of the family areas had mats hung for privacy in addition to waist-high partitions. Snug under my cedar covers, I was slipping into welcome sleep when a sound caused me to open my eyes. In the dusky light mats were being hung by the slave woman with reddish hair. She reached up to fasten the tops to lines, enclosing our space, and then I saw lovely woman's thighs and more as her dress went up over her head. Facing away from me she pulled on a lighter garment that ended just above her knees.

A boy appeared, stepped on a box and crawled onto the sleeping shelf slightly above and next to mine. The girl turned and her necklace clacked as she adjusted it between her breasts. She slid under the mats and turned her back to the boy, so he was against the wall, as a mother cat would protect her kitten.

She began to hum softly. This became singing so quiet I could barely make out the words, though some of them sounded Spanish. Her singing was very soothing and I felt sleep closing in. Then I heard, "Sleep little baby."

Beyond the mat curtains were the general sounds of men gaining sleep, other sounds of someone gaining pleasure. Far away the faint roll of a wolf howl drifted over the sibilance of gentle surf.

I wondered if I'd heard the English words at all.

Any expectation of easy duty was dashed the next morning when I was rudely awakened by sharp pains and gruff orders. A stout old woman was jabbing me with the charred end of a stick used in the fire, urging me up. She hit a tender spot and I came up quick, jerked the weapon from her grasp. This caused the woman to scream some curse at me, to which I raised the stick as if to strike her. A man immediately rushed forward brandishing a knife.

I dropped the stick and looked around. Squintanasis was not present, though several sets of dark eyes were watching. I sat on my bunk, began pulling on boots. The woman spat some order and I acted as if I hadn't heard. She repeated her words as I tied my bootlaces. There were several men bracketing the woman when I finally looked up.

"So what will it be, lads? I don't understand what she says and you don't understand me. I think you better get Squintanasis."

Their answer came quick enough. They grabbed me and hauled me outside. I did not think it wise to resist too strenuously, which my present condition did not support anyway, so I let them force me along and into shallow water. They then picked me up by feet and shoulders and tossed me further out. It was shallow but plenty cold, and I came up sputtering.

The loud woman was there with the men, all of them laughing. So I did the first thing that came to mind, which was discard my bark shirt, laugh wildly and dive away from them and start swimming toward the island. I did not look back until I'd reached chest-deep water, then stood and grinned at their surprised faces.

"Come on in," I called, motioning to them. "Nothing like an early swim to start the day. Certainly the loud wench could do with a dunking."

Squintanasis walked up behind them. A few words were exchanged and my antagonists moved off, the woman snarling something over her shoulder.

Squintanasis crossed arms and looked in another direction as I waded ashore. I stood before him, shirt in hand, dripping, shivering.

"Go with womans," he said. "Get berries. Now go Suisha."

Suisha turned out to be the tall woman who wore the yellow scarf around her waist. With an assist from the girl who always seemed near her, a daughter perhaps, my bandage was changed. I was given dry clothes and sent off with the scornful woman who had rudely awakened me. For this day I became a berry picker in her charge. I was the only man with a half dozen women, two of them short-haired slaves. We walked some distance, then ate a meal of dried fish that had been boiled to reasonable softness and a few bites of the tubers that tasted like potatoes. I was then directed to a group of bushes laden with red berries. Soon enough I was chastised for picking the wrong red berries, the crone dressing me down in front of the other women. As if I knew anything about their strange fruit.

While picking the correct berries I wondered why I was doing woman's work. Our clothes were similar. I looked like a tall, bearded slave woman without breasts, incompetently picking berries. Had it been Squintanasis's idea, or did he simply agree with it? Perhaps it was a test of some sort. Well, all right then.

I brought a ripe red berry to my nose and smelled with a big intake of breath. Again. When I was aware of several women staring I held the berry up in the sunlight.

"By God, this is a perfect ripe one." I tossed the berry high in the air and managed to catch it in my open mouth. "Um, um." I went back to picking. Soon I was picking with both hands, tossing one into the air now and then to catch in my mouth. Of course I missed nearly as many as I caught, but my actions kept the crone away.

*Makahs display considerable ingenuity in the manufacture of the knives,
tools and weapons they use . . . Conical shaped hats are made of spruce
root split into fine fibres, and plaited so as to be impervious to water.*

Chapter 6

Hot dreams filled with blood stench, acrid spent powder, savage
screams and howling wolves creased the night. I woke feeling dis-
orientated, unable to move freely, things flying around out of control, weightless creatures with sneering wet faces. Back sticky,
strangely warm. With effort I pushed away confining mats.

I awoke trembling with cold. The woman and boy were gone.
Human shapes floating through my field of vision as I gathered mats
tight around me. The tall woman, Suisha, came near, pressed a cool
hand to my forehead. She shouted an order and someone approached.
I put a hand to my clammy throat. Fever.

More mats were piled on. My head was raised by a gentle hand
and I looked up expecting to see my sister. A bowl was pushed between my lips, warm liquid I at first resisted, finally accepted; a taste
of clam juice mixed with something chalky, yet tart. I lay back for a
time and was beginning to feel warmer when the women came again
and insisted I drink another warm liquid, even less pleasant, bitter
on the tongue, followed by a dose of oily water.

Fires flared up inside rainbow rings, through plank walls came
screams of children and birds. Staring at bands of light I made out my
fate etched in carved boards along shadowy walls and felt resigned,
even content with a sense I had been a slave for a long time, even
before being made a slave by my own people, and now my value was

coming to an end. There came an extreme loneliness and I wished the end to come efficiently quick. These thoughts brought strange comfort, an understanding that relaxed cold fears and caused my eyelids to close of their own weight.

A familiar voice woke me. Squintanasis and a large man stood looking down, also Tomhak, the three looking at me and talking.

They parted and Suisha moved close and peered into my eyes. I was growing accustomed to her penetrating gaze. She now sported a red sash around her waist and her lips glistened with the oil they used. Soon the men seemed to reach some consensus and left, followed by Suisha. Two girls arrived to give me more of the heavy, bitter liquid. One of the girls had tied her hair loosely back, a wave drooping over the side of her face as she bent forward, and I recognized her as the girl who sang quiet lullabies. Her cheeks were very smooth and I studied her face as if this were the most important thing I could do. I guessed she was about fifteen or sixteen. As I sipped from the bowl she ran a damp cloth over my forehead and throat. Her necklace clicked as she worked and the loose neck of her blouse revealed a swell of breasts. Though weak, I felt a little better.

"Know some English?" I whispered. This brought a flash to her amber eyes, but no answer. *"Hablo Espanol?"* She glanced at the other girl, but said nothing.

They left and I had risen to use the piss bucket when a clamor outside got my attention. A woman burst in and turned to yell angrily. She then hurried toward the chief's area as a stout man in bearskin vest charged through the doorway, growling and brandishing a mussel-shell knife.

The woman continued to yell her rage and the man growled the louder, jagged teeth bared and spittle flying, but Tomhak was between them now and soon got the fellow to lower his weapon. He then turned and spoke sharply to the woman and she was immediately still.

Tomhak ushered the man outside. The woman began pleading her complaint to Suisha, who I understood to be Tomhak's woman, and she took on a startling expression for it reminded me of the way my father would look when I went to complain about my older brother. Everyone else in the lodge went back to whatever they were doing. Soon I lay down to the sound of rain beating on boards and quickly sank into sleep.

During the next two days I improved so I was eating and walking around. The afternoon of the second day I was sent with several boys and two men from our lodge to a spring just down the beach. Where the water dropped off a rock formation onto a sandy area a pool had been built with rocks and clay. We stripped and bathed using their tree-smelling soap and dried with soft bark towels. The men's bodies glistened with grease like the paddlers who had conveyed me to this place, and they first flopped on the sand, rolling this way and that until their bodies were coated with the stuff, then ran into the surf and splashed around like aroused ducks while rubbing themselves. This maneuver removed most of the grease and they then bathed in the fresh water. As we were dressing another group arrived and two men rolled on the sand.

That evening Squintanasis and I attended an outside fire while I gave an English lesson. He seemed weary, and I realized he had been working on the canoe-in-progress all day. A great deal of building was going on in the village, several canoes in various stages of completion, young men fashioning new spears, more weapons and tools seeming to take shape everywhere, women weaving. I had watched a wooden box being formed by kerfing with a knife, then steaming and bending a wide plank for three corners, the last corner and bottom doweled to form a watertight container.

The next morning Squintanasis sent me with two young men to

feed the white dogs. We set off in a well-used canoe, followed by two girls in another canoe. The sun had burnt through morning mist to light a towering rock on the north side of the village, connected to the mainland at low tide, which marked the beginning of a spine that appeared to extend far out into the ocean. Two high atolls along this spine broke the swell and calmed the water on our side. On their tops stunted trees grew from whatever soil had collected.

We slid between several rock seastacks toward the treed island where the dogs lived, and they were already running back and forth on the beach, barking a greeting. Gulls and other sea birds floated over the whole area and rode the calm waters we paddled through.

The dogs were fed strips of seal meat and fish scraps. I did little, helping when I could. The boys didn't give me orders or try to communicate with me, though they seemed curious. As we were ready to leave the girls came out of the woods with armloads of leafy stems. The boys each took a stem and began chewing the leaves. When a girl dropped a stem I picked it up and tried one of the meaty leaves. It tasted of licorice. I followed their practice of chewing out the juice and discarding the rest. One of the boys said something and the girls glanced at me and giggled. I understood a few words – they were amused by my beard.

"Do-woks art-leit-kwitl," Father is bear, I said.

They looked surprised, then laughed.

As we were returning to the village, a larger canoe stood off our port side and the native in the bow raised his paddle and began hooting. The canoe rode low in the water and as they reached shore first I saw they had bagged two seals. These were quickly unloaded, and while I was helping carry our canoe high on the beach two of the hunters were already butchering the animals and some women had arrived to help. The man who had done the yelling was walking away from this task. He was quite massive and tall, all the more impressive wearing a sleeveless bearskin jacket. He was perhaps the biggest man I'd seen in the village other than the heathen who had cursed me on my arrival, though this man was light on his feet and had an air of confidence. He appraised me briefly and turned to some young men who had come to greet him.

Squintanasis put down his tools and left the canoe he was working on to intercept me before I reached the lodge. "Talk English words," he said.

"Who is that big man?" I asked.

"Chief Senequah. Second chief. Brother Chief Kakemook."

We had a good lesson that lasted the afternoon. "You want to learn our language well," I said. "Why is this important?" I found myself speaking in a mix of Makah and English, but Squintanasis seemed to understand.

"Trade."

"But what about Spanish? Russian? They have been around longer."

Squintanasis shook his head. "Spanish go. No trade Spanish now. Russian . . ." He shook his head. "Boston man come. King George man. More come. Klooklo trade, no klooklo trade. Chinook know English words. Know klooklo trade words."

I nodded. "Some good trade, some not good. Fur not so many now. Know words, get klooklo price."

"Know plenty fur. Far people trade me. Boston man trade many."

I cast a doubtful look at the rocky seastacks in front of the village. "Boston man come here?"

"Come Neeah. My people. Tomanawos say, go there."

"I don't think a trading ship would risk an anchorage here."

"One ship come, long time. Russian. No more."

"Were you here when Russian ship come?"

Squintanasis looked at me sharply. "Not know Russian come. Bad time. People die. Russian die. No come more. Boston man. King George man. Boston man say him English."

"Well, don't be calling me that. I'm Irish to the core. My father's father came straight from Wexford in sixty-one."

Squintanasis looked suspicious.

"Not to say there aren't decent English folks in Boston, I know a few."

"Boston man no English?"

"No more than you're Hoh."

Squintanasis raised off his log with an ominous look. "Just a way of comparing," I added quickly, "not that I'd ever call you one. You no Hoh, me no English."

"Makah."

"Right." I pointed a thumb at my chest. "Irish."

Squintanasis studied me a moment and slowly resettled. He used a stick to poke at the fire.

"You klooklo, Suisha say." He smiled slightly. "Seir (my) tomana-wos talk true. Hoh talk pe-shak (worthless). Hoh say kok-shal (dead), spear true. Too small, maybe kok-shal. Irish little trade. One seal."

He said this quietly, and I took it as a friendly gesture, even if seemed to mean I'd been a bargain he'd picked up.

"Soon maybe see who you are," he said.

I arrived at my bunk as the girl was putting up night mats around our space. Her boy was there and came over to me as I was taking off my boots and trousers. After pulling on my sleepwear, a wood fiber skirt, I accepted the figure made of twigs the boy offered. It was a crude likeness of a bird and he jabbered some explanation, which I pretended to be interested in as the girl turned away to shed her clothes and pull on her nightdress. I stole a glimpse or two, but tried to respect her privacy. Longish hair or not, she must certainly be a slave or she wouldn't be sleeping in such close proximity to me. Yet she was not like the other female slaves with their close-cropped hair and bowed heads. She seldom spoke, but her eyes were bright and she held her head high. And she was often in company with Suisha.

Under the mats sleep would not come and I listened for my neighbor's lullaby. This was a quiet lodge at night, beyond various snores and men seeking pleasure, most notably from the chief's area, Tomhak apparently a randy fellow, not that I could blame him with such a handsome woman at his side.

Finally the music of her voice came, so softly it seemed only for me.

Chapter 7

The next morning Squintanasis appeared only long enough to tell me I would be going with Gleka and the women again. This time there were four slave women, the crone in the lead. We trudged up the slope through wet mist and took a different trail toward thick trees. We carried two travois made of springy logs about eight feet long, lashed together with kelp ropes. Without a load they could be rolled in the lashings and carried like two poles. After about a mile the sounds of axes striking wood could be heard.

When we arrived several men were chopping up branches from trees that had been downed. One of the workers was the big savage who had spit on me when I arrived. Since then I had only seen him at a distance. He looked us over with an evil grin, showing bad teeth. Gleka shuffled us over to a pile of small logs several feet long and we began loading these onto the travois aprons. When mine was loaded I positioned the woven cordage over my shoulders and measured the trail back.

Just then a woman gave a startled yell. I looked back as the big native was hauling one of the slave women toward some bushes. The other men yelled at him but he ignored this. He slung the woman to the ground, ripped away her skirt and jumped on. Gleka was screeching at him and the two other men approached, but he roared a warning and they stopped. His broad back rose and fell behind a bush as he grunted and pounded away at the woman while she uttered short cries.

Gleka raised her hands and dropped them, turning away in despair. "Go!" she commanded me. "Go. Go."

I went, dragging my load with a vengeance. The ends of the poles straddled the trail and dug lines through the mossy ground, gliding best over the wet places as my worn boots took on water. Sweat ran down my back and into my eyes and I realized how weak I still was. Weak and helpless, with no more to say about my fate than that woman being pounded up in the woods. Fine rain began falling, cooling my face and numbing my hands. The rain made pulling a little easier, but the trail down the slope was muddy and my feet slid from under me. I fell backwards, scattering the pile of wood. As I was reloading, two women came into view pulling the other travois. They walked in single file sharing the load. They paused, then went around, knocking my load off again.

"Thanks ladies," I said. With my cargo again secured I continued on to the village. Some women came to help unload. They pointed at my muddy clothes and giggled while I used a stick to scrape my trousers and boots. Two boys sauntered up to also chid me. One used a stick to mock my efforts until a harsh voice caused them to bolt and run away.

Squintanasis stood in the shadow of a fire shelter holding a beautifully shaped longbow, different from others I'd seen here. His expression I thought strange, kindly, yet at the same time it revealed nothing of what he might be thinking. He turned away and several boys fell in behind him, also carrying bows, a shorter type common around the village.

I had rolled the travois together for another trip up the trail when the slave girl that shared my quarters appeared. She held a steaming bowl and offered it. The bowl contained warm clam juice and something else, perhaps an ingredient to guard against sickness while working in the wet. I watched over the rim and she dropped her eyes.

"Thank you," I said, handing her the empty bowl. She took it and hurried back inside the lodge. But I had seen the flash of a smile.

When I returned the women were busy. The one who had been worked over by the big savage no longer wore her bark mantle. On her knees, she slowly stacked short logs in a pile. Gleka gave me some food, her face drawn into stern ridges. I squatted under a tree to eat. The big native was nowhere in sight. The other two men ate under a different tree. No one said anything.

I made two more trips pulling logs and was relieved when Suisha approached and told me to go to my sleeping place. The lodge was busy, women bustling about washing and processing berries. I had just shed my wet clothes for dry when Howessa came to change my bandage, so I pulled off the nightshirt again. I was surprised the way the wound was healing, the redness nearly gone.

"Klooklo," I said. Howessa's round face tilted up and she smiled.

The following morning I peered out from under my mats, tensing for another attack by the crone, but Gleka was nowhere to be seen. The fires were being brought up, men were arranging what gear they would need for the day's tasks. Howessa and her sister, Winaseek, arranged baskets of berries on a long plank. The girl and her boy were already gone and the mats had been removed. I had been allowed to sleep later than usual. Then I noticed a pair of moccasins next to my bunk. Most of the men went barefoot around the village and moccasins were not suited to slogging around on wet forest trails; this seemed a good sign and I slipped them on.

Squintanasis came through the doorway. "Come," he said.

We walked down the beach for a brief, cold bath. I was then led to the canoe-in-progress and ordered to assist a dark, gnarly man who initially ignored me. The project still resembled half of a big, reddish log that had been stripped of bark, roughly shaped and partially hollowed out. It was hard to imagine the sleek, contoured craft it would become.

"Kekathl show," Squintanasis said, and turned to his tools laid out on a board. Kekathl handed me a bone chisel and club-like wooden hammer and indicated I should start chipping away at the charred area inside the craft. This area had been burned and it was necessary to clear all this away. I had barely begun when Kekathl jerked the tools from my hands to demonstrate the proper angle for the chisel. He then laid the tools in front of me and went back to chipping in another area. His short, stout legs and broad shoulders seemed well suited to crawling around in a hollow log, and his demeanor gave the impression he was not happy to be stuck with such an unqualified assistant.

I worked away for a time, tossing chips overboard, having the occasional coughing fit from the charcoal. I could hear Squintanasis slicing away on the outside with an iron axe that had a short handle, more a hatchet, obviously a specialized tool.

"Talk English words."

I looked up to see Squintanasis with curls of wood in his hair and on his forearms. "You mean now? When I'm working?"

"Work. Talk."

So we did, between my coughing sessions, until interrupted by the woman that had been chased into Tomhak's lodge a few days before. She came running out of the lodge next to where we were working, screaming, her savage man in close pursuit. He overtook her and sent her sprawling with a blow to the back. She threw sand and rocks, kicked wildly up at him as he slashed at her legs with a knife.

Squintanasis and another man ran toward the melee and with the help of a third native pinned the fellow to the ground, but he got a hand loose and grabbed the hair of the man holding an arm. Squintanasis put a knee hard into the man's stomach, which ended it.

But they weren't quite through. They carried the burly fellow to the water and threw him in, much the way I'd gotten a dunking. There were plenty of people around now, so though he came out sputtering the fight had left him. His woman went with a group of women to another lodge.

"Don't get on so good?" I asked as Squintanasis walked up.

"Klayass good warrior," he said. "Good harpoon. No good for woman."

Howessa arrived with some warm food and we sat next to the canoe to eat. I nibbled some fish, washing it down with spring water and a little berry cake. I'd been given water when the others seldom drank anything during meals. I hoped the auburn-haired girl had sent it with Howessa, but I had no reason to think this.

Throughout the village women were at outside looms and fish racks, while the men worked on canoes and other projects. The pit where I had seen shellfish cooking was being cleaned out and a pile of fresh clams sat nearby.

"People of Ozette seem very busy," I said in a mix of Makah and English. "Not so many canoes, you build more. Make weapons."

Squintanasis looked around. "Need make now."

"Work fast to make. Why?"

He didn't answer for a time, until I began to wonder if he understood what I'd said. Kekathl finished eating and climbed back into the canoe.

Squintanasis pointed at the sky and spoke in a mix of our languages: "Cha-batt-a Ha-tortstl." (Great Chief who resides above). "Speak Kakemook. Speak Senequah. Seir (I, me) tomanawos speak me. Say make many boat, many spear. See fire spear. Fight come again."

"Fight? Who do you want to fight?"

Squintanasis pointed out to sea. "Six moons ago hunters go

tooplah." He touched his chest and pointed over the slope. "Seir meet tomanawos high meadow."

I looked up the slope, imagining some distant place of worship.

Squintanasis rose and picked up his axe. "Nittinat come Ozette. Big fight. Kill warriors. Kill women. Children. Take slaves. Canoes.

"Take Nanishum," he continued in a lower voice. "Take Nokish, Sahyoul boy. Koodahk, Senequah small boy. Take slaves." He slowly turned the axe in his hand as if trying to decide what to do with it. "On mountain. Tomanawos say, Look, see wolf. I look, wolf come. Wolf never come for nothing. Tomanawos say, Hear Thunderbird wings. I hear thunder wings. Tomanawos say, Go. Go people."

Muscles along his jaw rippled. "Come high meadow one night, one half day." He shook his head. "Send arrows. Get Nittinat leg. Nanishum try jump out chap-ats (canoe)." He took a short breath. "Next fight, kill many Nittinat. Nanishum come home."

"Who's Nanishum?" I asked.

Squintanasis looked up so sharply I drew back.

"Daughter Chief Tomhak! Daughter Suisha. Nanishum princess." He started to turn away, then looked at me intensely. "Tomanawos say you come. Show Makah. Now work."

He turned to the canoe and vigorously swung the short axe. I climbed aboard and took up my chisel and hammer. The rest of the afternoon we talked English words while I wondered what Squintanasis had meant by "show." He measured words as my dear departed Irish mother counted out coins at the market, and he had mentioned fire spear. They had brought some muskets from the trading session at the Hoh, but I'd not seen any natives carrying one.

In late afternoon two canoes carrying ten natives arrived. About thirty people went to welcome the visitors, including Squintanasis and Kekathl. The arrivals looked and dressed the same as Ozette people, except for one downcast native who wore only a ragged breechcloth and had his wrists bound together. Kakemook appeared and the prisoner was escorted to the chief's lodge. When Squintanasis returned he told me the visitors were Makah from Neeah, their sister village. "The prisoner?" I asked.

"Elwha," he said. "Kill Ozette citizen. Must die."

My place for the evening meal was established next to Squintanasis. This was now beginning to make a little sense. I had been brought here for a purpose different from the other slaves – otherwise why would they have bothered with a wounded, thin slave, even for nominal cost? There was little interest in any of us really, until Squintanasis took my hair and looked into my eyes in a way no one ever had.

After the usual hand cleaning and a ritual thanks to the spirits from Tomhak, a thick seafood stew was served: shellfish, clams, octopus, seaweed, a fine meal to please any palate. There was flat bread too, and I was not encouraged to drag it through whale oil. I waited until near the end to drink water, in accordance with the others. After the meal Squintanasis and I went outside for an English lesson. The sun was just setting and Squintanasis paused to watch two teenage boys wrestle on the beach. One boy, a muscular fellow, got leverage and threw the other so he landed on his back on the sand. Squintanasis yelled something to the boy still standing and he yelled back, waved and grinned.

"Kanek. Chief Senequah first son," Squintanasis said. "Good boy. Strong. Good harpoon like father."

As we walked toward the remains of a beach fire, passing some fish drying racks and boys playing a stick and hoop game, I noticed the two old men who seemed to sit on the same log every night, staring out at the sea. They were just leaving their log. "Why do they sit there every night?" I asked.

"See tomorrow sky," he said. "See tooplah. Tell fishermen."

During our lesson I could not help but admire the speed with which Squintanasis was learning new English words. I could not keep up in learning Makah and practically choked trying to make the throat sounds. His brow would remain furrowed during our lesson, even if it lasted hours. If he was unsure about something he might look off for a few seconds, jaw out, angled arrogantly, but it was simply his mask of concentration. For all his strength and ready appearance, his affect was gentle, yet you knew this could change at any moment.

The next day began the same, the three of us working on the canoe. I noticed the fishermen's canoes were still on the beach, or rocking at their anchorage in shallow water, and thought perhaps the weathermen had said tooplah was going to be rough.

A shout got our attention. Chief Kakemook appeared with a gang of ten stout natives pulling along the naked prisoner by a rope around his neck. This man was made to kneel on the beach as polished clubs beat on wood, drumming an ominous rhythm. Kakemook began to speak, announcing what may have been a list of the man's crimes. Squintanasis and Kekathl put down their tools and walked slowly toward the crowd. I tagged along, glimpsing the kneeled man between the milling natives.

Kakemook raised a spear with a white shaft, then lowered it and drove the broad point into the prisoner's chest. The man made a gurgling sound and the crowd began a chant, something like, *"Go alone, not as a man, go alone to land of dead."*

Kakemook put his foot on the man's shoulder and pushed him back, ripping out the spear. The man lay twitching as his blood ran into the sand and the crowd tightened, their chanting growing more intense.

I turned away and went back to the canoe. In a shady place I sat and stared at the sand fleas jumping between my raised knees. I heard Squintanasis and Kekathl go back to work on the canoe, wood being scraped and chipped. Squintanasis had said he was a murderer. Was their way less humane than a public hanging? Perhaps not, yet it made me think of the ship, darkness and horror, visions of James and my shipmates. When he was drunk my father sometimes spoke of the terrible price of victory, and now I began to see him as the terrible price of survival. After a time I picked up my tools. I didn't look toward the beach.

After Kekathl and I set numerous gouges with our chisels, oil – oolichan or some such he called it – was poured into the fresh slots in the good-smelling wood and set afire. This coincided with our mid-day meal of seal meat and a little left over seafood stew. I could not take more than a few bites. I noticed Squintanasis watching me from time to time, but he left me alone. I was thankful for the work and gradually began to feel better.

In late afternoon a canoe of fishermen approached with one of the paddlers yelling and waving his pointed paddle. Their canoe was riding low in the water and we canoe builders walked down to the shore with some other natives.

Sayhoul had a good catch he wanted to show off. He ate in Tomhak's circle and his family lived in the lodge. I had come to understand he was a top fisherman. His canoe this day was nearly full of the delicious flat fish, shoo-yoult the natives called them, that were taken offshore. On top they were brown and rough, except for the bulging eyes, their underside smooth and white as fresh snow, like a flounder but much larger.

Sayhoul displayed some broken hooks to his audience and complained that fishing had been klooklo, but he could not hold the biggest ones. His hooks were cleverly made - strong wood bent into a hoop, with bone points then lashed into slots carved in the wood to form barbs so the hook would not pull out. A few of the fish weighing the canoe looked to be perhaps fifty pounds, but he indicated there were bigger specimens out there and his gear could not hold them. I examined their lines and found them certainly strong. Below the hooks a grooved rock was lashed to take the line to the bottom. By the look of the stack of coils in the line baskets these fish lived in deep water.

Several women came and the fish were being unloaded. I walked back toward the canoe and stopped at a fire pit with an iron pot hanging over it. Good smells wafted up in the warm air. Lost in thought, I did not notice a woman come near until she reached past me for the pot. She protected her hands with a mat, but as she lifted the pot off its holder the weight caused the mat to slip and her bare hand touched the iron handle. I grabbed the pot handle and helped lift it away from the fire to the ground, and realized she was the slave girl who slept near me.

"Hello," I said. "Me Aidan." She got a new grip on the pot and lifted it. I wondered if she had understood my greeting. "*Me llamo* Ai-dan."

She turned and flashed a smile over her shoulder. "Know," she said in English. "Me Neveah." She hurried away, holding the hot metal away from her body.

"See you this evening," I said, realizing how awkward this sounded. But I certainly enjoyed *seeing* her at bedtime, and hoped tonight I might get there before she and the boy were asleep.

This was not to be, as after the evening meal Squintanasis kept me up late with lessons, and I was too sleepy to care by the time I entered the quiet lodge and crawled under my mats.

They excel in the management of canoes, and are more venturesome, hardy, and ardent in their pursuit of whales, and in going long distances from the land for fish, than any of the neighboring tribes . . . A whaling canoe invariably carries eight men . . .

Chapter 8

In the dark early hours rain beat like a thousand drums on roof boards. Streams dribbled through smoke holes and hissed in the fires. Boards on the roof guided most of the water away from the vents while along the sides of the lodge small rivers gurgled against diverters fashioned from boards and whale bones.

I sat up in the dark and realized there was someone else awake too. Through a narrow space between the mats I watched Suisha bringing a fire up. She wore the yellow sash and unrestrained flaxen-streaked hair flowed over her shoulders. Reflected in firelight were small crisscross scars on her bare upper arms, similar to Squintanasis's arms and legs and most of the men here. I hadn't given it much thought, but realized most Makahs had these scars. As quietly as possible I headed for the door to relieve myself.

"Irish," she said. "Pathl-hukt."

She wanted me to fetch firewood. I added to the river running past the lodge, then made a dash for the woodpile, raised a cover board and pulled a few logs, replaced the board and made the entrance as quickly as possible, but I was already drenched. Suisha muttered, and I heard the words a-whatl-tsuck and beit-la sa-se-tuk-lee, which I recognized as foolish and raincoat.

I could have put on one of the tightly woven mantels that hung near the doorway instead of going out in such a downpour. "Slave often foolish before daylight," I said mostly in Makah. She smiled slightly.

"Get dry," she said. "Come sit."

I put on my day clothes and returned to one of the split sitting logs scattered around Suisha's fire. Her carved ivory ear ornaments moved little as she fiddled with the fire, as ridged as her demeanor. A few women in the village sported small bones in their noses, but other than her ivory ear decorations Suisha had no visible piercings. Finally satisfied with firewood placement, she indicated I should remove my shirt. She looked over the nearly healed side wound, clucked approval, squeezed my bicep. "Irish hau-ouk tah-kah," Irish must eat more, she said.

"I have already gained some weight."

Suisha took my hair, parted it, examined the cut on my scalp. "Klooklo," she said, and leaned back, giving me an overall appraisal.

"Pardon me, but you are not entirely Makah."

She understood well enough to cause her features to harden. "Makah," she said, and turned back to the fire. I decided the wisest course at that moment was to put on a rain mantle and get another load of firewood. On my return I went to my bunk.

My boots were the short, pliable type seamen often wear that can be tied tightly around the ankle, made of oiled leather, with a pattern cut into the soles for better traction on a wet deck. But they were getting thin on the bottom and I was making a repair with some tough hide I'd found next to one of the many storage boxes surrounding my sleeping space when my bunk neighbor, Neveah, rose quietly from sleep.

"Good morning," I said.

She looked up where the rain continued to beat down. "No klooklo," she said.

"Well, not much coming in on us." She looked at the piss bucket and I faced away from her and continued working on my boots. Her modesty in my presence was curious since most women in these close quarters gave it little consideration. She used the bucket and rose immediately, toting it outside.

I looked in on the boy, but he still slept soundly. Neveah returned with the water bucket and the rinsed bucket, hesitated. I turned away again and she hurriedly washed and changed to her day clothes. When I heard her humming I turned back as she reached to unhook the first night mat. She was fairly short and on tiptoes. She got the mat unhooked and I rose to help take down the other three. We rolled them up for the day. At that moment Suisha said something and Neveah went to her. Almost immediately she came back and said, "Suisha want you."

Shisha had some water simmering and she dropped in a few pieces of dried fish. I stood for a time, finally sat where I had before, not sure what she wanted of me. Suisha and Neveah spoke a few words and fell silent, watching the water coming to a boil. Suisha prodded the fish with a wooden spoon and scooped the tendered pieces into one of the long, shallow bowls held by Neveah. The three of us wiped our hands on a moist bark towel and quietly began eating. We were still the only ones up. On a morning like this there was no sense getting up early, not much would be done outside the lodge. Smoke and humidity would get thick enough to slice with a knife, but if you stayed close to the ground it wasn't too bad.

Finished eating, Suisha began speaking in a low voice. I did not understand all the words, but her meaning was clear: It was not wise to suggest any citizen of Ozette was not entirely Makah. Slaves were not Makah, but sometimes a slave was different. Neveah was different because they *knew who she was*, and because she belonged to Suisha.

I was different because I belonged to Squintanasis, and because as a regular slave I wasn't much use. Everyone knew cloud ship men were not much good as slaves. But as long as Squintanasis wanted me I would be klooklo, I would be taken care of. Did I understand?

"Yes," I said. "Thanks. You kind."

In a near whisper Neveah began speaking and I realized she was interpreting what I had said, though I'd tried to say most of the words in Makah. Suisha poked at her fire, a crooked smile on her nice mouth.

She said something and Neveah turned to me. "She say Irish clever tribe."

"Well, not all of us," I said in English. "I'm different."

Neveah blushed and covered her mouth. Suisha looked at her questioningly until Neveah translated. Suisha went back to her fire.

"Maybe Irish tribe crazy too," Suisha said, or something to that effect. I understood well enough to chuckle, which caused Neveah's eyes to get big and Suisha to focus on her fire to hide the grin.

Squintanasis came as I was finishing up the new innersoles for my boots. He said we must go and help someone move, or that was what it sounded like, and I couldn't imagine what it could mean.

Indeed he meant we would help someone move all their belongings from one lodge to another. In the rain. The person changing residence was Hon-she, Klayass's woman. Apparently she was tired of her bear-shirted husband trying to kill her and had found a kinder man two lodges over. I got this in short bits as two other slaves and I, with Squintanasis, hauled heavy boxes of her belongings out of Klayass's lodge while he sat staring fiercely into a fire. I decided Squintanasis was orchestrating this because with him there Klayass was not crazy enough to challenge the operation. The other family spaces were occupied and children crowded round an old man who was telling a story. I recalled being very young and the stories I'd heard at home on such days, stories that evoked wild animals and ghosts and exciting moments of the Revolution, and I wondered if these children were hearing about such things. I had begun re-telling some of these stories myself, and these children wore the same rapt faces as they listened to the old man.

We tied on rain mantles and the good conical hats, but still got wet. My feet were numb. I had removed my boots at the beginning of the task and felt mud mixed with cold sand between disconnected toes. Toward the end the rain stopped and as we carted the last load the sun came out.

As we were moving Honshe's belongings, I noticed a person over against the slope crouched in a meager shelter of two boards held up by sticks. I came to realize this person, wrapped in no more than a couple ragged mats, was an old woman. She made a sound occasionally, nothing intelligible. What I could see of her face was extremely weathered, deep washes gouged out by a flood. A shaman lurked nearby, watching her, walking by and prodding her with the blunt end of his feathered spear, but not making any chant or song nor offering any assistance.

For a meal we went where Squintanasis slept. A row of slaves sat back against the wall and waited while we ate. This was Kakemook's lodge, the main chief, and he looked the part. Although barefoot like most Makahs, he dressed in fur seal shirt with a fringe of what appeared to be otter, seal skin skirt, bear skin vest trimmed in white fur and long, intricate necklaces of tiny carvings, shells and teeth, more elaborate than the ones Squintanasis wore. Bone jewelry impaled his drooping earlobes. The chief and several other men joined us around the cook fire for a meal of whale and various types of shellfish, which is what I stayed with, while extending my feet close to the glowing coals. No crab had been served since I'd arrived, and I wondered why.

After Kakemook and Squintanasis concluded their talk the chief was called away on some business. I asked about Honshe, if Klayass would go after her again.

Squintanasis shook his head. "No allow," he said. Then in a mix of Makah told me Klayass could beat Honshe until she left, and then he could not interfere with her again. Her children would go with her since they were still young, and her family property, and she would no longer be Klayass's woman. We finished, cleaned our hands and went out. Squintanasis looked at the sky, out at dark, choppy swells. Around us natives were cleaning up after the downpour, turning canoes over to drain, scraping out fire pits.

"What if Klayass goes after Honshe's new man?"

Squintanasis gave me a level look. "No allow," he said.

We went to help Kekathl straighten out the canoe-to-be. It was loosely covered but had acquired water that had to be dumped out by carefully rolling the heavy, bulky form on the simple frame that held it. It was too wet to do any burning, so I was sent with Kekathl to one of the lean-tos where lumber was stored. We came back toting a chunk of cedar log that we placed in a V-frame affair that held it steady. Kekathl arranged his tools and went back to his usual posture of ignoring me. Squintanasis was slicing away, shaping the outside of the hull with his short axe. I looked around for something to do.

Nearby Neveah and Suisha's youngest daughter, Winaseek, were uncovering fish drying racks and I walked over to lend a hand. I took an end and Neveah held the other end of a mat as we shook the water off. Not much water had penetrated to the fish and the sun would soon dry them. We exchanged a few looks as she rolled up the mat. As the distance between us grew less Neveah appeared to blush, which surprised me and caused me to feel my unkempt beard. I had removed the hat when the sun came out and knew my hair was a mess. I was determined to wash it properly this day and acquire one of the wooden combs I'd seen both men and women use.

"*Chet-a-pook! Chetapook!*" I looked around to see two boys near the water jumping up and down and pointing out to sea. "Chetapook!" they yelled, and far off I heard a familiar sound, like the roll of a cannon, and beyond the rock islands saw a plume of spray above the swell.

People were running in every direction. I turned to ask Neveah what was going on, but she was gone. Men hurried down to the beach dragging sealskin floats, carrying harpoons and other gear. Squintanasis hurried into Kakemook's lodge. An assembly was taking place on the beach, women and men, the men taking off their clothes, excited children nearby jumping up and down. Squintanasis reappeared with a harpoon and coils of line. He started for the beach, looked in my direction, motioned to follow and started for the group on the beach again. I looked behind me, but no one was there. Squintanasis turned and motioned more emphatically. I hurried after him.

Even before we got there Squintanasis was shedding his clothes and indicated I should do the same. Naked men were being slathered with grease and a woman began slapping some on my back and shoulders. Another woman covered my front and legs. Some of the men were now putting on bearskin vests and hide breechcloths. I looked around hopefully but no clothing was offered. There was a well-worn rain mantle nearby and I grabbed it up. A hat was shoved on my head. At Squintanasis' direction I got in a canoe and we were pushed off. Three bigger canoes were already ahead of us, the first, Chief Senequah's. Each carried eight men paddling as fast as they could. Our smaller canoe carried just two forward paddlers, including Squintanasis, me, and a stern paddler. Squintanasis handed me a short rope and some sheared sealskin. I tied the rope around my waist and hooked the skin under my crotch as I'd seen the others do.

A smack on the shoulder – I turned to accept a rectangular bowl; I was to be the bailer.

I realized we were going after the whale and measured our small craft against waves crashing up the rocky flanks of the shear islands ahead. The shaft of Squintanasis' harpoon extended well past me with the butt wedged in the stern. Two floats were wedged between the thwarts and another ahead of the next man. We were moving well, but the larger crafts in front pulled steadily away.

We passed Dog Island to a chorus of barking and the main swell hit us, the bowsprit surging high. We all wore the conical hats, a procession of dunces paddling madly for the open sea for the purpose of bagging a creature bigger than all of us and our canoes combined.

By the time we cleared the rock islands I was kept busy bailing. There was little wind, but we were in a canoe used by shoreline hunters. We surged up out of troughs with bare inches of freeboard. Salt spray showered us, seawater ran back and forth past my knees. The grease applied to my body kept me reasonably dry and I was working hard enough to stay warm. We kept digging into the next swell with all the power three paddles could deliver.

A blow sounded ahead and I looked up to see Senequah's conical hat with its double crown topping of a chief, then as we rose his whole silhouette, his arm cocked back, hand gripping the fifteen-foot harpoon shaft. He hurled the harpoon, a huge tail, swirl, then line and floats shooting out. Senequah yelled orders until he suddenly fell back as the canoe shot forward. The second canoe, tied to the first, was jerked along at a terrific rate.

The third canoe gave chase and we followed. Soon the first canoes were a mile ahead. Then I couldn't see them anymore and was beginning to lose track of the canoe that had been just ahead. For some time I kept my head bowed against the spray and bailed as fast as I could.

Finally I looked up and saw the third canoe, then the other two, and I realized they had stopped. As we drew near I saw in two canoes men standing, poised with their harpoons, one of them Senequah, the other Klayass.

A harpoon was hurled, a shout, both canoes back-paddling frantically as a huge tail reared up and slammed down, causing men and pieces of wood to go flying. The first canoe sped off again. This happened so fast I wasn't prepared for our canoe lurching forward as everyone began paddling more madly than before.

We approached the wreckage as a man was being pulled into the third hunting canoe. Shattered wood rose on the swell, carved bow piece, men treading water. By my count three were missing, then a diver surfaced. He shook his head and swam toward the hunting canoe. We began pulling men into our craft.

With two extra hands the hunting canoe set after the one still attached to the whale.

We wallowed in the trough of a wave as our four extra passengers positioned themselves as equally as they could in our small craft. Floats were lashed to each side to keep us from foundering. Another bailer took up a bowl ahead of the paddler in front of me and we slowly made a turn toward the land.

Impossible, I thought. In spite of the floats water sloshed over the gunnels as we climbed a wave. With two bailers we could barely keep up with incoming water. It didn't matter that we were running with the swell, we simply had too much load for the small craft. I bailed faster.

Once when I glanced up I thought I saw something. A while later I heard a shout. Two canoes were drawing near. The first one came alongside and the man behind put a hand on my shoulder, stood on a thwart, and with excellent timing jumped into the other canoe. Two others did the same. The next craft came close and the other man jumped in, followed by one of our crew, who was replaced by a sturdy fellow from the other canoe.

The stabilizing floats were brought on board and we turned back out to sea.

I couldn't see anything but endless swells, but Squintanasis seemed to know where we were going. For some time they paddled and I bailed. We crossed a current line with grass and debris, many birds about, our craft pitched about by chop, eventually passed through this into smoother swells coaxing our efforts to became metered, smooth as the endless green hills.

Finally I saw canoes ahead.

We came up on the others as a long fluke raised gracefully in the air. The whale gave a cry like a human sound of intense despair. A chill ran up my spine and caused a buzzing in the back of my head. I was frozen, unable to move. I could not equate it with the cries of dying men that still haunted my dreams, or any other death of my witness. This was the saddest sound I had ever heard.

We stopped and floated with the other canoes. No one did anything. The huge animal drifted next to us, held up by floats. Seagulls cried shrilly overhead, water lapped against cedar.

Finally Senequah raised his paddle and issued an address. I didn't understand much of it, but Thunderbird was evoked, several more names that could have been gods or men, I did not know. All paddles were raised like fingers pointed at the sky, and a phrase repeated by each person. They seemed to be paying their respects. I held up my bailing bowl.

Senequah said something and immediately a man stood with a line in his mouth, the end attached to a slim length of sharpened white wood. He dove and swam down around the barnacled head of the whale, the diver's color changing to bright copper in the blue-green water so full of light. He swam deeper and worked the shaft through the gapping lower lip of the whale's mouth. After what seemed a long time the diver surfaced to get a breath as water ran off his greased back. He handed the line to a person in the canoe and it was passed back so three could pull together to close the great mouth.

The diver went down again and began stiching the mouth shut. He surfaced several times to take air and finally the job was finished.

Lines were attached, floats adjusted, poles inserted in chocks and small sails rigged. We began to tow the huge animal toward shore, a misty dark line to the east. A westerly breeze filled the sails and the paddlers began to sing a chanting rhythm that kept time with their paddles digging in and being pulled back.

I noticed each billowed sail was different, an angle cut, a streak of paint or two, so you could tell, I realized, who was coming from a considerable distance.

Two blackfish whales appeared, bracketing the floating whale and our canoes, and several men yelled greetings at them. The blackfish went down and crossed under us, large quick shadows, came up again and blew spray over us, repeated the maneuver. They made a game of it, changing places, direction, the paddlers shouting encouragement as the huge creatures exploded through the surface in a roil of glistening ebony and glowing white, a giant eye looking right at you, down again and feeling the swell of water under our tiny craft until fear was displaced by a trance-like state of wonder.

The two whales breached clear of the water in front of us and peeled off to the right and left, crashed dramatically into a swell, a final swirl in their dance. Squintanasis turned to exchange words with the paddler behind me. He saw my amazed expression and with a grin said, "O-o-aris klooklo hunt. No shark come."

Relatives? In that moment I could believe anything. Certainly these fleet, toothed whales were superior to any shark in the sea. Yet we were towing an animal they ate too. They could have easily torn the whale apart below the surface, taken what they wanted. I looked back to see if anything had changed, but the great whale followed along as it had, all the floats in place, lines slackening and tightening as we climbed a swell and slid down the other side. The blackfish came back briefly, on either side, disappeared again. But now I believed they were close by, watching, escorting us, and I wondered what would happen if they took the lines and pulled our whale. In the moment it seemed possible.

The sun slid below the horizon, cooling our backs. Bags of drinking water were passed around, a few bites of meat. Two more canoes met us and attached lines to the whale. Several hours into darkness we neared Ozette to the sounds of drums and lights from beach fires. I made out the silhouettes of drummers beating their sticks on lodge roofs. We arrived to a cheering crowd. In the tide's half flood stage we were well short of the beach and many hands came splashing through shallow water to help carry the canoes to their berths.

Sudden sounds of anguish when the names of casualties were announced. Several women fell on their knees, one clutching a baby, children being held by their parents, more people wailing than could be immediate family. Yet I realized all here were immediate to each other, as they were in my home circle of cabins where all shared a neighbor's tragedy. The unfortunate hunters under the great tail had been driven to the depths and were no more.

Yet there was work for the living. Lines were attached to flukes and scores of people helped drag the great animal as high as possible up the rocky, kelp-strewn beach, giving their greatest effort to the rhythm of each wave. People strained on the lines while women wailed in the background. Kakemook's voice rose above all, evoking Thunderbird and wolf and urging each Makah to consult their tomanawos. It was then I realized a tomanawos was a private god or spirit to each person, and he was asking them to beg forgiveness for something; it sounded like they had done something wrong with the whale hunt and must make amends.

The butchering commenced, beginning with a ritualistic removal of choice parts from saddle and hump to be given to the chiefs. A few enfeebled or lame folks stood at the edge of the waves, shouting advice to the workers.

I emulated the natives, rolled in sand, then kneeled in the surf and rinsed off most of the grease with salt water. I trudged to the spring to wash again, rinsing away the salt itch, and drank deeply of the good cool water.

Wearily I entered Tomhak's lodge and scrounged a few bites of fish and seal meat, a handful of berries. I was still hungry but too tired to prepare more food. A baby's happy bubbling caused me to look toward the end of the lodge. A boy was rocking the baby with his toe tugging a line that held a suspended crib, causing the crib to rock back and forth with little effort, as I had seen women weavers do while working. The boy was using a shell knife to smooth a shaft about five feet long; a miniature harpoon to stalk shallow water prey. There were no adults in the lodge, everyone at the whale, even his pregnant mother. Neveah's boy slept under his wool blanket. I slid exhausted under my mats.

Chapter 9

I awoke to birds squawking and screaming so loud I thought they were inside the lodge. No sooner had I raised up to have a bleary look around than Suisha and Howessa arrived to check my bandage. Suisha untied the binding around my waist and as I watched she poured on a little warm water to soften the scab. Howessa peeled the dressing back; bluish places and a little red, but it was seldom painful.

"Klooklo medicine," I said.

Suisha ignored me and slapped on a foul smelling paste, a little more on my scalp. Howessa tied on a smaller bandage. Their hands were cold and both women smelled of salt and whale oil. Suisha's youngest daughter, Winaseek, was back in a corner of their living space. I hadn't noticed her around much lately and wondered if she was ill.

"Maybe Squintanasis come," Suisha said, and they left. This meant I should wait for Squintanasis, but he may not come right away.

I propped a chunk of seal meat over the morning fire and went out to visit the spring. Thin fog slid slowly through the village and the skeleton of the whale appeared like a giant insect emerging from the sea. Dozens of gulls and crows screamed over the carcass. They would pick the bones clean, then perhaps the bones would dry in the sun before being dismantled and put to the many uses I had observed around the village; wedges, clubs, knife handles and weaving needles, even deflectors for rainwater. All along the beach women, including Neveah and Suisha, worked around fires where great chunks of whale blubber dripped oil into troughs and meat roasted. Vertical feathers were sunk into the flesh along the tops of thick chunks of meat, a decoration; so placed at the point of minimum heat they would last until the meat had rendered and was mostly cooked.

On my way to the spring I went by the place where I had seen the old woman seeking shelter under the boards. She was gone, the meager shelter as well. At the spring I washed and brushed my teeth with a spruce root toothbrush I'd fashioned. The natives used various tools for this purpose, some of spruce root like mine, others of wood or dried kelp they first boiled and made into various utensils and lines. I returned to the lodge for my seal meat and brought it with some cold spring water to a log where I could sit and take in the busy scene.

I noticed Neveah's boy staring at me and motioned him to come closer. He was naked except for a small mat wrapped around and fastened near the throat, a mantle many parents used for their children, quick to install and it allowed the limbs to work freely. He accepted some seal meat and leaned against the log next to me. He was a quiet boy, about three years, well made and healthy appearing. I assumed he would grow up a slave since his mother was one. Yet she had a better life than the other slaves. Suisha had said we *know who she is*, and I'd been thinking about this, what it might mean.

I took the boy's hand and we made our way down the beach past high tide line. The ebbing water exposed wet kelp and rocky beach beyond the sand. We waded small tidal pools looking for prey. The boy squealed with delight while trying to catch baby fish and crabs underneath rocks I turned over. After a time I looked up to see his mother coming. I waved and she waved back. When she called his name the boy ran to her on short, chubby legs.

In the afternoon I pulled on moccasins and worked with Squintanasis and Kekathl on the canoe. Two lodges down Chiefs Kakemook and Senequah were giving forth, a crowd around them issuing a sad chant. A masked head decorated with ferns rose and fell, a shaft of feathers, a fist holding a rattle as a shaman worked in the midst of those mourning the hunters who had not come home.

We finished for the day and went to wash at the spring. I asked Squintanasis what Kakemook had meant about asking forgiveness, if that is what he had said.

"No make preparations," Squintanasis said. "Strange time whale come. No clean body, stay in water. Speak tomanawos. Spirits no like. Men die."

After a few steps I inquired about the old woman against the slope the day we were moving Honshe. He pointed up, "Go to Cha-batt-a Ha-tortstl. Head go. Now body go."

"She died?"

Squintanasis spoke with affected patience. "Good Makah long time. Time come die. Be memolose. Make mischief. Be with family spirits."

I did not ask if the shaman had killed her. From Squintanasis' tone I inferred I had already asked too much.

"Build boat, maybe two moons," Squintanasis said, showing off his command of English. We resumed our routine of working on the canoe while I gave English phrases, then a long English lesson after the evening meal. This left no time to get further acquainted with the intriguing Neveah – by the time Squintanasis called an end to the lesson she and the boy were usually asleep. Except for a celebration feast the day after the whale was butchered we had no break in our schedule for over a week. A dozen people came from another village to join in the feast and everyone was expected to eat lots of whale meat. I found the meat not too bad if cooked enough. This was hard to come by as the natives preferred their whale meat barely done, so that night I loaded up on steamed greens the women had prepared, especially nettle stems, which I found delicious.

While people were still eating a group of boys from about ten all the way up to Senequah's son, Kanek, began a game to test their skill with the bow. Two lines formed and a wood hoop about knee high was rolled from one group to the other. A boy would let an arrow at the hoop while it was rolling. I soon understood it was worth more points if the arrow struck the rim rather than going through the circle, no easy feat. Competition got pretty heated, until one side finally won. Kanek urged Squintanasis to give a demonstration with his bow, but he declined. He was at a fire in a game with chiefs Kakemook, Senequah, Tomhak and others, one man hiding something in one of his fast-moving fists while the rest watched intently, trying to keep track of the object.

Another game with the older boys was begun with hoops, but this time lances or harpoons were used, starting about the size of the one I had seen the boy working on while he rocked the baby. Kanek and another boy were bigger and stronger than most of the group, their lances longer and heavier, and they were so superior throwing these through the hoops the others soon tired of the game.

Kakemook gave a speech thanking the whale for the gift of its body, and as various gods were invoked I fell asleep against a beach log. Such placidness was not to go unpunished however, as Howessa woke me with shouts of an event about to take place. In our lodge the woman of the segregated family was in labor.

From my bunk I watched the process, and it was not unlike the way some natives and white women birthed at home. Suisha was warming her hands over the fire and rubbing the woman's belly. As labor became more intense the woman leaned over, grasped a thick board and squatted over a bed of shredded soft cedar. A stick was placed in her mouth and family members held her arms on each side, supporting and moving her slowly up, then helped her press down – her eyes squeezed shut, again and again, face wet and her teeth digging into the stick. Finally the baby was caught in the soft bed of cedar. Suisha cut the umbilical and tied it off. A woman from her family began to bath the baby as others wrapped the new mother in warm blankets, fanning steam at her and using more blankets as the afterbirth drained out. Suisha kept talking to the woman, praising and rubbing the blankets wrapped about her. Finally the cleaned baby was given to the mother and all seemed happy. Tomhak went to the mother and spoke over her and the tiny baby. The smell of birth was in the big lodge. It reminded me of home, of neighbor's homes. I lay back, hoping my thoughts of that far away place would not keep me awake for long.

During periods of rain we adjusted boards on the framework over the canoe and continued working. These folks had a cause to focus on, an enemy, folks to fetch home. But it was unlikely life here ever slowed to the pace of the Oohlnes.

"Damn!" Due to my daydreaming, the bone chisel had skidded and I'd run a thick cedar splinter into my palm. I took hold and pulled it out, watched the blood well up.

"Damn?" Squintanasis's head appeared above the side of the canoe, interested in this new word.

"Doesn't mean anything." I pushed on my palm and blood
flowed.

"Irish say damn."

"It's nothing, a bad word. Mind if I go take care of this?"

"Much English word say nothing. Say person name, go here, say
place, go there. Look person, talk, know who talk. Say what do, person know where."

"We're a damned jabbery lot all right," I said, pain feeding my irritation. "So no teach HBC means Here Before Christ rather than the
damn Hudson Bay Company! No teach No more help than a damn
jiggermast! No teach Bloody *drunk* I was on bloody Boston Common
and don't *give a damn*. And I'll bloody leak all over your damn boat if
you don't give me leave."

Kekathl grunted. Squintanasis looked amused.

"Go Suisha."

In the lodge I looked around for a mat remnant to stanch the
bleeding until I could wash the wound in salt water, which would
sting a bit but stave off infection, then a wash in spring water and
a wrap. Suisha was not there, but Howessa rushed over, a nurse
by calling, then Neveah was there, adding to my embarrassment.
Neveah cleaned the wound in fresh water while Howessa rummaged
in her stash of herbs. They smeared on some familiar dark salve and
wrapped a bandage tight in no time. As I expected, the salve stung
fiercely for a few seconds, then gradually my wound became numb.
My blood had fouled the water bucket, so Neveah set out to replenish
it. Howessa indicated I should lie on my bunk and I willingly took her
suggestion.

It was a warm afternoon and it seemed to me I'd earned a nap. I
could work with the bandage, but such a wound should have a chance

to heal a little before being rushed back to active duty. And by Suisha's own words I was a different sort of slave, perhaps a property worthy of some consideration. These dreamy thoughts were shattered by a scream.

Abruptly I was on my feet. Howessa and I looked at each other.

Another distant scream cut short. Mixed though it was with other sounds of the village, sea birds, surf, the crackle of new wood on a fire – I knew who it was. I bolted out and headed for the spring up on the slope.

They were struggling, the big savage Nootche and Neveah. He had her down on a mossy patch, pinned against a log. She was hitting him as he ripped at her clothes, laughing as he pinned her thrashing legs.

I grabbed a downed limb, brought it hard on the back of his head and it broke to pieces, rotten wood flying. He roared and started to get up. I caught him under the chin with a swift kick, but forgot I was wearing moccasins until pain shot up my leg. The blow knocked him back and he rolled half under the log, but scrambled out and drew a knife. I dodged his slashing knife and made a hobbled jump over the log. He came but lost his balance getting over and I went in with a solid punch that caught him behind an ear. He went down again but was not done. I looked frantically around, grabbed up another limb and smacked it against his forehead as he was trying to gain his feet. The blow knocked him back but the limb shattered – *a sea of rotten limbs!* I got in another blow with the stub – barely dodged his knife.

I retreated to a tree and he came with bloody face, roaring a sort of war cry. We played cat and mouse around the tree. He got hold of my bandaged hand, pulled me to him. I blocked his first lunge but was no match for his great size, knew the next thrust would put the knife in my chest, shut my eyes –

He bellowed, his grip loosened and I pulled away.

Squintanasis had his arm bent up behind his back. "Nootche klark-shitl," he said calmly, twisting the arm tighter. "Kartsop Nootche." Cut Nootche.

The big fellow cried out in pain and his knife fell to the ground.

Squintanasis gave him a hard shove down the slope. Nootche bellowed rage but kept going. Squintanasis came back and confronted me.

"Hit Makah, kill you."

"He's a swine."

He drew his knife and put the point under my chin, our faces close. "Kill you!"

"*Bloody do it then – do it.* If that's the sort you call your own you'd best kill me now, 'cause next time I'll surely kill him if I can."

We stared into each other's eyes a few moments. He leaned back, lowered the knife, turned to watch Neveah gather up her torn skirt, the bucket. She hastily scooped up some water, started down the trail, paused to say something to Squintanasis, continued on.

Squintanasis put the knife away, aimed his jaw into the upper reaches of a fir tree, his thinking pose. He turned and put a hand on my shoulder, slid it down over my bicep. "Nootche hahouk Irish."

"Irish pretty stringy, maybe Irish eat Nootche instead."

He turned away, but I glimpsed a slight smile. "Work boat."

He left me standing there. I wasn't sure, but thought he had decided some new thing. Maybe he'd decided before today. I never for a moment thought Squintanasis would kill me. Until that moment, as I watched him walk away, I had no thought such knowledge was in me. This gave me a start because these were the exact words my mother would say when she told me things while we were alone. I was young then, yet sensed the importance of what she was saying, as if I knew she would soon leave. Clearly I remembered being in the cabin alone that morning, eating breakfast, potatoes and a small, green apple, and looked at the spoon stopped halfway to my mouth. I carefully put the spoon down, jumped up and jerked the heavy door open and ran, ran . . . to the place where my mother had collapsed and the water bucket had spilled and rolled down to the spring pool.

This reminded me of something, other knowledge, and though limited it was something I wanted to speak with Squintanasis about.

I limped down the trail after him.

Whale oil serves the same purpose with these Indians that butter does with civilized people . . . Next to the halibut are the salmon and codfish, and a species called the "cultus" or bastard cod. Mussels of the finest description cover the rocks about Cape Flattery . . .

Chapter 10

"How make?"

"With fire," I said. "But I'm not sure I can do it."

"Have fire. Make."

"I can't just make them. Fire must be small and very hot. Must have iron. Must have tools."

I drew a hook in damp sand, complete with eye and barb. Squintanasis traced above the lines with his finger, seeing the finished fishhook.

"I will probably need some sort of bellows too," I said, feeling uneasy. I had spent a little time in Severson's blacksmith shop in Boston. He liked our family, and Father's home-brewed spirits, and taught me a few things. I thought I could fashion fishhooks from the square iron rods these people had brought back from the Hoh, but my experience at the forge was limited to a few tool repairs, wagon rigging, cleats for my little boat. Could I even create an adequate forge?

"Work boat," Squintanasis said and marched off toward Kakemook's lodge.

As I was assisting Kekathl, Kakemook and Squintanasis went into Tomhak's lodge. Kekathl worked steadily away inside the canoe. He had me cleaning up and fetching tools, a bag of water, small tasks. I knew this was not out of sympathy, rather chores befitting someone that would run a splinter practically through their hand while making simple grooves to hold burning oil.

The cooking fires were being brought up when Squintanasis appeared with a satchel and a handful of iron rods.

"Make," he said.

The satchel contained a wooden mallet – of no use – an iron hammer head that needed only a handle, drivers and pins, two rusty side plates from a pulley block, brass railing trim, a small metal wedge, broken knife blade, spanner, file and an iron Parrell ring. Not enough to outfit a smithy shop, but perhaps enough to get started. "I need a suitable place for a fire," I said. "A small fire, very hot. Bleached driftwood would be best."

Squintanasis led me to a spot between two lodges where a fire pit had been in the past. Part of the framework for a rain shelter remained.

During the evening meal a plate of warm bear meat was put down in front of me. I looked up as Neveah hurried away. If Squintanasis had noticed he gave no sign. But other men in our circle were giving me too much attention; they must have heard about my run-in with Nootche. They had seen Squintanasis and me during the afternoon, knew he wasn't going to punish me, and wondered what we were up to. Questioning looks moved between Squintanasis and Tomhak, who pretended not to notice and called for more berry cake, bringing a sharp reply from Suisha. No matter, Howessa quickly filled her father's request.

The English lesson did not last long that evening. Squintanasis noticed me holding the bandaged hand up and seemed to take pity. The wound had started throbbing, though the pain was perhaps less than I pretended. It had been some time since I'd arrived at my bunk early enough to see nightclothes time, and I had more on my mind than common English words. In the lodge I found the mats already rolled down. Damn.

I pushed a mat aside and there she was, nightshirt in hand, hair flowing behind bare shoulders. Without a stitch she was as beautiful as I knew she would be. Her eyes glowed through smoky shadows and I thought of the golden-skinned dancers who came down to the docks in the city of much light on the Southern Continent. I stared a bit longer than I should have, finally turned away while she put on her nightdress.

When I heard her slip under the blanket I sat on my bunk to get out of my day clothes. I had washed my feet earlier, gingerly dabbing at the swollen right toe, and put moccasins back on, so I was set. Everyone in Tomhak's lodge cleaned up pretty well in the evening. Although some wore oil-soiled and dirty clothes, most washed their bodies daily. Tomhak himself was quite fastidious, a good example of chiefly hygiene and good manners. I wondered if this was something well-groomed Suisha demanded, a price for his randy bent.

The mats felt pleasant this night, softer than usual. I propped up on an elbow and had a look, carefully felt the material; someone had replaced my inner mat with a softer one. Indeed. My slave mind raced. I lay back and elevated my bandaged hand. Sighed, not too loud.

"Aidan have pain?"

"Um? Oh, not much. Did not mean to wake you. Most pain inside head."

"No pain there," she whispered. "Slaves talk you. New slave be with Squintanasis. Go to whale. Have magic."

"Really? And what about your magic of the English words?"

"Ah. Father Spanish man. Teach English, Spanish for Chimakum, my people. Say me know trade, know language. Help people. Teach when small, like Kishkani. Three language my house. Before you, teach Squintanasis English words. But long time, no remember. You come, remember more."

"Where is your father now?"

"Die. Snohomish come, fight, take slaves. Sell me Makah at Neeah."

"How long?"

"Four winters. Maybe my people pay. Go home. Suisha good me. Squintanasis good me. He get Nanishum back."

"What? He get Nanishum?"

She didn't say anything for a few moments and I wondered if she had understood.

"Thank fight me," she whispered. "Sleep now. Ask gods give Aidan good luck. Arbi make good koo-yaks."

Tomorrow make good hooks. We hope. And how did she know about that?

The fire itself was easy since I had cedar curls for tinder and harder wood to use for the base. By the time I had glowing coals the last roof boards had been lashed in place, and none too soon, since rain came hard, big drops beating the boards. The shaping rocks were secured to a length of sun-hardened driftwood log that had been dragged next to the fire and was heavy enough not to move around during hammering.

I had an iron rod in the fire and was fiddling with it, trying to keep it in the hottest pockets of low flame. It took too long to get to workable redness; a concentrated pocket of heat was required. I found Squintanasis at the canoe and gave him a list. It was his turn to look bewildered, but he quickly recovered and went off in search of the materials.

An hour later he delivered what I'd asked for and I set to work making a bellows. It is one thing to know how a bellows works and quite another to make one. After an hour of struggle I borrowed some of Squintanasis's tools. Past midday, he came to check on my progress, finding me sitting in a pile of shavings, struggling with a sealskin float and various cedar boards.

"Make?"

"No. Don't know if I'll ever make the damn thing!"

That evening I did not answer the call for the evening meal. A little later, in the waning light from a rosy sunset, I had something that worked sort of like a bellows. It was made from a small skin float attached to two boards in a wedge shape with deerskin hinges that had a wooden spout on the hinged end. When the top board was raised air was drawn in, and when you pushed it down air was blown out. A slender disc of wood had to be held down to block the main intake while pushing the angle board down in order to force all the air to exit the spout. I heard footsteps and knew who it was.

"Make?" Squintanasis asked.

I looked up at him. "Maybe. We'll know in the morning."

Someone had saved a dish of food for me and placed it near a fire to stay warm. Neveah was scurrying about and refused to look at me. I sat and began eating fresh, broiled fish wrapped in tasty green leaves. Tomhak, Squintanasis and the others had finished their meal and sat in various family areas talking and working on gear.

"Thank you," I said as Neveah hurried past behind me. She did not reply, but Suisha had heard and cast a sly glance my way.

During the evening English lesson I kept correcting myself. I couldn't seem to keep my mind on the task. Finally I nodded off while Squintanasis was repeating a phrase and he called a halt. Neveah and the boy were asleep, and as soon as I was under my mats I joined them.

In the morning I began learning how to use the bellows, blowing air on a pocket of coals. Soon I had red hot, malleable iron. With the iron hammerhead that now sported a new spruce handle, I began working the rod over the stones. At first my motions felt awkward, inefficient. Gradually I became more comfortable with bellows and hammer and the wet mat that served as a glove. Bending and rounding a few inches into the shape of a hook proved fairly easy, the eye a little more difficult. I banged the hot metal around the secured Parrell ring to form the eye. The barb I cut with the old knife blade while the iron was still soft, then gently tapered the end to a sharp point.

My first hook was barely serviceable, the next one a little better, and by afternoon when I'd finished my third hook I was developing a method. Each hook had been quenched in water for added rigidity – this also caused brittleness. I had no experience about the best heat to quench the metal for adequate strength and minimum brittleness. I could only hope to do well enough for the hooks to hold a fish without bending or breaking. I sharpened the points with the file. A few children watched from a distance, two men paused for a time, all drifted away without saying anything. When Squintanasis came to check my progress, I handed him my best hook. He turned it over slowly. Finally he smiled and put a hand on my shoulder.

"Eat now," he said.

I looked around and realized the day was drawing to a close.

During ritual hand washing and then the meal, Tomhak impaled

Squintanasis with expectant looks. The other men in our circle were doing the same, but Squintanasis kept his head down and we continued quietly eating.

The women brought flat bread and a sweet sauce that tasted of honey and a compressed fruit I did not know, and when these treats were being eaten Squintanasis casually drew from his pouch my best hook and handed it across the circle of staring eyes to Tomhak. The third chief held the creation up to be sure all could see. He tested the point and laughed when it drew a drop of blood. He passed the hook to the man on his right, who examined it with quiet mutterings and passed it along. During this examination process Squintanasis continued eating. I sat to his left as usual, trying to be as casual as he was, which was difficult when you could smell contention wafting like wet smoke from the fires. I began to think men of his tribe, these brothers, wanted him to fail. Was it his white blood? Perhaps resentment for his indefinable magnetism and the high regard the chiefs had for him? Maybe I was the cause – the *different* slave who was using up their precious iron.

The hook went to the next circle and was finally claimed by lean, dark Sahyoul, his face an approaching storm, among the best fisherman in the tribe. Squintanasis and Sahyoul exchanged a look, and Squintanasis produced a second hook that he passed along to him. Sahyoul accepted the hook in calloused, scarred fingers. Squintanasis then ignored the expectant looks directed his way and went back to dessert.

At the fire that evening I was a poor teacher, sleepy and distracted.

"Home village many?" Squintanasis asked. "Strong tribe?"

"Yes. Big land. All together many."

"Father chief? Have many slaves?"

"We are not chiefs. My father makes things of stone. Big fire pits.

No slaves where I live." This was true, yet it was not. It was not something I could explain to Squintanasis.

"Big River people say Boston Man have slaves."

"Not Boston Man, but south of us there are slaves. These are like Boston Man. The slave owners I mean. The slaves are Negros." How could I explain?

"Big Chief own slaves?"

"Well, if it's Mr. Jefferson, yes he does. Slaves built his house. Both of them."

Squintanasis studied me, and I realized how this must sound to him. "It is like this land," I continued. "Each tribe has own laws. In Massachusetts – that's the land where Boston is, my tribe – it's against our law to have slaves. But other places not against law."

Squintanasis frowned while using the fire stick to move a log around, finally asked, "Who do slave work your tribe?"

I had to smile at this. "All do same work."

"Have woman there?" he asked.

"No. Well, there was someone. But she's probably with someone else by now, and I don't think she would take me anyway. Her family are like chiefs."

We sat looking into the fire. Squintanasis prodded the log some more and I thought of my brother sitting before our fireplace, poking at the fire, always rearranging. He often insisted I fetch more wood from the pile outside so the box was kept full. He feared cold.

In the morning Sahyoul and the two who always went out with him cast off in their large canoe even before I'd returned from the spring. They were halfway to Dog Island, pointed paddles digging in for a run into the open ocean. The thunder of surf had a deep pitch this morning, the swell high. Perhaps this would hamper their fishing. Birds screamed over the whale skeleton. Pickings had become meager, but for a local feathered group it was their morning ritual.

Squintanasis came and stood next to me. "Build boat," he said.

A little offshore fog. I had been here enough days to expect sun by mid-morning on a day like this. When the brightness did come I put down my scraping tool and looked out to sea for some sign of a sail. It was too soon of course. Around me yellow light illuminated steaming cedar roofs as people busily went about their tasks. Women and girls wove outside the lodges during fair days, some at long mat looms, others working on baskets.

A man and woman arrived at the whale skeleton and began removing selected bones. I recognized the man as Klayass. He was directed by the woman, a robust figure in sealskin skirt and cedar mantle who put the bones into a sling basket. Nearby two young men tested their strength by standing in place, arms locked, trying to dislodge the other's balance. Beyond them a small canoe with three boys set out with their undersized bows in search of whatever they might find. Low waves sparkled among the rocks at low tide, a few women near the water with clam baskets, sea birds drifting overhead, their cries mixing with the screams of small children running over sand and pebbles, playing their own games. If I was to be a slave I could have done worse than landing in this place.

I noticed Squintanasis watching me and quickly looked around, trying to remember what I was doing. With the slightest of smiles he went back to work.

It was late afternoon when shouts brought our heads up. Sahyoul's boat was inside the island and I saw his raised paddle, demanding attention. Squintanasis gave me a serious look before laying his tools on the board and walking toward the water. I could see heads and tails of shoo-yault (halibut) poking up over the gunnels of Sahyoul's canoe, which rode low in the water.

Their craft nosed into sand with Sahyoul chattering excitedly. Two fish I reckoned might weigh a hundred pounds, two more over fifty. Sahyoul was pounding Squintanasis on the back, laughing, waving his arms at other natives gathered around admiring the fish packed into his craft to the point that one more might have swamped it. Squintanasis shoved me, and then other men did, shoving me by the shoulders, but they were happy. The hooks were klooklo, and I laughed with them while silently thanking whatever gods might be listening for the good fishing day.

"Wash hooks fresh water," I said in Makah. "Dry good."

Squintanasis repeated this in correct Makah.

After the meal that evening Squintanasis indicated I should follow him and we walked down the beach past the weathermen sitting on their log, staring out at tooplah.

He asked if the hooks I made would work for the salmon that were coming to the rivers. The first of "their" salmon were due any day, but the biggest type did not spawn in their river that ran from Sweet Water, so they could not be netted or speared. Some fishermen caught the big ones beyond the rock islands, but they were very strong and often broke their bone and wood hooks. They traded with the Quileute who had a good river for big salmon, but it would be klooklo if they could take more of them in the ocean. I knew about salmon of course, which were abundant in my home ocean. "I will have to make smaller ones," I said. "Small," I held my thumb and index as if making a measurement.

Squintanasis shook his head and produced one of the hooks he still had in his pouch. "Klooklo," he said.

"But salmon are smaller. Hook must be smaller."

Squintanasis spread his arms fully and shook his head. "Sam-on."

Well, I was getting it now. These salmon were really big. As we walked along I was already picturing the hooks I would make; they would be slightly narrower but deeper of bend for better leverage.

The salmon I knew were scrappy fish that often jumped high in the air when hooked. There would be sudden yanking and times of slack line so the barb must be high enough to stay in.

"Maybe make harpoon tip too," I said.

Squintanasis stopped. He indicated throwing a harpoon. "Kaithladose?"

I nodded. "For fur seal, yes." I wondered then why I would say such a thing, why I would volunteer to make another tool for them to use when I had never made one before and didn't know the forces involved. I could produce something out of iron, precious iron, and it might fail. Someone could be injured using it and I would be blamed. Squintanasis would also be held responsible.

I shrugged. "Maybe not." I shook my head. "Maybe not klooklo. Maybe break." I pretended to break something over a knee.

Squintanasis straightened and looked around in that stiff way, considering. "Make," he said. "Seir," cocking a thumb at his chest, then pointing at me, "Irish. Make. We go." He made the motion of throwing a harpoon.

Sensing reduced risk, I readily agreed. "We go. We use. We make work. We get seal. Get kaith-la-dose."

"Work," he said. "*We* make *work*. *Get* kaithladose. *Get* karschowee."

"We get them all," I agreed, including his mention of hair seal.

"We *get* chetapook!"

"Whoa." I shook my head. "No chetapook. Not talk about whale yet. Whale maybe too big. Not sure about whale."

"Ah." He continued walking, chin out and head up, thinking large thoughts.

I matched his pace and kept quiet, thinking perhaps I should have done so a little earlier. "I think," I said, "we should do a little fishing. I'd like to get an idea what I'm up against. I'll make some hooks tomorrow and we try them. We fish."

"Spear."

"Let's take this a step at a time," I said carefully. "First I make hooks for your salmon."

"Arbi more hooks," Squintanasis said. "Maybe three days fish. Maybe five days go Sweet Water."

I took this opportunity to shut up.

In the morning I made three more halibut and cod hooks in front of an audience of children and one weathered old man leaning on a bleached walking stick with a natural knob handle in the shape of a horse head. I was gaining a following.

A pleasant surprise when Neveah arrived with lunch. The audience, sensing the show was over for now, dispersed. This was a fine meal of fresh fish, berries and flat bread, with a little bear meat on the side. She even brought a bucket for washing and a skin pouch of drinking water. I insisted she eat something with me, and she went to the lodge for more food, returned to shyly take a seat on the log that held my shaping iron and stones. I moved a short log used as a chair in front of her and sat with my food tray on my lap. She kept her eyes down and chewed without showing her teeth. I was aware of each movement of her round, brown arms extending from the woven cedar shirt, the shape of her ankles and calves. In the bright of day and at such close proximity she seemed as lovely and exotic as in her purely natural form in our dark sleeping quarters. She wore more ear ornaments than usual today, made of small bones and abalone, a tiny curve of copper. Her long, ever-present necklace hung outside her blouse.

"No work today?"

At first she didn't answer, and I realized it was because we were still eating. Even an informal lunch had its rules.

"Maybe soon," she said quietly.

I thought she must mean when the fishing boats came in. She and Howessa cleaned and cut up part of the daily catch to put on the fish racks. I waited until she had finished eating to speak again. "Thank you for such a good meal. I guess my liking bear meat has become a village joke."

She kept her head bowed and I realized she was blushing. "All slaves want now," she whispered.

"What?"

She flashed a brief grin. "Say, Irish eat bear, go Squintanasis, make hooks. Bear magic. We eat bear too."

"Um." I looked at my tray and picked up a morsel, offered it to her. "I saved you a little magic bear."

She giggled and shook her head.

"Boston man eat bear. In our little enclave, where my home is, we usually share when somebody gets one. They eat lots of berries and roots during late summer and fall. People like to drain off the fat to cook other things. Makah don't seem to like bear much."

"No tooplah in bear," she said. "Tooplah best food."

A sudden shout caused us to look down the beach. It was Kanek, running and holding his spear over his head, yelling something like, "*First! Kanek first!*"

People converged on him. Women left their racks and weaving, men left their projects. Neveah got up to go. "What is it?" I asked.

"First salmon," she said over a shoulder and hurried toward the crowd around Kanek. I followed. Suisha arrived, then Kakemook, Squintanasis. As I came closer Kanek went down on a knee and offered his spear to Suisha. I heard him say Winaseek, Suisha's youngest daughter's name.

The chief and Suisha seemed uncertain, while Squintanasis looked vaguely amused. Winaseek was summoned, and a conversation ensued that was much too complicated for me to follow. Neveah moved back from the crowd and tried to answer my questions: "This never happen, not know what do. Kanek get first salmon our river. Now must have ceremony. But Kanek no married. Mother die long time."

"What does it mean?"

"Kanek want Winaseek make ceremony. He want marry her. She almost maiden. Kanek want her, she want him. She want make ceremony for him. But no wife now. Have no stone knife make ceremony. Kanek have no mother make ceremony. Not know what do."

"Surely there must be some qualified person –"

"Chief get first salmon, klooklo. Maybe good fisherman. Sahyoul maybe, he wife know ceremony. But Kanek get first salmon."

Kanek was still on one knee, holding his spear, but now it was Winaseek before him. They looked longingly at each other while the older folks discussed the problem. Finally a decision was reached. Suisha glanced around and motioned to Neveah, who went quickly to her side.

They went into Tomhak's lodge and soon emerged again. Suisha held something wrapped in dark cloth. Suisha, Kanek and Neveah marched off down the beach with an entourage of about twenty people, including Winaseek. Apparently they were off for their river, which emptied into the false bay a brisk half-hour walk from the village.

I went back to work. In the afternoon my audience thinned. The old man came back, leaning into his walking stick, his cheeks like fired mahogany in the light from the dropping sun, and one small boy who didn't seem to have anything else to do. I fashioned two salmon hooks that resembled the picture in my mind, and after quenching I handed one to the old man. He turned it slowly between scarred fingers, hefted it, held the eye up to his eye. Knocked it against a stone. With a slight nod he handed it back. "Kar-tark," he muttered. Hard.

Suisha and the rest came back with Kanek leading the procession. Cradled in his arms was a headless fish opened like a butterfly with flesh the color of blood.

Squintanasis had business with the chiefs that evening so I got to bed early. Through flickering shadows inside our space Neveah whispered what had happened: "Suisha send Kanek, me. Get klooklo ferns close river. Green. Young ferns. Fish lay so look up river. See Kanek, me get good ferns. Suisha clean fish with ferns. Cut with stone knife. Suisha know. Take head, bones. She call gods. Put bones in river. Head look up river, bones where belong. Body come to Makah."

"I saw when the fishermen came in, the fish was roasted and they all ate some."

"Yes. Ceremony done. Now more fish come. Many fish come maybe. Kanek *show who he is.* Chief's son. Maybe get chetapook soon."

"How old is Kanek?"

"Sixteen summers. Chief's son. Marry Winaseek maybe."

"How old is she?"

"Twelve summers. Feel change. Soon maiden. Not eat much so ready for Kanek."

I thought I must have heard incorrectly. "Do you mean she is so smitten she can't eat? What we might call a love fast?"

"Winaseek be small for Kanek."

Could it be that the girls here dieted like Boston girls? Maybe that is why I thought Winaseek was ill. I had noticed all the girls around marrying age appeared quite slim, but they were still growing. Not that there was much obesity in this village. Some stout ones, yes, strong, certainly in better condition than some of my tribe. I extended my hand and she touched my fingers. "Neveah small too," I whispered.

"*Oh.*" She jerked her hand away and hid under the covers.

Chapter 10

I smiled up at the puzzle of drying clothes, flesh, stowed gear and thought about Gretchen, what she might be doing, who she married; I was sure she had, probably my brother's friend, Quinton Chittenden, whose family had the means to help her father avoid financial ruin which would ruin his identity completely. I didn't mind now thinking about the two of them together, it was best for her family. Perhaps best all the way round.

Chapter 11

Swells slammed the rock islands sending sheets of water and foam up the cliffs. The wind came up during the night and she had not yet settled. I paddled hard as we rode up the next moving hill, tipping over the crest and trying to keep the canoe straight for the fast downhill. The craft's flat bottom kept it from digging into the side of a wave and perhaps capsizing, but I wasn't used to the way it slid around. Squintanasis manned the stern, in control. The underwater ridge extending out under the islands caused the swell to rise steeply and soon we got into confused chop that tossed us about. Yet with only two of us aboard we road high and took little water.

Patches of vegetation and other debris floated in twisted strings and curled down through columns of bluish green light. Small fish moved under us, the flash of their scales like many falling coins in the water. Off the bow a swirl and a seal's head appeared. Squintanasis showed him a harpoon he'd brought along and the seal went down.

We baited our new iron hooks with kloo-soob (herring) that were often present in front of the village. The women went out in canoes to scoop them with concave rakes into loose woven baskets. They attached lids and anchored the baskets with stones in front of the village and in the morning the fisherman would pull up the baskets and take as much live bait as they needed for a day's fishing. We had several dozen flopping in a basket of wet sea grass. I hooked my kloosoob through the head and ran the line through so I could sink the point near the tail. I gently swung the fish in a circle, my fingers next to the small rock weight, and let the line go, sending it out about thirty feet from the canoe and playing out another twenty feet of line. Following Squintanasis' actions, I took a loop of line around the shaft of my paddle and we began rowing. We paddled slowly and it gave the bait good motion.

We had covered only a few canoe lengths when the paddle was yanked from my grasp. I grabbed the line and it ripped through my hands. I heard Squintanasis chuckle as the fish changed direction, took more line, then the line went limp and I thought I'd lost the fish – but it abruptly shot out of the water in a mighty silver leap and crashed down with another surge that made line fly out of the line basket. Squintanasis threw a mat remnant at me and I used it to shield my palms as I put pressure on the line to stop the fish. He came out of the water again well off the boat and I glanced in the basket to see only a few coils of line left. At that moment Squintanasis grunted and swung around and I saw his line racing around the paddle shaft.

As I struggled with my fish, gaining a little, feeling his head swing and the weight of him trying to take line back, I glanced at Squintanasis and saw he was playing his fish off the canoe paddle, holding the flat part of the paddle against the gunwale and maintaining the loop around the shaft for leverage as line ran out. His fish jumped but he kept the pressure on and the strong line held and the hook did not break.

He was already working his fish toward the canoe while mine was still well out beyond my floating paddle. Squintanasis led his fish in and as it came close to the boat he picked up a short harpoon with a club-like handle, line attached, and drove it through the fish near the head. After a brief struggle he reached down, gilled the salmon and dragged it over the side into the canoe. He picked up a carved fish club and whacked the fish across the head. The tail curved up in a dying quiver. I kept glancing at the fish, certainly the largest salmon

I'd ever seen, perhaps sixty pounds.

More give and take, blood now dripping from my palm, while Squintanasis calmly went about covering his fish with a wet mat and re-baiting his hook. He tossed his line back out.

"Hook klooklo," he said. He began paddling slowly in the direction of my floating paddle. I was determined now, gaining line as fast as I could, which was not fast, but I felt I was winning. We came along-side my paddle and Squintanasis picked it up, laid it over a thwart.

I had him now, close to the boat. A silvery flash as the fish came grudgingly to the surface. He looked huge, bigger than the one Squintanasis had in the boat. I started to ask him to harpoon my fish, but his line was raking over the paddle shaft again, he had another one on. I grabbed the harpoon in my right hand and tried to pull the fish closer with my left, but he seemed to look right at me and abruptly went into a fast roll, shook his great head and was gone in an angry swirl. I pulled in the line and examined the hook. A small piece of flesh remained on the hook and it was bent slightly, but it hadn't broken.

"Need fish in boat," Squintanasis said casually, deftly stopping another run by the fish he was fighting by using his paddle shaft as a restraint. "No eat in water. Get in boat. Eat home."

"First one practice. Practice is Irish way."

He looked puzzled and I shrugged. He didn't need to learn every word, I would hold some back for moments like this. I bent the hook back using the paddle handle and re-baited. Soon after I took a stroke with the paddle Squintanasis led his fish alongside, deftly harpooned it in the head and pulled it aboard. This one wasn't as big as his first, only about forty pounds.

We headed back to the village with the canoe low in the water. Nine beautiful big salmon crowded us for room. I had managed to boat three, two of them harpooned by Squintanasis. But we were still using the same hooks we'd started with, so although my palms were crisscrossed with line cuts I was relieved.

At the village the men were quietly impressed and the women chattered as they dragged fish out of the canoe and began splitting them. Their flesh was a pale to deep rose. We turned the canoe over and washed out fish slime by lightly rubbing wet sand over the dull red interior.

"No work today," Squintanasis said. We picked up the canoe and stowed it near a lodge. I headed to the spring to clean my damaged hands and slimed clothes. Later, during English lessons that Squintanasis did not consider work, he told me the Quileute would wonder if Makah did not offer seal and shooyoult for the big salmon from their river. This seemed to please him.

For the next week I was kept busy at the forge making fishhooks and spear tips. I also repaired two iron knives and an iron pot handle. Besides the children and old man I had gained a new audience member: Squintanasis arrived with Kanek and told me he would watch my work, maybe sometime I could show Kanek how to work with iron. The second day I let the young man bang some hot iron into a flat shape, but then he inadvertently grabbed the hot end. I sent one of the boys to fetch Howessa or Neveah.

While Howessa was bandaging Kanek's burned hand a commotion got our attention – people down the row of lodges were scattering as Klayass ran through them, jumping over a fire, wild-eyed, bear shirt flapping. We crouched defensively as he huffed past with his new woman, wielding a double-pointed seal harpoon, in hot pursuit. Klayass bellowed – for assistance I presumed – and dodged just in time to avoid being impaled as the woman hurled the harpoon, which sailed past his head and pierced the side of a lodge. Down the way two men and a big woman jumped on her and forced her to ground.

Klayass kept going.

At the forge we searched each other's face, as if seeking an explanation. In my best Makah I said, "Maybe Klayass get klooklo woman."

Kanek burst out laughing.

The next day Kanek returned with his bandaged hand and the rest of the week he came when he wasn't called to some other task. He was an enthusiastic young man and we joked about his mishap as I showed him a little about working iron. I told him I would let him do more soon, but the next day he was summoned for fishing and I didn't see him for a week.

After evening meals Squintanasis and I continued the English lessons and I would add a few more Makah words to my vocabulary, sometimes sitting next to the remains of the forge fire, other times on a bleached log half buried in sand. Two canoes were dispatched to the Hoh village to get more iron. I had requested Squintanasis try to procure more stock, if available.

During an evening meal the following week, low singing began behind a corner of the lodge that had been partitioned off with boards and hanging mats. This was so unusual I began to look around. The men all sat in their usual places, but several young women were missing, including Neveah. Soon Neveah returned and began serving food.

The volume of singing increased and a procession emerged from the enclosed area. One girl had a blanket over her head, perhaps Winaseek. There were two girls in front of her and three behind. They sang loudly and marched outside.

After we had gorged on broiled salmon the women brought fresh cherries. Men began to raise their heads and talk quietly. Squintanasis pulled out a pouch of hooks and handed them to Tomhak.

At the end of the meal, as the washing bowl was being passed around, the third chief began to speak about Squintanasis and his assigned slave. He waved the pouch in our direction, causing me to feel self-conscious, and emphasized – rather loudly – the good things we were doing for Makah. More new hooks would be distributed among the best fishermen. Soon there would be enough shooyoult for the winter season, and more for trade. Tyee (big) salmon were being caught now where they were feeding on the reef. More kwish-hey-tuks (blueback, sockeye salmon) were appearing in their river since the successful ceremony of the First Salmon. Soon hah-did (coho) salmon would arrive at the reef. Much yelling supported Tomhak's words, flexing of muscles, raised fists, knives, fierce looks sent my way. I hid my shaking hands.

That night I lay listening to the singing up at Tomhak's end of the lodge. Winaseek and her friends had returned and were behind the makeshift partition, their young voices rising in a long repertoire to a climax, a pause, beginning again. I waited until it seemed everyone else was asleep and slid the pouch from under my bottom mat. I dug a hole with a sharp stick. When I looked up Neveah was watching. I put a finger to my lips. She imitated my motions, grinned and watched me bury the pouch Squintanasis had given me.

"Maybe memelose come take," she whispered.

"Who?"

"Dead people. Make mischief. Come from ground in night. See you play in dirt, come take."

"They have no use for these," I said. "Squintanasis will make a curse if they fool around with them."

"Big medicine," she whispered, with a slight mocking tone.

The singing stopped for a minute. "Why are all those girls with Winaseek?" I asked. "Where did they go earlier?"

"Wash. Wash many time. First blood come."

Winaseek's first menstrual, as Neveah portended. "How long

does this go on?"

"Go to end," she said. "Now wear dentalium (Haiqua, money shells). Listen for spirit come with maiden songs. Maybe Suisha say, can marry. Maybe spring. Kanek know."

"She is rather pretty."

"Take Kanek," she said quickly. "No take slave."

"Um. Would you?"

"*Oh.*" She quickly disappeared from my view.

Squintanasis hurried us through a cold snack and out into the misty morning where preparations were already underway. Six other people would accompany us to Sweet Water: Four women – including Neveah and another slave, a male slave, and spear-toting Kekathl. He was barefoot, as was Squintanasis and the male slave.

Neveah pushed her conical hat back and let it hang from the chinstrap. She smiled at me and started up the trail. We trudged up the slope and were well up on the flat before we began to feel the sun's heat. The trees changed from wind-ravaged, gray-mossed evergreens along the slopes next to the sea to tall, green-mossed fir and dark spruce, cedar, deciduous trees and many kinds of bushes, some with berries that I knew. Small dark squirrels and smaller chipmunks were everywhere. Squintanasis carried his strung long bow and across his back a quiver full of arrows that extended above his head.

We made good time with light loads. Jays set up a warning from a thick stand of firs and we paused so Squintanasis could check the trail. I took up the pace directly behind Neveah. She looked good walking ahead, her step light and sure.

Several deer bounded from a meadow, but they were quickly gone and Squintanasis did not slacken his pace. We encountered marshy sections and I removed my moccasins. After an hour or more I glimpsed a patch of water through the trees.

Squintinasis held up a hand and we halted. He made an emphatic motion and everyone except me moved immediately into a thick group of trees off the trail. When I caught up, Squintanasis motioned us down, then in a crouch moved away and disappeared into undergrowth. I studied the others hunkered there under tree branches amongst moss humps, trying to understand what was going on. Loads were carefully placed on the ground. Kekathl laid his spear over a downed branch and his fingers rested on the knife in his waistband. Wind hushed through treetops and brought various bird voices from the direction of the lake. Another sound.

Soft footsteps sounded nearby, abruptly glimpses of bodies appeared through the underbrush and trees, coming toward us on the trail. They drew opposite our position, moving past, four men carrying weapons.

The last man suddenly reappeared in a gap between leafy branches. With a shout he covered the dozen yards where we huddled and just as quickly the others were with him, menacing, brandishing club, knives, a musket raised and pointed in our direction.

One spoke words I didn't understand. I glanced at the others in our group, but they seemed frozen in time. The words were repeated, something on the order of *"Gog tok shen."* No one responded. The one who had spoken stepped forward and kicked the male slave under the chin, sending him ass over teakettle into the brush.

Kekathl snarled and jumped up, knife poised. The kicker yelled a response, his knife up and ready – next to him a hammer slammed down with a metallic snap – misfire – and in the same instant the musket holder had an arrow sticking through his neck, part of the feathers buried in his throat. The weapon left his hands and he fell backward with a surprised look. As he was falling another arrow socked into the first man's shoulder and he uttered a cry and went down on a knee. But the arrow was nowhere to be seen – it had gone through and left torn flesh. I grabbed up the fallen native's musket. Kekathl uttered a blood-curdling yell and went for the other two with his knife. They instantly turned and ran. Another war cry as he bounded after them and I ran with him, yelling too, both of us chasing them down the trail like madmen. I knew the musket in my hands would not fire but it felt familiar and made a good club.

A voice stopped Kekathl and I ran into him, ended up sprawled on the ground. Kekathl looked down with brief disgust, muttered something and headed back. Squintanasis stood in the trail with an arrow notched in his bow. We followed him into the brush where the women surrounded the wounded native. All held knives pointed at him as he knelt on the ground, one hand gripping the bloody wound in his shoulder. Kekathl started forward with knife raised, but a word from Squintanasis stopped him.

Squintanasis retrieved the arrow that had pierced the native's shoulder. He came back and very deliberately wiped blood off the arrow on the wounded man's shoulder and neck. He put down his bow and knelt in front of the native. He spoke quietly, was eventually answered, and they had a brief conversation that I did not understand, the language being different from Makah.

Squintanasis said something that sounded final to the wounded man, then rose and moved his head slightly. The native got up holding his wound, hurried to the trail and soon disappeared.

Kekathl glared at Squintanasis and with contempt said *"Quileute shab."* He turned away and spoke harshly to the trees, *"Shabah Quileute."*

I understood shab meant feces. "Enemies?" I asked Squintanasis.

He moved his mouth in a casual way and shrugged, meaning maybe or sometimes. Great, I thought, just a casual encounter with one dead and another wounded, glad it was nothing serious. Squintanasis was looking at the musket in my hands. I offered it to him. He hesitated, indicated I should keep it.

There was no powder in the pan and I wondered about the load. I retrieved a pouch from the dead native and found makings inside. I pulled the ramrod, unloaded and reloaded the musket, put a few grains in the pan and closed it, put the makings back in the pouch and attached it to my waist. Squintanasis had been watching me. He nodded, indicated we should get our packs.

We were soon headed down the trail as if nothing had happened. The dead native was left where he fell. The slave who had been kicked uttered a pitiful groan. The women had stuffed his bloody mouth full of meaty leaves and made him walk between them so he couldn't fall behind. Nothing had been said, but he was in their charge now, to be ministered to while we warriors remained alert for further skirmishes, and I hoped there wouldn't be any.

The lake opened up before us, a large body of water, the far end out of sight beyond the far trees. A dozen teal rose and flew off over a reed bed. Everyone veered off through the brush except Squintanasis and me, and the slave with the damaged mouth who was allowed to rest under a tree. Squintanasis explained that the Quileute would return for their dead tomorrow so we wouldn't be camping. He and I would go hunting while the others gathered what they could. Small, upside-down canoes appeared moving above the underbrush and the women and Kekathl brought them to the lakeshore.

Squintanasis and I headed down a trail that led beyond the north end of the lake. Soon we took a lesser game trail into thick trees and brush.

It felt odd to be walking stealthily behind Squintanasis with a loaded musket in my hands. I thought of home, my father's musket from the war, how he had trained each of us to shoot, Sis too. Father expected my brother and me to bag several deer a year to feed us.

The occasional bear was acceptable, but we had to travel and camp out since the animals seemed to know when it was time to get out of the area. My older brother was the more enthusiastic hunter, so I asked my sister to go with him while I brought home fish and sold or traded the extras I caught. Gradually I learned the shoals and pockets where fish congregated. I liked it out on the water in my little boat.

This musket was similar to the one I'd learned with, though not all that accurate with loose military balls made for rapid fire. At home, Seversen cast tight-fitting balls in his blacksmith shop that were accurate enough for hunting, but this weapon would serve at close range. I imagined how easy it would be to shoot Squintanasis and strike out on my own. With a musket, good knife and extra clothing I could procure food and look for a white settlement, although I didn't have any idea where such a settlement might be other than a long way to the south.

Even while thinking about such options I knew I could not shoot Squintanasis. It was inconceivable. I wondered what it was that made him seem so much more than my owner. Maybe because I sensed things would be worse without him, the way you might regard an estranged family member. This made me wonder about his family; he didn't seem to have a close one.

Squintanasis stopped and gave me a direct look, strange, mystical, as if he knew what I had been thinking, and I felt like a child who's been caught doing something naughty.

"Bokwitch," (deer) he said quietly. "Get." He held up three fingers. He pointed at a thicket within a stand of trees ahead, then a direction for me to flank around to one side.

As quietly as possible I moved to a deep, narrow trail that had been made by the animals that lived in the area, with views of open patches between trees and bush. I settled into a sitting position in the recessed trail and positioned the musket barrel against a knee, left hand under the stock. I added a few grains of powder to the pan, drew the hammer to half-cock and sighted down the long barrel.

Small sounds filtered through the foliage. Time dragged and I wondered if perhaps Squintanasis had been wrong about there being deer in the thicket. Then right in the thick stuff a small branch snapped.

A sharp thonk followed by total eruption in the thicket, deer bounding out everywhere like startled birds, bounding so fast so many ways I couldn't get a bead on anything, bouncing down the trail at terrific speed until they were on top of me and the musket went off with sparks and a boom and I was hit, pinned, trapped down in that slot of a trail by a warm, hairy body; pungent, sweet animal smell. Hooves I could not see thundered past and faded with the distant crack of breaking branches.

I lay there for a time, a feeling of relative safety, and finally struggled out from beneath the deer's body. I looked up at Squintanasis standing nearby. He moved his mouth in that inconsequential way. Then he looked around as if to avoid embarrassing me further with that look of his, as if he were having pity on me.

We hauled the two deer Squintanasis had downed out of the thicket and bled the three animals by cutting a slit in the throat, then positioning their hindquarters uphill. He gave me his good iron knife and went to get the women and Kekathl. I began gutting the deer I had shot. They were not large animals and I thought we should be able to carry them back to the village in one trip. The others soon arrived. The women put down their loads of cattails and reeds. Neveah put her hand over mine and I looked into her dark amber eyes. She smiled slightly and I relinquished my grip on the animal's leg. This was woman's work.

I returned Squintanasis's knife and followed him to the main trail along the west side of the lake. We settled down in some lush ferns a few yards off the trail.

"Quileute come, fire spear," he said in a near whisper, speaking to me in his usual mix of Makah and English.

"Do you think those three will come back?" I asked.

pounds but the weight caused my bare feet to sink into the ground and they didn't want to come out again.

After a mile or so a slave woman ahead of Neveah tripped, her load of grass tumbled over her and she was tangled in the harness. Neveah went to her and I loosed my load to lend a hand. We got her upright and I helped Neveah regain her load high on her back. As I struggled with my own load she moved in back of me and pushed the deer high up for best leverage.

Another mile and I had to rest, leaning against a tree and slowly sliding down, spent. Squintanasis said something and the others rested also. Certainly they were tired, yet I knew they would not have stopped if I hadn't. Such endurance! Squintanasis carried both his bow and the musket, which he now attempted to hand over to me. When I refused he looked surprised.

"Women cut and take," he said, indicating my load.

He was going to have the women carry my load!

I struggled to my feet. We continued on. The smell of heavy salt air renewed my strength. By the time water came into view my shoulders ached to the point of numbness and my legs were driven forward by force of will. At the village I fell in a pile next to Tomhak's lodge. Two natives peeled the bundled deer off my back and I just lay there, a cheek on cool, sandy ground. A sand flea hit my eyelash and I just blinked. The sonund of surf had never been so realxing.

A hand slid under my neck and began to lift. Neveah. She held a ladle of water to my mouth, which I eagerly accepted. As I struggled to sit higher her hand pressed my bearded cheek and she pulled back slightly. But then she purposely touched my beard again and moved the back of her hand over whiskers until she was smiling. I took her wrist and moved the back of her hand to my mouth and kissed it. She recoiled, relaxed, so I did it again. A blush rose on her cheeks and she jumped up and ran away.

Bird spears are made of three prongs of different lenghts, barbed, and fastened to a pole ten or twelve feet long. This spear is used at night, when the natives go in a canoe with fire to attract the birds. The manufacture of whaling implements is confined to individuals who dispose of them to the others and are peculiarly expert...

Chapter 12

"Traders home," Squintanasis called from the lodge entry, abruptly ending a rare afternoon nap.

As I trudged barefoot down the beach in his wake, he flung an arm in the air and yelled in that Makah way when they wanted everyone's attention. Two canoes were making their way through the rocky south channel near Dog Island.

The traders brought a variety of iron and copper materials acquired from the Hoh, and a little iron they got from the Quileute, along with boxes of red and white clay; these would be mixed with oil and perhaps chewed salmon eggs to make body paint. From overheard pieces of conversation I'd learned that paint recipes varied somewhat from family to family and all cosmetics were taken seriously. Squintanasis passed objects to me for inspection as we helped unload the canoes. The flat metal pieces formed shapes in my mind, and they had more metal rods too, and some brass. Brass resisted corrosion and might work better for arrowheads used around seawater; perhaps I could make a form for them out of iron. Kanek arrived and showed great interest in these new items for the forge.

As I stood on the beach among a group of Makah men and a chief's son, it felt as if we were engaged as equals unloading the canoe and discussing the possibilities. Yet this was based entirely on Squintanasis's regard for me, which stretched like an invisible thread through the village. Knowing this kept me alert for any sign I should pull back. It is a short distance from warming yourself at a fire to getting burned.

Squintanasis was talking about our encounter with the Quileute men at the lake. The traders confirmed that the hunting party had arrived home bedraggled, full of rage, and the Quileute chief had been upset. The wounded man had been shown no sympathy. The chief was not happy with the uncalled-for aggression while Makah were in their village for trade. The traders did not think anything would be done about the man who had been killed. To show his good faith the chief added several metal pieces to the trade.

During the evening meal I stole glances at Neveah over in her circle. She was aware of my attention, yet politely kept her head down. But she noticed.

"Irish eat many," Squintanasis said in a low voice, speaking English.

"Hahouk for yesterday's hunt," I answered.

After a two-hour English lesson Squintanasis became quiet for a time. He looked out across the placid swells to the long island where wool dogs occasionally howled, sea birds circled, dove, paddled and cried in their languages. Crows still scavenged the beach at the end of this long summer day. Several dozen puffins foraged in the shallows, their orange and red beaks bobbing ahead of black bodies. James had called them web-footed parrots, and tried to squawk like a parrot. Back home Sis would be preparing food about now, dipping a spoon in a pot on our good iron stove and tasting like mother did. Or she might have the big pot hung in the fireplace full of venison stew. Her bread would be to one side, warm enough to emit a new-bread smell. Father and brother Michael would be coming home and smell the food as they opened the door. Maybe they'd been building a fireplace together. There was plenty of mason work if you were willing to trade labor for goods instead of coin. But Father was called for cash jobs too, and by now my brother would be skilled enough to go alone when Father was into the spirits. I didn't like being around him then. The subject of my mother's waning health always seemed to come up, how she was never as strong after I came.

Crimson rays angled up from a clear horizon promising a good day tomorrow. The weathermen had already left their log for the night.

"Sooeni, mother," Squintanasis said. "Father's people bring death." He paused. "Come cloud ship," he continued. "Much trade. Iron. Cop-per. Beads. Long knife."

I guessed Squintanasis had been thinking when I had asked regarding his father and now decided to answer. His story unfolded in the mix of language that passed between us. This is what he told me happened twenty-six early winters ago at a time when the moon is large and wolf speaks every night saying whale and fur seal will soon come:

A ship wallowed into the lee of Dog Island after a storm had lashed the coast for several days. Looking where Squintanasis pointed, I thought it a miracle a sailing ship had navigated between the rocks, and I was told this was the only cloud ship to ever come to this village. There was damage to the sails and masts, and from shore the men moving on deck looked haggard and strange. It was a huge vessel to the natives watching from the village, yet in their sister village Neeah ships had come before with strange men that had wonderful trade goods, such as blankets and iron knives, and more stories came from people of the far north who knew of these cloud ships from long ago. This appeared to be an exceptional opportunity for the people of Ozette and they sent out canoes to welcome the strangers and invite trade.

The tall, bearded strangers had much to trade and wanted fur, but not just any fur, they wanted sea otter. A crude communication was worked out and goods began flowing back and forth. On the second day the crew was invited ashore for a celebration in their honor. The captain and eight crewmen attended, bringing with them a smelly liquid that burned the tongue and caused frightening dreamshapes while awake. They also brought another new thing that at first was invisible.

Competition for the wonderful goods the white men brought caused jealousy among the chiefs. When they ran out of otter they traded their best fur seal mantles, and what they had in mink, fox, even rare lynx and some tailored bear fur used in rituals. Then they brought intricate watertight baskets and conical hats and blankets made from the softened inner bark of cedar trees. When the men from the ship tired of these the chiefs offered slave women. A boastful warrior without young female slaves offered his thirteen-year-old daughter, Sooeni.

The next day the seamen returned to the ship and that night a driving rain rode in on a howling westerly and the first person, a young slave girl, became sick. The next day two more people fell ill. In three more days the virus had spread through the village. People were dying. This combined with the relentless, violent storm was taken as a sign that Thunderbird and tooplah were angry. The Tyee Chief, O'lachnish, uncle to Kakemook, called a meeting of all tribal leaders healthy enough to attend. The men conferred across low fires as coughing and death rattles echoed against pounding surf. The leaders agreed: This cloud ship must have been sent by angry gods. They must act quickly to save as many people as they could.

An hour before dawn, during low tide, thirty warriors carried canoes down the beach and eased them into shallow water.

The sleepy seaman on watch made a sound as he died. Men came from below and fired muskets point blank. The battle raged on the dark deck. The fight was intense and soon over. As Squintanasis told this part I felt a shiver up my spine and clearly saw and heard the fight in the dark.

The bodies of white and red alike were piled on deck and the ship set ablaze. One of the dead was Sooeni's father.

People of the village gathered on the beach to bear silent witness to the burning ship. Some, too sick to walk, were carried out wrapped in blankets. After the returning warriors joined their families, mourning songs filled the night.

In a few weeks the burial trees above the village could hold no more bodies. There were not enough healthy strong men left to dig graves. The last old canoe that could be used for high burials carried O'lachnook's son. Three days later the chief died. In desperation the dead were piled into a lodge and it was set ablaze. Another week passed and bodies were dragged down to the edge of the surf at low tide and offered to tooplah. Such sacrilege caused the men to cut themselves and women to wail all day and all night. Sooeni wailed for her mother, who had succumbed to the sickness.

After the moon came around again the dying stopped.

A hard winter set in. Snow and ice. Hunger. In front of the village tooplah still held a bounty of food and in the forest above roamed elk and deer. But the men who were able did not hunt. They sat in lodges staring into empty cooking fires while dispirited women scavenged the beach. Tribal members and kin to the north could have helped, but feared the spirit wrath that struck down people like grass before a blaze.

Squintanasis said relatives watched as one man ran into the sea and swam straight out until exhausted. Winter storms ruined two carelessly secured canoes and most of the wool dogs were killed for food.

In the spring following this time Sooeni bore a child. She was one of those who had not been affected by the invisible wrath. The new chief, Kakemook, came to the family's lodge to see this first child to come to them since the terrible curse. When Kakemook saw the newborn he turned and spit twice into the fire. With contempt the chief gave the baby its name. He said, Squintanasis, which that night I learned means white baby.

When Squintanasis was six years old his mother died.

Sand fleas jumped around my moccasins and out on dark Dog Island a few gulls screeched at each other as they settled in for the night. The last bloody light along the horizon silhouetted few figures on the beach. One of them was Squintanasis, walking along the edge of gentle surf. Every day of his life, I realized, his name reminded everyone of the terrible disease that had wiped out half the village.

I got up and hurried into Tomhak's lodge. Using a sharp stick I dug into the dirt under my mat and took out several objects hidden in the buried pouch.

When I caught up with Squintanasis on the beach he barely acknowledged me, just kept walking slowly along. I tripped over a piece of driftwood. Squintanasis took no notice. I held out three brass objects.

He stopped and looked at my open palm.

"The bigger one is for a seal spear," I said. "The other two are for you to try on your arrows."

Squintanasis picked an arrowhead out of my palm and held it up so it silhouetted against what little light was being reflected from sand and clouds. He turned it slowly back and forth, hefted it, judging its weight. He did the same with the spearhead. Finally he nodded and brought out a pouch, dropped the items inside.

"Klooklo," he said. He walked away, paused and looked back at me.

"Talk tomanawos," he said. I watched him walk slowly up the beach, carrying the guilt for a crime he had nothing to do with.

Songs of the Makahs are in great variety, and vary from that of the mother lulling her infant to sleep, to the barboarous war cries and discordant "medicine" refrains . . .

Chapter 13

In the morning Squintanasis prepared to lead a group of ten well-armed men and several women up the slope, headed back to the lake. Several of the men were slaves. In a mix of English and Makah, I questioned him about the need for such caution when the traders had said the Quileute chief assured them the previous conflict was unsanctioned and there would be no reprisal.

Squintanasis held one end of his bow against a foot to string it. He swung a full quiver of arrows over a shoulder. "Chief Quartzehet good chief," he said. "Many good trade. Speak truth most time." He gave me a small smile.

Kekathl was there at the edge of the group, looking hopeful, two spears clenched in one fist. After they left he headed dejectedly toward the unfinished canoe. I went into the lodge for a burning stick to start the fire in the forge. The fire was almost right when a native brought new iron materials and laid them on the sandy ground under the shelter of the roof boards. That's when I noticed the spanner was missing. I didn't use it for its original purpose, but, lacking a forceps, it was handy to steady the iron rods in the notch of a rock while I beat them into shape. I looked all around but the tool was gone. I scavenged the littered beach until I found a forked stick that would serve the purpose.

About mid-morning rain began to fall, but it didn't reach the fire and only the occasional gust let some moisture reach my back as I worked.

The hunters did not come back for three days. It felt odd to be eating in the circle of men without Squintanasis there. No one paid me much mind and I enjoyed gorging on fresh red salmon and stealing looks at Neveah, hoping for some reaction.

I had made a half dozen iron spear tips and turned most of them over to Tomhak, who made his usual show of passing them around for inspection before doling them out to favored harpooners. I held back the two best ones for Squintanasis.

On the second day at the forge children and the old man began to move back and a shadow fell on my working space. I looked around to see Chief Senequah standing there, copper and blue bead earrings, open bear skin vest exposing a broad chest and intricate necklace. He reached down and plucked a spear tip off the flat stone I used for a table. After a careful examination he picked up another and put them in a pouch at his waist. He gave me an approving nod and walked away. This was the closest the second chief had come to speaking to me.

During our meal on the second evening without Squintanasis there was talk in the circle of an upcoming ceremony, something to do with wolves. This would occur after the salmon and before the fur seal came. Many words new to me were said and there seemed to be much planning involved. It seemed the ceremony would not be held here but at Neeah, a half-day's canoe journey up the coast. One of the men left and came back with a new type of body paint, which the others showed great interest in.

Without the evening English lessons I got to watch Neveah prepare for bed every night, a guilty pleasure perhaps, but that made it the better. She would look the other way while holding her necklace and whispering some prayer, then undress and pull on her sleeping garment. She would then turn and catch me looking at her, a flash of white teeth before she slid into her bed. This had become our little game and I looked forward to it all day.

That night I told her about the missing spanner.

"Maybe talk slaves," she said.

"A slave would have no use for a spanner. Maybe it was one of the boys."

"How look?"

With a stick I drew the outline on the hard dirt floor. "I don't want any of the boys to get in trouble," I said. "It is not very important."

Her look remained serious. "I get. No tell chiefs."

"No, of course not." I asked her about the festival at Neeah.

"We go kwar-te-puthl, maybe more," she said, and continued in a mix of Makah and English. "Help make Klukwalle. Big medicine."

"October? That's three months, unless I've totally lost track of time. It must be important to be planning already. What's a Klukwalle?"

"Most big wolf ceremony. No Klukwalle Ozette now. Those go be at Neeah. Sad time Ozette. Many dead from Nittinat so go Neeah this time. Suisha say Irish, Neveah go help."

"I'm really quite busy here."

Neveah reached and patted my head. "Suisha say, you go." Then very quietly, "Maybe work together Klukwalle."

I looked up but she was hiding under her mat. "Since you put it that way," I said, and heard her muffled giggle.

The next day wasn't all spear tips and fishhooks. My audience of children was growing, boys mostly, though an occasional girl stopped to watch, and the old man with the walking stick usually arrived about mid-morning. The children were fascinated to see hot metal shaped into something usable, and as a lark I made one of them a copper bracelet, using narrow flat strips I'd cut hot with the knife blade, fusing the ends and quenching. It wasn't much, but went over so big I had to make several more and promise more for the next day. As I was trying to get back to my regular work, the children, there were more than ten at that point, were chattering away and crowding in so close I feared burning one of them as I banged away with the hammer.

I told them I must be alone to do some work then, but tomorrow I would make a few more bracelets. I moved my arm in an arc over them, in the style of Kakemook when he was being profound, and whispered gravely, "Klooklo."

They jumped up and down in a kind of cheering way and I had to laugh.

And then Nootche appeared, a stinking hulk. He said something like a curse in Makah. I had only glimpsed him around the village recently, but apparently our skirmish had been eating at him. I turned back to my work. He kicked me in the back and I went off balance, almost upsetting the forge. Instinctively I swung around with a length of flatiron, barely missing his face with the hot end. He pulled a knife and moved in. To my surprise the children started throwing rocks at him and yelling. The giant kicked at them, connecting with a boy about eight who went flying.

In a rage I slammed the hot iron against his shoulder hard enough to knock him to a knee. He lashed out with the knife, cutting through the hide trousers. I connected with the side of his neck and kept hitting him with the hot iron until he was lying on the sand, bleeding from his head. I resisted the urge to finish him for sure and threw the iron down. Besides the children an audience had gathered. Their look was stark; a slave had struck a tribal member in plain view.

I backed up a step. My first thought was that this could be it, something so quick and simple would result in them killing me. The boy who had been kicked was still sitting on the ground, holding his stomach. I picked him up and took him into Tomhak's lodge. Several natives followed me inside.

Tomhak was working on a spear. When he saw me with the boy in my arms and the people fanning out around me he stood slowly. His broad face etched into serious dark lines.

I laid the boy down on a bunk and approached the chief. I told him as best I could in Makah what had happened. He put the spear down and spoke to one of the people near me. The native stepped forward and began giving his version of what he had seen. About then children piled through the doorway and flowed around us, all talking at once.

"E-yahh!" Tomhak commanded. Everyone fell silent. He strode forward and the group parted. He went to the injured boy and spoke quietly with Suisha and another woman who were ministering to him.

We followed the chief outside to Nootche. Tomhak went down on a knee and put a hand to the side of Nootche's neck. Grains of sand fell from a fluttering eyelash. The chief pushed Nootche over on his back, looked around and gave an order to a youngster, sending him off at a run.

The children began chattering at Tomhak and he seemed to be half listening. He studied me a few moments, his usually placid face a complex of uncertainty. He pointed at his lodge and grunted an order for me to go there. I told the nearest native to get all the iron under cover and walked toward the lodge.

Neveah came running toward me, trailed by Howessa. She stopped a dozen feet away, looking past me at Nootche lying on the sand like a slain walrus, a crowd gathered around.

"He wanted to continue our talk," I said in English.

Her lips formed a firm line and she hurried past me.

Without looking back I continued to the lodge. I sat on my bunk and worked on a new version of a spruce root toothbrush I'd started the day before. Something would have to be done about me, I knew. It seemed no one liked Nootche, but I had learned he was son to a cousin of Chief Kakemook. Swine or not, he was family and I wasn't. Now the chiefs were in an uncomfortable position. I had become more valuable since activating the forge, but still, I was a ko-thlo (slave) who had attacked a citizen in full view of half the village.

Tomhak came in with two large men in tow. One of the fellows put a stool down in front of me and the chief sat with his men flanking him. Neveah entered and kneeled next to the chief, her face pale, not looking at me. Chief Kakemook appeared in the doorway, filling it. Two more men followed him in and another log stool was put next to Tomhak's. Kakemook sat.

Neveah looked very frightened, holding her gaze at Tomhak's calloused feet.

"Strike citizen," Tomhak said. I understood, but Neveah translated in English. They wanted to be clear about whatever they had in mind for me.

"Slaves killed for this."

Neveah uttered a halting translation. I remained silent, looking into Tomhak's dark eyes, aware of Kakemook's stare boring into me.

"Told Nootche try kill you," Tomhak continued, a weariness creeping onto his voice. "Boy hurt, Yawkaduk's boy, good boy, maybe throw harpoon." He paused with a slight shake of his shaggy head. "Nootche not good. Not good Makah. But law broken . . ." he glanced at his cousin sitting next to him while Neveah translated.

"You not make trouble," Chief Kakemook said, picking up his cue. "Make hook. Make boat." He raised an arm, brought his hand down to a meaty knee. "Good has come from you. We know. Go Squintanasis. Squintanasis decide punishment."

Tomhak nodded agreement, looking relieved.

With that the chiefs rose and left with all the people who had followed them in. I sat there for a time. Neveah and I blinked at each other. "So?" I said.

She tried a nervous smile. "You stay here for Squintanasis come. Stay in lodge."

"That seems fair," I said. "Will you stay with me? We could get under the mats together."

"No!" She came part way to her feet, then caught herself. "You tease!" she accused in Makah. "Kakemook maybe kill you. Squintanasis maybe kill you."

"Squintanasis won't kill me."

"No know! You beat Makah."

"Twice," I said. "Well, Squintanasis helped the first time."

"He beat. Cut you. Makah law."

"I trust him."

She stared at me. "Will you dress my wound?" I said.

Neveah huffed and looked away. I reached and touched her arm. She grabbed my hand and squeezed it, briefly put it to her cheek, then jumped up and ran for the door.

"Hey!"

She stopped but did not turn, head cocked slightly, a heel off the ground and the fingers of one hand splayed.

"Thanks," I said.

She went out quickly, leaving the door flap swinging. I found a small woven cloth and tied it around my leg. The cut was not very deep.

Chief Tomhak came in a while later and I asked permission to continue my work at the forge. He struggled with this a few moments, finally waved a hand, indicating I should go back to my task.

My audience of children was waiting.

And there, lying on my working log, lay the spanner. I held it up and looked questioningly at my audience. One boy stepped forward. "Slave Docka bring," he said, and pointed behind him down the beach. "Run that way."

I looked at the spanner, back at the boy. "Why did he run?"

"Docka say, too many medicine. Beat Makah, still alive. Irish have too many medicine. Docka don't want so many."

Well, Docka might be right – I did seem to be treading the outer limits of slavedom.

During the evening meal I felt calmly detached. I wasn't on the usual edge when Squintanasis wasn't nearby, even with reprisal looming. I hadn't completed a single fishhook or spear tip that afternoon, but Tomhak sported a new armband made from four strands of woven copper, Howessa had a new copper anklet, children were running all over the village showing off their copper bracelets. Bracelets and fishhooks, throw in a few spear tips and arrowheads and I might survive my transgression yet. Squintanasis was bound to punish me, but I was ready for whatever he had to do.

That night I let the partitions down as if I had been doing it every right. Neveah would notice that I had taken her little task. She always went out and cleaned herself last thing before getting into bed. I was sleepy, but determined to stay awake until she turned in. When she brought Kishkani inside our space I called him over and pushed a copper bracelet over his small wrist. He seemed puzzled at first, then wide-eyed, then gave me a clumsy hug and jumped up and down, holding his wrist high.

"Ho-she-ark-shis," Neveah said.

"You're welcome. I will make one for you tomorrow."

She smiled, shook her head.

I understood: Children and chiefs were one thing, but it would not be acceptable to make her a bracelet when I hadn't made them for all the citizens.

"Docka give property?"

"Yes," I said. "All klooklo."

Neveah got the boy settled in, glanced my way, turned her back to me and slowly pulled her loose dress over her head exposing trim legs, buttocks and back. She took her time slipping into a pullover of soft bark, taking our game a little further. She shook her head, fluffing shimmering hair that now fell to her back. The nightdress did not extend quite to her knees. That night I fell in love with the back of a woman's knees, so smooth and well designed, so feminine.

She slipped into bed and turned her face toward me, a gentle smile. Her features dimmed and glowed from firelight glancing off the mats. She started to pull back and I whispered, "Don't go yet."

She wasn't smiling now, waiting for me to say something and suddenly I was frantic. I couldn't just say what I was thinking.

"You're very pretty."

She did not move or reply. I wondered if she understood. "You beautiful."

For a few moments she did not respond. Then a hand appeared and extended toward me. I reached out and she held my fingers. Her small hand was strong and moist from the oil she used at night. She just held my fingers, not moving. Finally she let go and disappeared into her mats.

I lay back and gazed around in the gloom where meat and clothes hung. This place was quite cozy really, once you got used to the smells, night sounds of wild men, wolf howls from the hills. Wind gusted and rain increased, blowing fresh through wall cracks, whistling out roof vents and drawing curling wisps up from low fires. Stray drops hit my cheek and arm. Just a squall, I thought, it won't last.

"Aidan not sleep so good now."

"Wa-shél-lie (west wind) bring rain," she whispered back. "No wolf speak. Aidan sleep klooklo."

"I rather like the wolves to speak. We don't often hear them back home." I'd only seen wolves once, a group of three running up a snowy hillside, the one out front in a rocking chair gate to break trail. I watched and at the crest they stopped and looked back. All three looked right at me as if they knew I was there all along, though I was being quite still. As we watched each other I wondered what it would be like to be close to one. As close as Neveah and I at this moment.

Chapter 14

The heavy rain passed and the sun came early. Vapor rose from wet lodges and canoes turned upside down to drain. I assisted two other slaves retrenching around Tomhak's lodge, smallish fellows sporting a few streaks of paint and dotted tattoos. They seemed to look to me for guidance in our task, which struck me as amusing. The fire pit also needed cleaning before I could begin work at the forge.

I was at the forge in late afternoon when a few hoots from men working on canoes greeted the hunting party marching down the slope, bent under big loads. A gutted black bear with its feet tied together over a pole was carried on the shoulders of two stout men. There were several more men with deer weighing them down, and women packing high bundles of long water grass and reeds for weaving, baskets of fresh berries, tubers, bunches of nettle stems. They told the gathering audience more reeds and grasses were bundled near the lake to be picked up later, and more meat. Squintanasis announced there would be a celebration in two nights and they would dress the bear.

I waved to him from the forge and he raised a hand. Tomhak took him aside. I went back to work. Before long the children moved back a little, signaling his approach. I put down my hammer, took a breath, turned and faced Squintanasis.

He motioned with his head and began walking. I caught up with him and we walked down the beach. Surf matched the rhythm of our leisurely pace.

"Punish."

"Yes."

"Tomorrow. Blueberry meadow."

He wasn't going to do it in front of the village. Who else would be there?

"Nootche hurt boy. Go Neeah. No more Nootche."

We stopped. Squintanasis aimed his chin up the slope, scanned the beach with sharp eyes that eventually came to rest looking into mine. "Nootche no good," he said in English. "Any other must kill you."

"Your English getting klooklo," I said.

His eyes brightened fiercely and he turned away.

In our beds that night Neveah extended her hand again and I took it. "After go with Squintanasis come here," she said. " I get medicine."

Before first light I lay listening to an unusual stillness. The last wolf voice had drifted away. No bird sounds yet, they were waiting for the first dim light. Surf thundered as if far away. It would be a fine day.

We made our way up the slope, moving through a gossamer veil swirling around mossy limbs. Animals moved at the edge of visibility and squirrels chattered warnings as we passed. A porcupine paused in the trail ahead, moved aside when we were only a few feet away. We cut off on a smaller path and soon entered a clearing full of low berry bushes that still bore fruit. At the edge of this meadow we stopped in a grove of cedar trees.

During the morning we stripped cedar bark. This was normally woman's work, but Squintanasis toiled along with me, not talking.

With a good start you could rip off a strip of bark eight feet long or more. It was wonderful stuff for weaving; the largest trees became canoes and the inner bark was worked until soft enough to cover a baby's bottom. We took our time, stacking the strips neatly. By midday we had a pile above our knees and used lengths of the stuff to bind the long bundle.

Squintanasis opened the lunch pouch and we ate in silence. I knew it was time and didn't eat much. On the *Lucky Wind* I'd once received ten lashes for striking the second mate. It would have been more but they wanted me able to work. I hadn't thought about that for some time.

Squintanasis brushed off his hands, braced them on knees and looked off into the trees, jaw muscles rippling. "Must see blood," he said.

"The more the merrier."

"Shut up."

"Now that is one of my favorite –"

"Shut up."

I tossed the bones from the venison we had eaten and wiped the berry container out with moss still damp from dew. "It's all right," I said.

Squintanasis drew his knife. There was a stinging sensation as he made several shallow cuts on my upper arm. He told me to raise my skirt, which I had worn for the occasion, and cut my legs. He took some on his fingers and smeared it across my forehead and neck, lifted my shirt and made two cuts on my back, smeared more blood on my skirt. Then he dug down in the moss until he hit clay and used his thumb to grind some of this into my whiskered jaw, neck and head, matting the hair. He ground more dirt into my clothes and made a small cut on my chest; a few drops of blood ran down over my stomach.

He looked me over, cleaned his knife on a stump and put it away. We tied two lines to the bundle and began hauling it back toward the village. Before we got to the slope Squintanasis stopped and told me I was to look like I'd been beaten. Now I would drag the bundle of bark alone.

The bundle was bulky and heavy with moisture, but when we hit the downhill part it became nearly weightless. But I bent into the load, staggering, straining, a pathetic creature pulling the result of his woman's work after his ritual beating. Squintanasis marched slowly in front, head and jaw up. He looked marvelous.

Where the sandy soil began in back of Tomhak's lodge I fell in my traces. A curious group gathered a distance away as Squintanasis slowly marched around me, paused with head up, walked away.

Neveah helped me into the lodge and to my bunk.

"Stay," she said and hurried away. She returned with a bowl of warm water and began cleaning my wounds. I saw her brow gradually crease into a frown.

"It was hell," I said.

She muttered in Makah. "No deep."

"I have lost much blood."

"You tla-tla-wik!" (jest) she hissed.

"How can you say thus? I've been cut and beaten."

She began cleaning dirt out of my hair.

"Better not clean it all off today," I whispered.

"No cut. No mark. *Oh!*"

She shoved the course cloth in my mouth, eyes wild. I caught her wrist, pulled the cloth away and kissed her hand. She started to laugh, stopped. I held a finger to my lips and she tried to be quiet, almost succeeded. I glanced toward Tomhak's area and saw Suisha frowning at us, yet her mouth looked amused.

"He didn't want me to miss the party tomorrow," I whispered, which set Neveah off again.

Finally Neveah went to help Howessa and I lay back on my bed, hands locked behind my head. The cuts still stung a little, but I was happy to have an afternoon off. The miscreant slave left alone in his dark lair to brood about his sins.

The next thing I knew I was being prodded awake by a large, bare foot.

"Work Kekathl," Squintanasis said. "Build boat."

"But I'm cut and beaten." I sat up. "Should I be seen working?"

Squintanasis looked down, hands on hips.

I sighed, began pulling on moccasins.

It takes a long time to make a whaling canoe. A huge cedar tree is reduced to a light form less than an inch thick on the sides and thirty or more feet long, using simple hand tools and fire. Kekathl and Squintanasis worked by eye and memory developed over generations. Our boat was far from finished, but the final outside shape was nearly complete. She would be light and fast, able to carry six paddlers and helmsman with a harpooner in the bow. Eight would paddle when necessary.

I removed charred wood, scraps from bone chisels, sharpened the two iron chisels with a rusty file, fetched and carried on demand. But I wanted us to finish before the others under construction. Of the two other canoes being built one was ahead of us. That afternoon we washed together at the spring.

"Morning teach fire spear," Squintanasis said.

"But I have to help finish the canoe."

"Fire spear."

"We could be done in a month. Maybe less."

Squintanasis shook his head and rinsed himself by tossing water over his head from the bucket. His muscles glistened in the falling sun. "Fire spear. Maybe me hunt soon. Kekathl make boat. Irish teach fire spear."

That evening as our meal was winding down, I said, "Before we can do any shooting we have to take inventory. See what weaponry and ammunition you have. Not always shoot."

"Many," Squintanasis said, and showed me eight fingers.

I shook my head, decided that wasn't appropriate and shrugged. "It isn't as simple as your spear or arrows. We have to have a look." Other people were watching us now, including Tomhak. I made a point of keeping my eyes down as I spoke.

"Get fire spear. Make bang-smoke."

"Where are they?"

"Chief get fire spear."

"Tomorrow we see," I said.

In the morning Neveah and I woke early to the sound of children playing at the other end of the lodge. She insisted on cleaning my cuts properly. "No cut much. Nootche gone. No care now."

"Make me pretty."

She slapped a wet cloth in my face.

I'd barely started eating what was offered for breakfast when Squintanasis appeared. I took a few bites of food along and followed him into Kakemook's residence, the largest lodge in the village. There were many elaborate carved boards along the walls, the usual clothing and smoked food hanging everywhere; small copper utensils and a teapot were dangling like ornaments, and there were high stacks of the cleverly made wooden storage boxes, some decorated with colored carvings. Kakemook sat in his inlaid chair at the far end of the lodge, being ministered to while binding a long harpoon shaft. Squintanasis talked to the Chief as his short, buxom daughter, Nocheebe, groomed his hair. His wife, Cocumbishee, sat nearby weaving a basket.

The conversation became fairly complex and I couldn't follow it, but finally Kakemook directed us over to a corner of his cluttered lodge where eight muskets stood propped against the wall. Two nearby powder kegs were covered with a cedar mat, but underneath one side the kegs were damp from a wall leak. I moved the kegs a little away from the side of the house and re-covered them with the mat, tacitly thankful that all that black powder was stored here and not where I was living. Two fires burned in the lodge and the nearest was only a few paces away. I wasn't familiar enough to suggest the chief alter his safety measures.

The balls were in four containers, two from ours or another ship, two batches in small native baskets. On further examination I discovered that six of the muskets were French Army Charlevilles, the type many colonists used in the war, and two were standard English "Brown Bess" type, like my father carried as one of Washington's volunteers, and my brother was probably still using to procure food. The balls in the two largest baskets seemed to be a loose fit in the sixty-nine caliber Charlevilles. They dropped easily down the barrel, just right for a rapid-fire military musket when lead would coat the inside of the hot barrel, but seldom accurate beyond twenty paces. The last basket was full of small shot for a fouling gun, of little use for our purposes. A few patches were stowed in the stock closet, but no purses of patches and no fine pan powder. The Brown Bessys were seventy-five caliber and I could not find any appropriate balls in their collection. The balls for the Charlevilles were too small for the Bessys.

I sat on a powder keg and considered what to do. There were plenty of makings, if not all of the right size. They were expecting me to train some of them to shoot effectively, must get Nanishum and the boy back and so on. To increase reliability, we could grind some pan powder out of the regular stuff. The Bessys would be fine if I had the slightly larger custom balls we used at home in the military muskets, or if I could make a mold and melt down some lead, but I did not know how to make a mold and with the meager tools available wouldn't even attempt it.

So what to do? They expected all these weapons to see action. I would have to use the fowling shot in the Bessys. I dare not try to teach rapid fire, so there would be four shooters with four loaders. They would have to know how to sharpen flints and place pan powder properly; keep it dry in thick fog and torrents of rain; recoup quickly from misfires, keep moisture and dirt out of the flash hole. Squintanasis's bow was beginning to look like a more efficient weapon in this climate.

All right, I needed three shooters and re-loaders. And since I didn't feel up to trying to explain the drawbacks of a scatter-load I would have to shoot the Bessys loaded with fowling shot. And I would insist Neveah be my loader and translator.

"I train six to shoot," I said. "Seven including you. But in battle you will not shoot. Only three will shoot, plus me of course. The others are replacements should the primary be hit."

Squintanasis patted his chest. "Shoot," he corrected, unwilling to make this final concession.

I shook my head. "You too good a bowman." I demonstrated pulling a bowstring. "You will do much more damage with your bow than these muskets can do, for sure at anything beyond thirty paces. And all those in the tribe anywhere near your level should also use a bow. And the harpooners should use spears. These," I pointed at the muskets, "these are for the weak who cannot shoot the bow or throw the spear or swing the club as well as you and Senequah. Like me," I pointed a thumb at my chest. "Not trained for bow. Shoot musket. You," putting my thumb against his chest, "use bow and club. You great warrior. Great warrior better with no musket."

I had never planned a battle or led men into mayhem, but what

I proposed seemed logical, and it was in my best interest for these folks to do well. I was surviving here and didn't want to be a slave anywhere else.

The training process began smoothly enough, lulling me into thinking this would be a simple game and I would gain stature with little effort. Kakemook's son, Misak, was one of the assigned shooters, his loader a cousin, a boy of about fourteen. Misak, in his mid-teens, had a deformed left leg and arm, and I perceived he was selected because Squintanasis had taken me at my word regarding who should be a shooter. Misak could never be a great whale harpooner, a skill his father was revered for, but he was soft spoken with a quiet determination and I liked him immediately. Perhaps the most enthusiastic trainee was Senequah's son, Kanek, who enlisted his sister, Kloo-kles-a, as his loader. The great fisherman with twisted leg, Sahyoul, insisted on being the third shooter, assisted by his young nephew. I was the fourth, my loader, Neveah. She was frightened at first, not knowing what we planned to do to her, but when I explained she beamed at being assigned such a responsible task. We then both acted like it was simply a practical matter because she knew some English words and in battle communication was essential. I told her it was also her dexterity with weaving moves, ramrod, etcetera. Squintanasis just gave me one of those piercing looks.

After I explained the pitfalls of unstable black powder to Squintanasis he assigned the chore of grinding some into flash pan consistency to an old woman who was nearly blind; I winced, but could not refute the rationale.

"Tell her use hard wood," I said. "Make slow. No stone."

Loading patches came from the pages of a ship's log, written in Russian, which had been thrown in amongst the rifles and powder. I found it under a basket of berries in Kakemook's lodge. Soft paper to make loading cartridges would have been useful, but there was none in the proximity. My father had said a good rifleman didn't need them if he ran out, knowing from experience how much powder to dump down the barrel, but I thought my little group should be protected against overloading.

After some thought I searched the beach until I found half a small clamshell just the right size to measure a load. I decided we should have at least a dozen of the same size and went to find Neveah. She was working on the fish drying racks. Howessa protested when I said Neveah's services were needed, but when I told her in my best Makah it was for the fire spears, she grudgingly let her go.

Neveah came shyly, an act for Howessa. I explained how the shells had to be exactly the size of the sample I gave her. She must use sand to measure the capacity, they must be dried. The shells must be very clean and dry inside.

"Know," she said quietly, and indicated the sun in the sky, which was shedding warm light on us. "Know dry. Shells. Dry. Know."

She gazed at me so intently I felt lost for a moment, lost in one of her eyes a lighter brown than the other, intense, liquid. I pointed at the shell in her hand as if to show her something else, but when she held it out, concentrating, brow furrowed, I took her fingers and held them until she realized it was a trick. She suddenly laughed, pulled her hand free and, clutching the shell, ran toward the beach.

Chapter 15

Hauling our armory and a snack Sahyoul had insisted on, the lot of us trudged south along the beach past rock carvings of whales, moons and stars, faces etched in interwoven lines into rocks exposed to wind and salt. A hundred paces beyond a large tidal rock we arrived at a gouged channel in the high bank with a small stream trickling out. For this first session I wanted only primary shooters; loaders could join us for the next practice. Several curious men and children tried to tag along, but I stopped and said our first training session should include only the designated shooters, and of course Squintanasis who was determined to be there.

Along the cut-banks bracketing the stream were piles of drift logs. I placed small chunks of sun-bleached driftwood for targets. To build confidence, I made the first setup only twenty paces.

I started off by showing them how to make sure the weapon was clear, then loading one musket at a time, everyone taking a turn. They practiced sighting over the muzzle bead and everyone took several dry runs. Enthusiasm was building to "make fire spear speak."

Kanek wanted to be first. I had explained the firing delay, but might as well have said nothing. He took aim, pulled the trigger, flint hit frisson, pan powder ignited and, thinking the round had fired, he made a recoil before the real one hit him. When the actual charge went off he nearly downed a low cruising gull, causing a few excited comments from the rest of the group.

I went through the sequence again.

Kanek put the next round into the woods. I explained the sequence a third time and fired a round. To my surprise I actually hit one of the pieces of driftwood, which brought approving murmurs among the hopeful marksmen and eager requests to be next.

Misak took a turn and barely missed. Then Sahyoul fired his weapon and was also close to a target. Kanek was next, and under pressure to do as well as the others. He did keep the ball within the pile of drift where the targets were lined up.

Squintanasis had been silently watching all this and now stepped forward to take a turn. He held steady on pan ignition and nailed one of the little pieces of driftwood on his first try. This started a clamor among the others and it became a hellish competition until Neveah arrived to announce that Chief Kakemook wanted the booms to stop because it was time for singing and food was in the fire, or the like. The afternoon was sunny with a light northwest wind, ideal weather for a party.

I motioned to Neveah and we walked behind the enthusiastic group of shooters toward the village. Squintanasis remained stoic and the others deferred to him since he was the only one to have actually hit two targets. Neveah touched my hand, quickly jerked her hand away. I smiled and moved my head, beckoning her closer. She sidled up, suppressing a smile. I bumped her, causing her to look surprised and stumble on the sandy gravel.

She shoved me back and I pretended to lose my balance and stagger to one side. She put a hand over her mouth to suppress a laugh, but enough got out to cause Squintanasis to look back at us. We refused to meet his eyes.

The village was bubbling with preparations. Though it was only late afternoon a large beach fire was underway. Inside the lodges smaller fires heated pots and hot rocks to be used in baskets. Women rustled about in grass and hide skirts, children assisted their mothers-aunts-grandmothers while the very young ran naked on the sunny beach, involved in their own games. Singing wafted out of smoky lodges. Few men were present, and soon our group dispersed to prepare themselves.

Neveah touched my hand before hurrying to help Howessa and Winaseek. I was left to care for the weapons. I carried four at a time over to Kakemook's lodge and put them back in the area where they were kept. The Chief was in there, along with several relatives and slaves, shouting orders as preparations were being made.

I knew there was whale oil for lubricant, but was at a loss for solvent and brushes. I searched all around the area hoping to find a brush to clean the barrels properly, until one of the relatives tending the chief came at me with demands, wanting to know what I was doing messing with the chief's belongings. I tried to explain in Makah, but this just made him more confrontational, to the point of pulling a knife and threatening me.

"E-yahh!" Kakemook bellowed, a word I recognized that meant stop, and my aggressor straightened and stepped back. They exchanged a few words and Kakemook frowned, then motioned for me to approach. I moved toward him and in my best Makah explained what I was looking for.

At length Kakemook shook his head and spoke; his meaning was clear: Not have. You make. Tell Kekathl or Squintanasis to make.

He moved a hand in an arc. "Take what need. Care fire spear. Care iron. Ai-dan high slave. Tell Squintanasis what need. Squintanasis speak for you. Teach fire spear. Klooklo." He held a palm high over his head. "Give Makah koo-yak. Fire spear. Now high slave."

Great. It sounded like I'd received a new commission, from Different to High. And how do we make a brass barrel brush? And where do we get solvent? I sat on the powder keg, looked around in remorse. Tomorrow would be another practice, and the day after that until they could hit something. Maybe old reliable urine would cut the lead in the barrels. Or we could have one of the medicine boys spit down there and sing a chant. Shaman seemed to appear when needed and fade into the population when things were going smoothly, eagerly serving at the chief's pleasure or if someone wanted to pay them for a special service.

My wandering gaze fell on a crock under the chief's raised platform. Rum can take the lining out of your stomach – could it also cut the lead in gun barrels?

The chief wasn't keen on giving up any rum, but I told him it was for the fire spears and we didn't need much. To be sure it was used only for that we'd mix some urine with it. He talked in a roundabout way for a time, indicating two more crocks against the wall, finally relented. I poured out a half pint from the first crock into a wooden container with a fitted lid. Kakemook ordered the one who'd threatened me to piss in it. I had hoped for a sip or two before that was done, but Kakemook was no fool. Now I had to come up with a tough brush.

Carrying the fouled rum, I found Neveah at one of the fires and explained what I needed. Howessa joined us and the two women discussed it, and soon hurried away to seek additional council. Later, Neveah found me in Kakemook's lodge cleaning the muskets. We had fired only three, but they were all dirty. She said old Thomtarsh, the most respected weaver in the village who specialized in spruce root, was working on the problem and I must take one of the weapons to her lodge so she could check the size. By tomorrow she would have a tool for me to try. Now I should get ready for the party, it would be klooklo.

"Maybe you could loan me some paint," I said.

Neveah became serious. "Cut hair," she said, meaning my beard. "Yellow on throat." She touched my forehead. "Blue here." She nodded. "No more."

"What about some red and black like the other lads wear?"

A flash of dark eyes and glance toward Kakemook. "You no Makah," she whispered. "No allow. Kakemook beat you." She shook her head for emphasis, then her mouth made a casual twist. "Blue. Yellow. Show respect."

"What's a high slave?" I asked in an equally low voice.

Neveah shrugged. "No know high slave." She grinned and gave my whiskers a tug, "Cut hair."

She hurried out of the chief's lodge and I wondered what I was going to do about shaving. I went to find Squintanasis. He seemed amused as I tried to explain to him the need of a very sharp knife. I also needed Boston Man shaving soap, but since this wasn't available I at least would have to have a mirror.

Holding the amused expression, he said, "Neveah say cut hair?"

"Well, for the party, yes. So I might get some paint."

I followed him back to Kakemook's lodge. They exchanged words briefly and Kakemook gave me an appraising once-over. Then he waved a casual hand and said something to Squintanasis. We lifted a cedar box off the one under it and a little rooting produced a leatherbound shaving set with a small mirror, ivory-handled razor, soap cup, tiny scissors, plucker and whetstone. This was a travel set worthy of a captain or at least an officer. I resisted asking where it came from and thanked the chief for his great generosity.

I filled a battered iron pot with water and placed it over one of the food fires. While that was going I used a mussel shell knife to cut my beard to shavable length. I carried the pot of hot water and equipment up the slope to the rocky outcrop, above the usual bathing area, where the spring stream came out of the hillside and I could be alone. I hung the mirror on a branch and had a look. Startling. The image in the mirror was not I but some vagrant off the wharf with nothing but the stinking clothes on his back.

No, I was more: a language coach and firearms instructor who had been elevated to high slave by influential people. And an attractive young woman had some interest in me, though as I stared into the tiny mirror I could not imagine why.

The soap cup was a minor miracle and hot water with it felt luxurious. I began shaving to the sound of singing as groups warmed up for the feast. Razor cuts streamed down my cheeks like an awakening. I wanted to leave them there, my own glorious red streaks, keep your paint. I rinsed my face in cold spring water, dried it on my clothes and rinsed again.

The remaining hot water I poured slowly over my head while scrubbing with the smelly soap. I had seen mothers washing their babies in urine diluted with warm water to cut the smoke glaze from inside the lodges, and Neveah said everyone used it sometimes for shampoo and then rinsed well, but I did not abide this practice for myself. I put my head under spring water and rinsed until I could no longer feel sand. My hair had grown enough to flair a little on my shoulders, no longer slave length. I worked a wooden comb through it until it was free of snarls.

From a nearby cedar I worked off a narrow piece of under-bark, trimmed it to consistent width, and tied my sun-streaked brown hair back. I tied in a sprig of hemlock too and used my knife to trim the ends of the cedar strip.

The mirror was no larger than my palm so it was difficult to see more than a small part of myself at a time. I washed up under my arms and in my crotch, brushed and straightened the buckskin skirt and my repaired wool shirt, slipped them on. They had been cleaned only a few days ago.

I crouched and stared into the mirror. I'd filled out from a rich diet of fish, fresh meat and greens and felt stronger. The sun and wind off the ocean had darkened my skin, accented creases across my brow. The eyes looking back were more intense than I remembered. The hair tied back looked like theirs with the dash of hemlock. I wondered if Neveah might like me this way.

Not a little self-conscious, I crept into Tomhak's lodge and sat on my sleeping mat. My battered boots were replaced with moccasins and I put on the soft cedar vest Tomhak had given me. The vest seemed a little snug, and I straightened, tensed muscles. From the cedar box holding my meager stash I took out the length of woven leather I'd put together from strips cut from a scrap of soft deer hide Squintanasis had given me and tied it around my forehead.

To a background of singing I strode straight and slowly from the lodge, around a cook fire attended by busy women, past my cold forge, through a group of children playing, across the graveled sand to the edge of soft waves.

And nobody noticed. Sea ducks cruised in the low swell and small fish dimpled the surface. An eagle banked and swooped down in a long arc to grab a dead fish off the water.

"Ai-dan?"

I turned and she was standing there, petite, well made, dressed for the feast with something in her hand, a shell with paint inside. Blue paint. Neveah stared, eyes large, started to speak, then turned and hurried away.

"Wait. Stop." She did so but did not turn toward me. I went to her, resisted an urge to put an arm around her shoulders, asked what was the matter. She shook her head and stared at the sandy ground. "You different," she said.

"Well, you're not. You always look good."

She grinned, but kept her head down.

"You make me feel that way too you know."

She shook her head, then raised it and looked at me. "Want paint now?"

Facing each other on her bunk, she applied a line of blue paint to my forehead. Her mouth twisted in concentration, eyes large. She painted with her right hand and steadied with her left, made a vertical line on my cheek and moved back to consider her work. I took her left hand and felt her resist, then relax a little. I pressed her palm against my smooth cheek. Sudden tears filled her eyes and I let go of her hand. She leaned back and looked at me.

"Me no maiden. Kishkani worth more."

"We are slaves now, but not forever." I took a breath. "I will make us free. Your son too."

Her look was sympathetic, disbelieving. "No my son. Kishkani Trikishka's son. Chief son kill Trikishka at Tatoosh when I at Neeah. She try stop him take boy away. Chief mad to son. Call him crazy. Tell me, Trikishka slave, boy slave, you no maiden, you take boy. Go Ozette. Give you Tomhak. My son go fishing long time."

Drops ran down a cheek and I wondered what had happened to her. I resisted an urge to hold her. "It doesn't matter," I said. "Listen to me. Somehow I will get you out of here. Even Squintanasis said the spirits told him I would leave soon."

She moved back a little more and looked weary.

"Please believe," I said. "Never mind about it now. We are here and it is time to feast. Do I have enough blue paint on my face? Well?"

"Maybe yellow on neck."

"Well, come on then," I urged. "Make me pretty. Then we're going out there and have a good time. You will bring food and sing and we will eat much."

She managed a smile and picked up the applying stick. Her expression grew serious again and she drew thin blue and yellow lines down the side of my neck. When I told her to call me Blue Warrior she flashed a smile. She had two narrow yellow lines on the sides of her face and I said we would be the jay and the butterfly.

Screaming interrupted us. We rushed out of Tomhak's lodge and watched a middle-aged man being dragged by the hair down the beach, rolling and flailing with sand and pebbles flying, screaming in all chords as the head shaman, thick fingers locked in the victim's long hair, dragged him without mercy. Reflexively I started to go to his aid, but stopped when I realized no one else was going to help him. "What the hell is that about?" I asked.

"Headache," Neveah said matter-of-factly.

"Headache? I'm sure he has one, but why?"

"Cure," she said seriously.

"The man has a headache and that's what they do to him?"

"Good cure. Maybe work."

The man was still screaming, kicking his feet in the wet sand near the waves. "I see. Well, I can assure you, if I have a headache I won't talk about it."

"Cure," she insisted. "Pull hair hard. Headache gone."

"Uh-huh. Because after the treatment they don't talk about it anymore."

She slapped my chest and we headed for Kakemook's.

Chapter 16

About a dozen visitors had arrived by two canoes in the afternoon and had the attention of Senequah and Kakemook and other high-ranking Makahs. They were barefoot and dressed similar to the people of this village except two of the four women had prominent bones through their noses, and two of the men made a show of carrying their muskets until they were sure all had noticed, when they were then given to the women to stow in their canoes.

Near the chief's lodge, half an elk had been split into several pieces and impaled on a large rotary affair over an outside fire. Fat bubbled out and dripped into a collecting trough and sparking flames. Women fluttered about over this and another fire where whale meat smoked and spit. Singing was non-stop now, accompanied by plank drums, whistles, rattles and humming, people inside and out keeping time with their feet while they went about their chores, children darting through the workers like bees at a picnic. It was a small celebration for the successful hunt Squintanasis had conducted.

And near the entrance to the chief's lodge, next to the welcome carving of a man, sat mister bear. Bear was propped up in a make-shift chair with lines holding up his head and front legs. He was draped with cedar ropes arranged like bandoliers, and between his dangling rear legs he wore a buckskin breach cloth. On his head had been tied hemlock sprigs, some feathers and white down. Flowers and ferns lay across his lap.

I stared for a time, finally asked, "Why?"

"Bear good," Neveah said. "Come celebration. All part bear good. Some maybe eat him. Like eat bear. I hear."

I had to laugh.

"Bear honor party," she continued. "Maybe get skinned tonight. Bear spirit stay three days. Maybe see Irish eat him."

We crowded into Kakemook's big lodge where the dancers were already into their warm-up steps and the chorus was giving forth. Next to Chief Senequah his son, Kanek, he of the great energy and wild shots, sprang to his feet and shouted for quiet – this happened almost immediately. Kakemook began to speak, sweeping an arm for emphasis as he described the successful hunt that had brought such a bounty of food. Squintanasis had slain a bear and all the hunters had given good account of themselves. Thunderbird must be pleased with the Makah and would soon provide more great bounty from the sea, and so on.

Neveah was pressed against me by the many people still pushing in until there simply wasn't room for more, yet more kept coming, crowding the tight circle in front of Kakemook and the entertainers. I grasped her hand and pulled her through the mob toward the door-way. We made it finally and laughed while breathing salty night air. To my surprise Squintanasis appeared then and said something to Neveah I did not understand.

Neveah followed him a short distance and they exchanged a few words. Squintanasis walked away without looking in my direction.

Feeling confusion oddly like anger, I went to her and asked what had been said. Her eyes were molten in flickering firelight. For a few moments I wondered if she'd heard me.

"He say feast klooklo," she said in a near whisper.

"He does not do as well yet with English words as you."

She shook her head. "You tease everything." She suddenly looked at me very intently. "Squintanasis speak for you. Speak for you chiefs. You high slave."

"I asked you about that before. What does it mean?"

She moved a shoulder. "Maybe better than slave. Never know high slave."

"It sounds like something made up."

"Maybe. Chiefs listen Squintanasis. Talk chiefs many things. Big medicine. Tomhak say, get tomanawos only twelve. Go to mountain. Go too high, no trees, where Thunderbird live. No take tooplah, take mountain, be with wolf. Tomhak never see this, so high no trees, say Squintanasis best hunter to land. Stay mountain half moon. Sleep bear cave. Speak to wolf. Wolf say, ha-aéd (cougar) come. He come, Squintanasis kill. Take skin, eat heart. Share to wolf. Come home warrior."

"He killed a cougar at twelve?"

"Great warrior. Most persons no see ha-aéd in life. Ha-aéd mother to He who scream in woods. Most persons fear go far in woods. Dark. Wild man wait there. Persons belong tooplah. Friends in tooplah. Best food in tooplah."

"But Squintanasis is branded somehow," I said. "He's part white."

She slowly shook her head. "Squintanasis get poison blood. No marry Nanishum. Much sadness."

"He wanted to marry Nanishum? Tomhak's daughter? Nanishum that was kidnapped?"

"Nanishum love Squintanasis," she said quietly. "He love her.

Poison blood. Poison blood father bring to Makah." She shook her head. "No marry. Only marry slave. Squintanasis no take slave. Only want Nanishum."

She gently took my hand. "Squintanasis much wolf spirit. Great hunter. Much sadness for chiefs."

It put me back on my heels and I felt a new pain.

"Squintanasis say feast," she said, her voice dropping low again, causing me to turn toward her to hear. Her face glowed in the thin orange light from the horizon. "Feast now. He give something you later. Want happy now. He say, you sing." The gentle pressure of her hand pulled me out of my trance.

"Me? Sing? Oh, I don't think anyone wants to hear that."

We pushed our way back into Kakemook's lodge. With some urging I did briefly try to sing and was crudely laughed at for my grotesque pronunciations. Great chunks of elk were passed around for us to tear at, whale too and I had to let them see me eat a little, the inevitable bowls of oil for dipping, sweet berries, cherries, greens of various kinds, masked intruders yelling and throwing things at us, jumping up on the high seats with the box drummers, people drumming on the plank drums on the floor and shaking rattles while eating with the other hand. The party was quite informal, people helping the singers while chewing mouthfuls of food. Finally the crowd began to thin. People left still pushing food in their mouths.

Howling outside where mostly naked young men and girls raced up and down the beach like lunatics, children and the village clown chasing after them, everyone screaming and making animal sounds. Near the water's edge two young men wrestled, hurling each other about.

The real wolves were quiet this night, no doubt repelled by the human madness.

Neveah and I strolled down the beach away from the activity.

Where we were in the lee of Dog Island waves gently combed the beach, but further down surf pounded and we could see the phosphorescent white line before it crashed down. Two people sat on a log and as we drew abreast I recognized Kanek and Winaseek. They were not touching, but obviously focused on one another.

"No bend fire spear eye," I said in Makah, causing Kanek to laugh.

"Maybe shoot true like teacher," he said.

"Better than teacher."

We went on. Neveah seemed both serene and strangely nervous, floating along with silent steps. When I tried to take her hand she jerked away, then grabbed my hand in both of hers and pressed it to her cheek, rejected it again.

A sound caused me to stop short and put an arm across her chest, stopping her. Three men sitting on a pile of drift, groaning and laughing at the same time. I put Neveah a little behind me, on the ocean side, and we continued on. As we passed the men I saw a crock and one yelled a greeting. They were quite drunk. I just waved and kept going, ignoring their invitations. They yelled something like a challenge, but didn't follow us. Another dozen paces and I began to relax. Her hand had been lightly on my arm and now dropped away.

We walked a ways without touching, passed the etched rocks, jumped the small stream at the shooting area. "We've never been this alone before," I said.

No answer. "Is that what makes you nervous?"

"No," she said.

We walked a little farther. "More fire spear practice tomorrow," I said. "I want you and the other loaders there."

"Maybe."

"What do you mean? Of course there will be practice tomorrow. There's much to do."

"Maybe."

I slowed my step, wondering what had changed her mood. "Don't you want to be my loader? Learn about fire spear?"

Neveah suddenly brightened. "Yes. Do you say."

"I'll talk to Squintanasis. I think the loaders should practice with the shooters now. Loaders must learn to shoot too. They are just as important. It is time."

The last of the twilight lingered, the cool air still full of summer. We heard the yellers and singers back there, gruff laughing of the drunks.

"It was a nice little feast, don't you think? All the food and singing."

A short laugh. "You a-whatl-tsuck," (foolish) she said.

After a sideways glance I said, "We're quite a way from the village."

"No far."

"Want to keep going? Make a run for it?"

"No." She smiled; her teeth glowed like phosphorescent surf. "Go back now."

I tensed as we passed the three men at the pile of logs, but they were too far gone to notice us, down on the sand, blubbering at nothing, the empty crock between them.

"They won't feel so good tomorrow," I said.

"Kakemook throw in tooplah. Get mad take lum-muks (rum)."

Kanek and Winaseek had left their log, perhaps to find a more private place.

We didn't talk on the way back, but it was enough to be with her on such a fine night. There were few clouds, stars shown brightly, as if magnified, and I gazed at the dippers, Orion, a sharp and clear North Star.

As we approached the village a tall figure separated from the lodges and people and came toward us. Squintanasis stopped a dozen paces away and waited for us. He said something in fast Makah I did not understand.

Neveah immediately hurried toward the lodges.

I frowned at him, irritated that he had interrupted the best evening I'd had during the whole of my reluctant career as a slave.

"Something wrong?" I asked. Squintanasis's hint of a smile irritated me further.

"Kakemook talk."

When we walked in the visiting guests were sprawled around the lodge, a knot of them near the chief. He ordered them to give us room so we could sit near him. The plank was blocked off the dirt floor to nearly the height of a chair.

"Irish eat good?" the chief asked of me in Makah.

"Well, yes. Hauouk klooklo tousuk." (Eat good elk.)

The chief nodded slightly at my use of Makah words, which I took to mean I said them well enough for him to understand.

He began to speak of my skill as a hunter, a hook maker and teacher of the fire spear. This he did with head nods and waves of a thick, scarred hand, extolling my various feats. As far as hunting skill, Squintanasis had apparently stretched the truth since it had been a pointblank shot and if the deer had been an elk I probably would have been trampled under the animal. Then he said something I could not understand and I looked to Squintanasis.

"Chief say, you high slave now. No hardairk barcooak." No woman's work.

"Chief Kakemook very kind," I said. "Aidan try be of value to Makah."

Squintanasis interpreted and the chief grunted, weariness etching his large face, and began speaking again. I could only understand a few words, but it sounded positive.

The hunting had been good, we had eaten well and the chief liked me. I felt lulled, and tomorrow we would all sleep in and then go to fire spear practice and Neveah would be there. The boys would shoot a little better and there would be even more talk in the village because the loaders would have things to say. As a high slave I would be treated a little better, but would never be offered a seat in a real whaling canoe. And as the fire spear teacher I would not have to learn how to shoot a bow or hurl a spear, all of which I accepted as the good parts of being a high slave. I had risen to in-between person.

Finished speaking, Kakemook looked around a bit furtively and said something to his daughter. Noocheebe came forth with a small crock. Kakemook directed her to pour rum into three wood cups. She handed me one first, an error or surprising honor that caused me to glance at the figures nearby in shadow. I felt an urge to bow, but held my cup and silently waited for direction.

The chief spoke briefly and Squintanasis interpreted the meaning, which was that we would have our rum and then retire and I would go to the small lodge this night. I must have looked confused because Squintanasis then explained – what it sounded like – was that my sleeping quarters would be altered somehow to express my new position, so it was necessary I sleep in a different place tonight.

Kakemook drank down his rum without a flinch and we did the same, followed by a few moments of silence.

The small lodge was considered sacred. I had often seen shaman near the little building on the slope. Visitors sometimes slept there. I was getting uneasy. The klooklo food began to rumble in my gut. I was a slave to these people, high or otherwise, a slave and white to boot. They were putting me in one of their sacred places for the night. I was beginning to suspect sacrifice or the like. Perhaps there was some sort of painful ascension to high slave.

Kakemook leaned toward me, rattling his elaborate necklace, put a hand on my shoulder and gripped it briefly, his face a solemn map of fatherly concern. He straightened and with a wave uttered what sounded like a dismissal. Squintanasis rose and we went out.

"Sleep klooklo," he said.

I watched Squintanasis walk away, then trudged up the path to the little lodge. The trail was dark under the trees, the small building a black shape, but as I approached there seemed to be some light, a small fire inside that glowed around the edges of the mat covering the entrance. Perhaps a simple ritual would be held to bring me into the high slave realm. So long as there was no hair pulling.

At the entrance I listened for a few moments, heard nothing, moved the mat and entered. Dark and a bit smoky, low fire in the center of the room, almost coals, the scent of seal oil and something more appealing. No one there, then on a low bunk I made out a form under a blanket. I stepped further into the room.

"Hell-o, Ai-dan."

"Hello, Neveah." I went and kneeled next to her. Her hair was combed out, flowing around bare shoulders, gleaming red highlights in the wavering soft light. A wool blanket was pulled up almost to her throat and though her eyes were molten and large, and her sculptured lips suggested a smile, she looked frightened.

"Are you here for me?"

"Yes."

"Should I get in there with you now?"

"You want?"

"You look beautiful."

Sudden moisture filled her eyes, spilled out.

"What is it? If you don't want to do this we don't have to. I'm a slave too. We can wait. I think we should be together eventually, but not until you're ready."

"Me no maiden," she said.

"You are to me. A beautiful maiden." No appropriate cloth appeared available, so I took off my soft leather vest, fumbled around for the cleanest area and used this to dab her tears. While I was so occupied she watched her hand that touched my arm and moved slowly up to my shoulder, over to my neck.

"Comb hair?" she asked.

"Sure." I reached for the cedar holding it back, but she grabbed my hand.

"Me do."

I turned around and stretched my legs out so my feet were near the small fire, sitting with my back to her. The blanket whispered. Bare legs brushed me and then pressed my ribs. Gentle fingers on the cedar knot, quickly undone, fingers moving my hair, fluffing it as gently as a summer breeze. Her necklace brushed my back with every movement. The fish bone comb began to glide through my hair as if the bones were still alive, a most sensual feeling. A nipple tiptoed against my back and she began to hum a melody I had never heard. I never wanted it to end, yet I had such a growing, overwhelming desire to please her – *please her*.

I reached back over my head and slowly our arms intertwined. I pulled her forward until her breasts pressed against my back and her arms wrapped around my chest and neck and still I wanted her closer, I wanted us completely inside each other as the wolf knows it is inside its skin. I pulled her head down until I could crush her hair over my face and smell it, breathe it like a life force. I quickly discarded my clothes.

She coaxed me up and into the bed and for the first time I felt the full heat of her body against mine. Her fingers moved over the ridges of scar tissue on my side, back and forth, exploring the spear wound, then her hand closed over the tender scar in an oddly erotic, protective way.

I kissed Neveah full on the lips. She was surprised but willing. I pulled back and let her catch her breath. The second time was better. On our third try I felt her passion.

"Spread your legs now." I was slow, careful, never so knowing.

"Put your arms around my neck." She did while looking into my eyes.

"Come to me."

I watched her, loving her, and soon her arms began to tighten around my neck. And then she was eager. Her embrace took my breath and I didn't care.

We couldn't stop kissing each other, everywhere, her nipples ridged in my mouth, and I could not stop giving her every ounce of strength in me, as if we had waited our whole lives for this moment and later, much later, I tried to calculate the hours of darkness we must rest so we could be that way again.

She was backed up tightly into me holding my arms around her and slowly moving my hands over her wonderful body with a hunger I could barely imagine. I thought I was the starved one, the non-native slave who could never have the resistance to ordinary emotion these people exhibited on a daily basis. Emotion was weak. It interfered with survival.

"You are my maiden," I whispered. "Mine."

Droplets ran over my hand as she kissed it. And then she turned her heat toward me.

*At certain periods, generally during the winter months, they have ceremo-
nies, or mystical perfomances . . . Into all these mysteries persons of both
sexes, and even children, are initiated; but the initiation does not endow
them with medicine or tamanawos qualities until they have gone through
the private ordeal, of finding their own tamanawos, or guardian . . .*

Chapter 17

Bands of sunlight caused me to blink as I opened my eyes. If the
sun was on this lodge pouring through the roof vent then it was
late, late for the tasks that were my assignment. I threw the blanket aside and lurched to a sitting position, began searching for my
trousers.

"Ai-dan?"

"Must go. Fire spear practice."

Her hand gripped my arm, stopping me from rising. "Sorry," I
said. "You have to get up too. It's a wonder –"

"Ai-dan," she interrupted. "No fire spear." Her light fingers traced
the lines the whip had made on my back so I had to remember what
we were talking about.

"What are you saying? They're probably all at Tomhak's with –"

"No, Ai-dan. No fire spear. Rest now. Squintanasis no come.
Nobody come."

I stared at her. "That can't be. He would have told me."

Her hand slid over my shoulder. "Squintanasis no tell. He not
know what you do."

"About what?"

"Me. He say, 'Maybe not want you. In morning, you say.'" She smiled. "Now morning. You here. No must go."

I relaxed a little, put my hand over hers and gazed into the remnants of the fire. Her fingers pressed my bicep. "You two thought of everything," I said. "I guess I'm the fool."

"No happy?"

"Of course I'm happy. My God. It's just that I seem to be the last to know anything that's going on. It's as if I'm a child."

She uttered a giggle. "No child," she said. "You big warrior."

I laughed, lay back down next to her, both of us naked, staring up at the logs holding up the ceiling, gulls screaming and distant children's voices. She threw the blanket over us and snuggled closer.

"You tired warrior?" she said.

"Oh, yes."

"Hungry warrior?"

"Starved."

She kissed my chest and raised up on an elbow. "I get food. You make fire?"

"We're doing pretty well without a fire."

She straddled me and pinned my arms down on the bed. "Make fire," she said. "Me get food. We stay all day. No work today."

"Who says?"

"Squintanasis say. Or you no want me. You no want me, you go. You go?"

"Not a chance. Get the food. We are holed up for the day."

Neveah laughed, a short sound like a startled bird, and bounded up on bronze legs. I watched her pull up the skirt and put her arms up so the soft cedar shirt fell over her shoulders and breasts and the top of the skirt to hide her wonderful shape and immediately I wanted her again. My father had told me it would be like this when you found the right one and after that no one could ever take her place.

"Skookum come, you make go," she said.

"Who's that?"

"Skookum spirit make mischief. No let come in." She was grinning. "Tongue make lightning in fire, big mischief."

"Anybody but you shows me tongue and I'll knock 'em senseless."
She laughed and hurried out.

This was the first fire other than the forge I had been called upon to make. There were two dark coals with enough heat to ignite some grass. Next some broken twigs caught and I added a few sticks. Outside I surprised a squirrel hiding in the woodpile of small, dry logs covered with a board.

Neveah came back with a little freshly smoked fish, still oily and delicious, a cooked grouse, greens and a basket of berries. She also had a little bear meat, which amused her. "My maiden must eat artleitkwitl too," I said.

"Aidan maiden eat artleitkwitl," she announced in Makah. She mixed English, Makah and an occasional Spanish word in a delicious way.

"Should we go wash at the spring first?" I said.

"*Bueno.*"

The place where I had shaved was conveniently near and it was good to be here alone together instead of at the main bathing place. She meticulously rinsed her face and hands in the clean cold water, then turned away to clean her legs and up under her skirt. She seemed as modest as a Boston woman. There was a luxury in watching her every move. Today we could do whatever we pleased and we began by sitting cross-legged in front of the fire I had made, enjoying the food Neveah had brought. We threw the grouse bones into the fire and fed each other bear meat and berries and I bent her head toward me and inhaled the scent of her hair. She pulled the hair on my chest and wiped my mouth with a cedar towel.

"Tell me about your necklace," I said. "You have many types of shells. What are these little skinny ones? I have seen other girls wear them."

"Dentalium," she said. "Winaseek wear many dentalium now. Maybe marry Kanek." Her fingers moved over the necklace. "Here haletosis (abalone). These good luck snails. Yew wood mother make. This good white stones from my village. Spanish coin from father. What coin?"

"Trade," I said, taking one of the square coins between my fingers. "What of these teeth?"

"Father's. Some come out. He say, take my teeth for luck. But they come kill him, make me slave."

"Sometimes luck needs time to work."

"Father nice me. Fight to me. Respect his teeth."

"Then I think you should keep them on your necklace."

She smiled. "No like Spaniard. Like father. He good."

"I'm sure he was. He bore a brave and beautiful daughter."

She modestly dropped her eyes, causing a flood of feelings that were still new to me. "How did you come to have a Spanish father?"

"Spirit send," she said quietly. "Spanish make trouble to s'Klalum. Fight. Father go tooplah. Cloud ship go. Father come in night. Very cold. Lose much blood. My people help. Mother care. Some time she no want Spanish man go. So Father stay."

"Did you see the ship?"

She shook her head. "My people never see cloud ship. Not know. Not know what people. Maybe kill Father. Mother say no kill."

"The ship never came back?"

"Cloud ship come when I small. Come our village one day, one night. Father hide. He no want his people. Want us."

I tried to picture this man. "Did he tell you his Spanish name?"

"Yes, we say him name. But hard. His name, Edweerdo. He laugh when we say. We call him E-wo-wo. He like new name."

I smiled at the picture in my mind, how this alien Spanish man who could speak English must have been regarded. "I do not understand how he was able to survive and your mother wanted him. Perhaps your people thought he was a god or something."

"My people know he no god. Want kill him. But mother say no, he not like others. Then when I small King George Man make trouble Nuu-chah-nulth (Nootka). Boston Man make trouble. They want kill my father again, but mother say no. He my husband."

I frowned. "Boston Man make trouble with Nootka? What happened?"

"Big fire spear make thunder. Many thunder. Kill houses, kill people. Village gone."

"What? What Boston Man would do this? Are you sure?"

"Great cloud ship, many fire spear like thunder come. Chief Maquinna say him called Gray. He send word, be careful this Gray."

This was shocking to hear. Captain Gray? It sounded about the same time Captain Stark had been with Gray, but he hadn't mentioned such carnage in his stories of that time, other than firing on the canoe in the middle of the night. Yet there had been rumors back in Boston . . .

In the afternoon we sat high on the slope watching the activity in the village and the ocean all the way to the misty horizon. The visitors that had come the day before were leaving, headed north. In their wake some boys paddled out to feed the wool dogs that howled and ran along their island beach as the canoe approached. I asked Neveah if there were more dogs someplace.

"Neeah," she said. "Good wool weavers Neeah. Most dogs stay Tatoosh. Most beautiful island. Cold."

"And spruce and cedar weavers?"

She shrugged. "Same. More seal hunter here. More whale hunter there." She grinned mischievously. "More high slave here."

"The garments made from wool dogs are not so many."

"Most blankets. Make child warm. Some people like in cold. More in cold."

"You like?" I said.

She cocked her head. "Rain make smell. Chimakum no have."

"What is this about Kanek and Winaseek getting married? Soon?"

Neveah nodded. "Maybe. Chief Senaquah son. Maybe first cheta-pook harpoon, like father. Tomhak more seal now. Squintanasis always seal, otter. Kakemook not hunt much now. He hunt fur seal. All good hunter get fur seal. Have short time."

"What about Klayass?"

She scrunched up her mouth, a quick shake of the head. "No be first harpoon. Nobody like much. Make trouble, don't like paddle much. Tomhak say he crazy. Suisha no like."

A rush of air caught our attention and a raven landed in a bent spruce very near us. Neveah hooked an arm under mine and pressed against me. The raven stared and made a guttural click. Neveah averted her eyes.

"What's wrong? I thought raven was good."

"Come look at you, life change. Maybe bad."

"Maybe good?" I said. "Since last night it seems to be looking up."

I felt her smile against my arm. "No, no laugh raven," she said sternly, her words muffled. "Raven get mad."

"Well, we don't want him getting mad at us." I smiled and raven glared back, made a clicking sound and moved along the branch, bringing him a little closer to us. "But I'm not sure this isn't an overgrown crow puffed up to look like raven."

"No, no," she said. "no insult Changer. Crow raven's wife, but she never equal him." As Neveah spoke raven cocked his head as if listening, responded with some sounds that did actually resemble strained human words. He moved a little closer along the branch, glared some more, then slowly spread his wings and took off, leaving the tree branch swaying. "S'long mate," I said.

"Hope him no mad," Neveah said.

"So crow is raven's wife. Is she a good wife?" I asked.

"Of course. Raven very wise. Before he Changer. Change everything the way now. Make animals, birds. Persons. Even make Thunderbird and teach eat chetapook. Then Changer make him raven, but he white. He carry fire from sea to land. Smoke from fire make him black. He stay black after take crow for wife. He let crow make mischief to everyone: eagle, hawk, even persons, but crow never make mischief to raven. Raven so wise get lazy because know how get plenty food. Teach crow, so then she have plenty time make mischief."

Neveah was watching where raven had disappeared beyond some trees.

"You know, in some places there are crows but no ravens."

Neveah shrugged an impatient shoulder. "Don't know those place. Maybe where raven put stupid crows."

I resisted laughing and thought perhaps I had just acquired some of raven's wisdom.

"I should see the woman about the cleaning brush for the fire spears," I said.

"I see Howessa for you-me, how say, *place*. You-me place."

Old Thomtarsh had done excellent work fabricating a cleaning brush from spruce root. She had woven two designs from the tough material with a method to attach them to a long length of willow the thickness of an arrow shaft. I had brought the fouled rum with me and poured a little on the brush and down the Charleville she had used for sizing, ran the first brush up and down a few times and had a look. Amazing. The brush was filthy beyond my expectations. The barrel was a little pitted but bright inside. I tried the second brush and decided the first design was the best. Thomtarsh promised to make more like it in klesehark, (one day). I hurried to Kakemook's to tend the others.

No one was in the lodge and I fell to the task. Neveah found me cleaning away and immediately began chastising me for working today. It meant I did not like her.

"This should be done before morning," I said. "We must practice tomorrow. You too. Lead coats the barrels and must be removed or the fire spears will not work properly. The salty air and heat attracts moisture to make rust."

Her eyes turned liquid. "They say you no like me."

"Nonsense. I will shoot anyone that says such a thing."

She sat in the middle of the lodge and put her face in her hands, despairing.

I leaned the musket I was working on against wallboards and kneeled next to her, put an arm around her shoulders. "I need to get this done," I said. "These people must learn to use these weapons as quickly as possible. Quickly, like the canoes being built. I cannot explain."

She lowered her hands and stared. "You get *vision*," she whispered.

"Well, no, don't get into that. It's probably nothing. I don't really know –"

"Vision not nothing." She touched the side of my face. "I help. Teach what do."

There was no refusing her help. So we cleaned the muskets together and I showed her how to lubricate them with whale oil while keeping the pan clean and dry. We carefully sharpened the flints. I went through the loading sequence and she loaded four of the five Charlevilles.

"Now you will have to show the other loaders how it's done," I said, causing her to straighten and her eyes to glow in the shadowy lodge.

I brought out the Brown Bessys and said these would be our muskets. I showed her how to load them with two-dozen smaller fowling balls, using the same clamshells to measure the charge and ramming everything home with paper patches torn from the Russian ship's log.

Finished, I leaned against a nearby bunk, my back sore from working in an awkward position. Neveah was on her knees in front of the row of muskets. She ran her hands down each barrel, over the complexity of the hammers and pans, the long, smooth stocks.

"Show," she said. "Neveah load-er." Then sternly, "They good load-ers or beat."

"Well, perhaps not beat. Some may need a little more –"

"Beat!" she insisted, nostrils flaring. "Load now. *Vision say.*"

I sighed.

"Load you klooklo," she said seriously.

"Oh yes." I suppressed a smile. "I have every confidence."

"Con-fi . . . how mean . . .?"

"I say our work here is done and you should take me to our little lodge and feed me and make me be your high slave."

She squealed with delight and jumped up like a startled deer. Off she ran with me chasing her.

We stayed in the lodge that evening and night. Neveah went for food and good spring water. I tried to help, but she wouldn't hear of it. I had to stay in our little nest. Of course I protested, tried to help, but she was so determined. And I was so weak.

The next morning was overcast, damp, a shower just finished. Gray light misted down on our musket squad as we trudged along the beach to the designated shooting area. With Neveah at my side I could scarcely think of anything but her. I believe we both understood that morning we must be together, it was stronger than family. At the same time, I had no idea how I would gain control of our futures.

Fire spear practice that morning was quite productive. Everyone shot a little better. The loaders quickly learned their tasks with some extra help from Neveah's sharp tongue, a tone I hadn't heard in full sail until that morning. And she did get the loaders squared away in short order, a credit to any first mate I'd ever encountered. When everything seemed to be going smoothly, the sun obliged by burning through the mist and we peeled off our rain mantles.

We returned shortly after midday to greetings from the natives outside working on their own projects. Children ran up and touched the muskets, ran away screaming as if they had done something prohibited. Neveah and I set about cleaning the weapons. It had been a good practice all around and we talked about this while we worked.

When we finished I stopped suddenly and gazed at Neveah. Around Kakemook's spacious lodge, deserted now except for two old women weaving at the other end. Thin smoke rising from dormant fires. Soft thunder of waves. Incessant gulls, eagle's scream.

I thought about my mother and other people in Boston who claimed an ability to look into the future, although this wasn't a popular subject in most circles after what happened over in Salem a while back. Neveah pressed her hand into mine. In her dark eyes I saw us huddled on a cold beach at the edge of the world. I told myself it was the madness of thinking like a slave, wrenching culture, falling into impossible love . . .

"Neveah, you must promise something."

She stared.

"If something happens, whatever it may be . . . if I tell you to run you must do what I say. You must run very fast and not look back. You must promise."

"Go where?"

"Just away. You must promise."

She stretched out and put her head in my lap, moved my hand over her cheek. "No leave you," she said.

Chapter 18

They had done a fine job on our quarters in Tomhak's lodge. Woven mats with intricate designs of dyed porcupine quills and other colorful materials enclosed our space. Our sleeping places had been remade with a larger bed where Neveah's had been. My bunk had been stripped and covered with two stuffed mats. On it sat one of their good boxes with doweled corners.

Neveah opened the lid and gasped. She began taking out gifts: Colored cloth, a wool blanket, a pair of new moccasins for each of us, several articles of wool and hide clothing, small containers of oil.

There was more, but my attention settled on the musket standing next to the box. While Neveah examined the other items I picked it up, felt its balance. The receiver was scrolled and the stock nicely carved with brass inlays and an ornate sliding brass door covering the patch box. The barrel was smoothly slender and the stock thinner than standard, one of the newer designs. It was a fine modern version of a Kentucky rifle, a smaller bore than the muskets. This type was made for hunting, not war, and was more accurate than the military weapons. A quick check of the contents in the box revealed no balls to load it, yet this was an unbelievable gift for a slave to receive, even a high one, whatever that was. It was smaller and lighter than the muskets and, with no balls the right size, the chief may have thought it was of little value.

I stepped back and shook my head. There was only one person who could have caused us so much good fortune. Suisha and her oldest daughter, Howessa, came to enjoy our surprise, and we thanked them for their contributions. I sat with crossed legs on a mat, rifle in my lap, nodded and smiled as Neveah showed me the items over and over, insisting I look, say something, until I was laughing and so was she. Her excitement was the best gift of all.

"Talk English words."

I followed Squintanasis to our place near the canoe-in-progress, a somewhat neglected project lately due to other requirements and assignments. We did lessons for a time. He abruptly stopped his pronunciations, intertwined strong fingers, stretched them backward while staring at the sandy ground.

"Thank you," I said. "Everything. Especially Neveah."

He did not respond.

"I know it was you," I said. "You have done me great service."

He continued to study the ground between his spread knees as if counting sand fleas.

"You speak good enough English right now to trade."

Squintanasis briefly raised his eyes to mine. The intensity was as unsettling as always, but in that moment I could only admire it. And now I wanted to do him a service.

"Boston Man," he said. "King George Man. Must know more."

I looked around at the activity, those massive, beautiful rocks rising so high above crashing surf. He was so capable at anything he focused on. Yet there was something more to his drive to learn English words.

"When will you be ready to fight the Nittinat?"

Squintanasis tensed and glared without looking at me, relaxed nearly as quickly.

"When fire spear people ready?"

"Soon," I said. "Tomorrow loaders take a turn shooting. If a shooter goes down the loader will take over. If I go down Neveah knows what to do. Each person will have to know the other's duties."

Squintanasis watched me a few moments. "Irish know?"

"I don't know shit from a woodpecker hole. But my father fought in our War of Independence, like I said. He took two balls at Trenton in seventy-six. Nearly froze before they got him home. My mother, before she died, she said he was never the same after that, just like a lot of them, and maybe if I fight Nittinat I won't be either. But he taught me a few things and I'm using them all up and then some."

Squintanasis plucked a lonely shaft of beach grass and stuck the juicy green end in his mouth. "Need more canoes. Two moons everyone work." He continued in a mix of English and Makah. "Two big canoes. Thirty Neeah warriors come. Maybe ten womans. Maybe three moons go."

"Winter soon," I said. "Bad weather. Now better. Maybe Nittinat kill Makah slaves."

"One Makah die, ten Nittinat die."

"Maybe go Nootka ask for help," I said, mixing English with Makah as he was doing. There was a chance of finding an American ship at Nootka, and perhaps Neveah and I could go along if they made such a trip.

"Makah cousin Nootka. Nittinat also cousin Nootka. Make trouble Makah – Makah business. No Nootka. No Boston Man business."

"Just a thought," I said. "You seem ready to do anything to get Nanishum back."

He jerked to his feet and towered over me, eyes wild and hands tensed. *"No touch Nanishum,"* he declared. *"Nanishum marry chief."*

I stood slowly and looked him in the eye. "You don't have poison blood."

For a moment I thought he might strike me. He turned abruptly and marched off. I ran after him. "Listen," I pleaded. "Let me do this for you. I can prove what I say."

"*Prove? What word?*"

Hurrying alongside his stride, I said, "I can show you do not have poison blood."

Abruptly he grabbed me by the loose shirt, pulled me to him with such force I was on tiptoes. "Show you," I managed.

"*Show.*"

He let me down. I started to reach for my knife, changed my mind and held out my hand. "Give me your knife."

Squintanasis leaned back a little, observing me defiantly. He slowly pulled his long iron knife from its sheath and laid it in his hand, handle toward me. I took it carefully, looked at him, moved away a step and drove the point into a log.

"Wait," I said. I ran across sand in the direction of Tomhak's lodge.

Soon I returned with Neveah running in my wake.

I pulled the knife out of the log and cleaned the blade on my forearm. I stepped close to Squintanasis. We looked at each other. I moved the knife up near his throat, to his shoulder, down a little to his upper bicep. I made a cut. When the blood welled I put my fingers into the wound and moved them to my mouth and sucked the blood off them.

"But you might think it not poison to me." I took Neveah's arm and guided her forward. I put my hand on her head, the sleek hair. "Eat his blood," I said. "It is not poison."

With fear in her eyes she stepped forward and put her fingers under the trickle from the wound and brought her fingers to her mouth.

Squintanasis was staring at me.

Neveah repeated her finger sucking after putting them into his blood again. Then she beamed madly and put her mouth on his arm and sucked the blood from the wound.

"She die."

I shook my head. "I would not risk her even for you."

Neveah had to sit on a log. There were flecks of blood on her lips. I sat next to her. Squintanasis slowly crouched before us. Keeping his focus downcast, he touched Neveah's hand.

"We say nothing," I said. "We will wait for you."

Squintanasis rose and looked down at us. Neveah still seemed overcome, but I met his gaze and smiled.

"Irish clever." Squintanasis backed up a step. "Talk tomanawos." I smiled. "Say hello for me." His eyes flared as he turned away.

That first night in our old-new bed we were subdued. The boy, Kishkani, was not present and nothing was said about this. Neveah acted particularly shy, although once under our real wool blanket and mats we began talking about the noises other people made and she got the giggles so we had to pull the covers over our heads. "Tomhak always make grunting noise at end," she whispered. "Dahchat visits his personal lover," I whispered back. "Who?" "The one that lives in his fist." "Oh. He boy." "Sahyoul sounds like he's landing a big fish." She hit my chest while trying to be quiet. "Myself, now, I'm turning into one helluva yoshault." "No – No tonight, too close. Me can't." "But you must," I whispered, "Every night. Every morning. Every noontime. Every – ouch!" She had accidentally hit the spear scar while pummeling me to be quiet, and then she was remorseful, striking my poor wound that way. So she let me rub her hair in my face and bury my mouth in the soft hollow of her neck, then between her breasts. Her necklace rubbed my cheeks.

We tried to keep quiet.

Crisper nights signaled the coming change of seasons. A run of beautiful salmon had Sahyoul and the rest of the fishermen heading into early light even as the rest of us were eating whatever was laid out for breakfast. These were smaller salmon than the earlier ones, bright as a polished sword, and I quickly made some smaller hooks for the fishermen to use. I asked Squintanasis if we might go fishing again, but he was committed to other tasks. He carried his harpoons and bow down to the beach in first light and went out for seal when he wasn't working on the canoe-to-be. An older native I did not know went with him. Each day they went out they brought in a hair seal, and one day I saw them drag two up on the beach for skinning and butchering. Squintanasis said he must hunt now to prepare for the fur seals that were coming. He tried the brass spear tips I had made and said they were klooklo.

The bounties of receding summer were a sign fall was near, time to prepare for winter, a busy time. Squintanasis said the winter hunting season was very important. There was the whale migration, but first the prized fur seals would start to come. On one trip Squintanasis and his silent partner were gone three days and returned with six otter and two seals. I was very impressed, but he treated the otter casually. They were given to a woman who specialized in removing the wonderful fur and Squintanasis said arbei she would cook them and we would eat them with the kau-ite, the bumpy little potatoes I liked.

Sometimes on dry mornings our musket squad honed their skills, generally making good progress until midday. Sahyoul's loader, his nephew Weekooth, named for the month of August for a reason I did not know since he told me he had been born in the spring, often shot in his place during this time since Sahyoul was busy fishing. He was a quiet boy and proved to have a good eye for fire spear. Neveah nearby, a good sky and light winds, the shooters and loaders in a satisfactory rhythm, loaders taking their turns shooting, the smell of burnt powder mixing with salt air. The mood with the musket squad was confident. We were done with regular fire spear training now and I felt strangely contented. Not that there wasn't tension, everybody knew we had been making preparations for battle. But I was teaching these people something. Odd. I'd never felt better about going to work.

Afternoons I fired up the forge and started with a copper bracelet or two for gawking children, another for Wikibokwitch perhaps, a boy in Tomhak's lodge, another for Winaseek or other high-ranking maiden. I made spear and arrowheads. One day I examined a flat piece of iron and figured I could make two knife blades out of it. I would start them tomorrow using my new confidence and experience with quenching.

Just the two of us on the beach a few hundred paces northeast of the village. Squintanasis had brought a carving along, a tiny whistle he was making for the upcoming Klukwalle. The man never seemed to have enough to do, now it was whistles. I thought about Neveah back in the lodge helping Suisha and Howessa after our evening meal, and I wished Squintanasis was impure enough take a woman tonight.

"Fire spear ready?" he asked.

"Ready as I can get them."

"Have vision. Get ready."

"No damn vision. Probably crazy. All this whale oil and sex. Don't believe anything I say. Don't even have a tomanawos."

He didn't respond and I looked up to chalky sounds of his whittling. He worked away at the whistle. It looked finished, but he kept fiddling with it.

"Maybe it's Neveah. How I've come to feel . . .never mind."

Squintanasis smiled slightly. "Maybe memolose make Irish crazy. Come in night take head. Much memolose under lodge. Many people die one night. Live gound. Come up take people's head."

"From a battle you mean?"

Squintanasis shook his head. "One hundred winters before rain come hard. All day, all night. Day. Night. No stop. Ground come down on village. People in ground now."

I thought about this a few moments. "You mean they were buried under the place where Tomhak's lodge is now?"

Squintanasis looked up the beach, nodded. "Too much water. Ground come fast. Four lodges under ground. Many memolose. Come play in night. Say, 'Don't worry to die. We take care you. We are you.'"

We were living on top of their ancestors. A slide had buried those people alive and the survivors had simply rebuilt on the new ground. Perhaps not so simply. I thought about our circle of six families back home and wondered what we would do if half of us were wiped out in a blink. Would we leave? Go where? It was our home. Most would probably stay, remake our enclave, and be more determined than ever to hold their ground.

"Make whistle?"

Squintanasis's voice brought me back to the present. "No, I'm not experienced with the whistle. Our whistles are different."

"How Irish whistle?"

"Well, they're shaped differently and sometimes there's a little pea or something inside. They just whistle. Except musical instruments that sound like a whistle."

He held out his newly finished instrument. "Sun seeds inside."

"I'm really not a person of music."

"Make Irish sound."

I took the small object, held it to my lips and blew – a gutteral sound came out.

Squintanasis chuckled. "No klooklo," he said. He took the whistle and shook it to get any spit out, shook some more so the seeds inside rattled freely, put the whole thing in his mouth and blew. The most incredible bird sounds came out of his mouth.

"Did you work with Kekathl today making the canoe?"

He nodded. "Neveah you woman?"

"Yes," I said, immediately suspicious.

"Chimakum. Quileute be Chimakum. Hoh be Chimakum."

"What? What do you mean?"

"Many time before, flood come. Tooplah high like hills. Go up mountain. Many person go in tooplah. Some land new place. Some Chimakum be Quileute. Hoh. Talk Chimakum."

"Well . . . you trade with those people."

He seemed amused. "Chimakum," he repeated. "Span-ish. Makah slave. Good woman you."

"Good woman," I said. "My woman." We were watching each other. "My woman," I repeated.

Squintanasis gave me an odd look and I had the feeling I had just passed another test of some kind, which caused the sort of irritation you would have for a friend who dared doubt you.

"Maybe Nanishum good woman you."

Squintanasis dropped his gaze and I saw his features relax. He rose straight up from a cross-legged position. "Have yew in water," he said, marched off. He was making another longbow. It was a protracted process and his specialty, making powerful bows that he could shoot dead accurate and were too long for anyone shorter than five-ten to handle well. I wondered if he did it just to irritate shorter fellow tribesmen.

As the weathermen predicted, that night the mild weather ended as a storm blew in and rattled roof boards. The wind grew intense and bluish light flashed through wall cracks; Ha-hok-to-ak's tongue, the lightning fish Thlu-kluts (Thunderbird) wore around his waist when he went whale hunting. Those two certainly seemed hungry tonight.

Up we went, grown men acting like monkeys, mainly naked, lying spread and clinging to roofs to keep them from flying away. Looking through driving rain during bright bursts of lightning I could see others on the roofs of their lodges, human anchors sprawled on wet boards as wind howled, thunder cracked, rain pelted and ran into our bare whatevers. I spit out rainwater and managed to maintain a grip on the slippery cedar.

Finally a respite in the middle of the night. Neveah dried me while I shivered. She wrapped me in two blankets and made me take hot clam juice mixed with herbs, as the others were drinking. I managed to swallow most of a bowl between chattering teeth.

"Damn it," I said. Then in Makah, "Want rum." Tomhak heard me. He went to one of his trunks and pulled out a crock. Winaseek poured some into a wood cup and brought it to me. Just like that. A couple of the men were eyeing me while I lapped it up, providing a moment's guilt, but it quickly passed. It was decent ship's grog, not pure rum, but it never warmed my innards better than that night. These chiefs controlled their spirits pretty well. Perhaps it was the lesson learned from that Russian ship.

"Thank you," I said, extending the cup in a toast toward Chief Tomhak. His look was complacent. He turned to a man who had arrived with a report on a lodge missing part of its roof.

In the morning all regular duties were cancelled while we repaired storm damage in a soft rain. A sudden gust now and then whipped around the lodges and swirled debris as we put unfinished canoes back on their blocks, secured side and roof boards with new lashings. The forge was a mess, but an hour of cleaning and rebuilding the pit restored it to good condition. My makeshift bellows was never left outside so was not damaged.

That night two people in our lodge came down with hacking coughs. Boards were moved on the roof so the sickness could escape. Shaman went from lodge to lodge to arrest sickness and usher it out through the vents. I told Neveah the shaman and clam juice would probably do the job, but this kind of sickness was frightened of rum, and as she could see, it had run quickly from me. "White man medicine," I said gravely, causing her to frown. Then she caught me trying to hide a smile and called me a raccoon in Makah, which means about the same as rascal.

The next day repairs continued to the lodges, but at a leisurely pace. Not long after the noon meal Neveah and I slipped away and took an hour's slow walk down to the river that emptied into the wide bay east of the village. The sun peeked between clouds and brightened the landscape. We made footprints on cool, wet sand above the ebbing tide and Neveah pointed out concentrations of clam beds, their type and when they would be harvested. She dug down and scooped out two white-shelled clams, opened them with a sharp-edged rock she carried in the pouch at her waist. She dislodged the meat inside, tipped the shell up and let the meat slide down her throat, handed me the other one. I couldn't take it in one gulp, but after brief chewing was able to swallow the raw clam. Neveah was amused by my expression.

We found a convenient log near the mouth of the river and sat watching dimples made by the small fish in the shallows, further out swirls by salmon waiting impatiently for the swelling flood tide. Soon they would enter the river for the arduous journey of reproduction that would end their lives and start another generation.

"Come with nets for these," Neveah said. "Not so good as blueback. Make good cakes. You like?"

"I'm sure I will. I was a fisherman back home, and sold them in the pub and along the common."

"Make hooks?"

"No, this is my first try at that. But I like fishing, and like to catch them for others to eat. My father taught me to fish. He was a fair hand at it, but he's tired now."

"Aidan sad to father?"

"Sometimes. I wonder about my older brother and sister holding things together. Taking care of him. I think he wanted to die."

She took my hand. "Chetapook want die, he die. Father want die, he die. Someday, all die."

I put an arm around her shoulders. "I saw a whale die and it was a tragedy. And then it was a blessing. Perhaps survival itself is the tragedy."

"You no die," she said. "Aidan child in me."

"What?" I stood. "What are you saying? We have only been together a short time. How can you know such a thing?"

"Know." She looked at me in a very serious way.

I sat next to her again. "But how can you? I mean, God help him, how can you possibly –"

She put fingers to my lips. "Yes," she said. "Child boy. Strong like Irish. Strong like Chimakum. Maybe be chief."

"What do you say? I do not–"

She put her fingers to my mouth again. "Mother Linyooahn, chief's daughter. Me princess to Chimakum."

It was a bit much to digest. I relaxed into a slouch on the log.

Neveah got out the snack she had brought: fish, a little bear meat, several small tart apples that had started appearing at meals.

"But we have only been together a short time," I repeated.

She shoved an apple in my mouth.

Fish swirled into the mouth of the river. How strange it must seem for a creature that had lived its life in an unlimited environment to meet the restrictions of a river. I put my hand to her cheek and turned her face to me. Such a pretty face and I knew every little part of it. I kissed her. "Our child will have good parents."

"Squintanasis say maybe you go, time in –"

"Shhh." I pulled her head to my shoulder and held her. In a low branch one of the white hawks that frequented this area waited patiently for the fish to come. Beyond, in the shadow of fir trees, the silhouette of an owl. Here it was believed owls were spirits of relatives that had drowned and somehow brought bad luck. In my culture they were usually considered good luck.

"Don't worry," I said, stroking her hair. "Don't worry about anything."

The hawk dropped from its perch. All but the white tail disappeared underwater. The hawk rose with a small salmon struggling against the grip of talons. Wings beat water as the fish fought to stay submerged. Hawk made it to shore and kept beating strong wings on pebbles and sand until the fish was dragged well clear of any chance of escape. Releasing one clawed foot, the hawk hopped higher, dragging its prey. It stopped, chest heaving, looked around with the arrogance of victory. Fish looked heavier than captor, but the hawk had judged right. Now it could eat the rich flesh and carry the rest back to the nest.

As we walked to the practice area, Sahyoul let it be known he was not convinced my plan for the fire spear group's deployment during an attack was right. He hated the idea of hiding behind a log while real fighting was going on. Twisted leg and all, he wanted to be in the thick of it. I asked him if he would rather quit the fire spear and go with knife and club. I added there were several others who would gladly take his place, to which he struck a threatening pose and marched off a short distance to stare at the horizon.

I told the group we would move the targets back to forty paces. I also made the targets a little bigger. This was an extra practice to keep everyone sharp and try different techniques.

Even grumpy Sahyoul warmed to the new challenge. He talked about his great eye for seeing surface fish the way the eagle sees. Nobody disagreed, but Little Misak out-shot everyone again, including me. I had suspected he had exceptional eyesight, and it seemed to compensate for the musket's inaccuracy. Since he seldom went out fishing he did not have the squint of most men here caused by many days of sun glare on water.

I didn't like shooting scatter loads in the Bessys, although Neveah loved taking a turn because it hit so many places at once. But this was not necessary target practice other than to check the wildly random pattern the two dozen small balls made blasting out of the barrel like a badly conceived fowling piece. I wanted to try a little different load in the sixties, and as I was about to shoot a group of mallards came zinging over, so I swung ahead of the group and blasted away. To my surprise two birds fell to the beach. For this I got a brief vocal ovation and Misak limped over to collect the birds.

Sahyoul cast an arrogant look around and said, "Irish shoot warriors in sky."

"Get from sky, eat better," I answered in Makah, which brought a laugh from the others. Finally Sahyoul smiled.

Then Misak sidled up and asked if he might learn to care for the fire spears like Neveah. "In case she do other work," he added, implying she would be called to woman's duties. Neveah did not like this, but I told her someone else should know the procedure, and it was a chance for Misak to *show who he was*. Misak did not have many chances at warrior tasks, something Neveah understood.

After a few rounds I called a halt to practice and put everyone to work digging what lead they could find out of the drift. Most of the balls were too deformed to be reused, but I thought it prudent to save them for the day when a mold might be available.

Back at the village, Neveah and Misak went together to care for the muskets and I was called to the chief's lodge. When I walked in Squintanasis and all the chiefs were in attendance – a formal meeting to discuss strategy in the event the village was attacked. It was humbling to be discussing battle tactics with these seasoned warriors. Chief Kakemook swept an arm as he talked, Chief Senequah preferred pointing. I understood that Tomhak would lead the second wave, or something of the like. Tomhak interjected a word here and there. Squintanasis said little, his brow furrowed in concentration as the others laid out a battle plan. The chiefs finished and Squintanasis spoke.

"Canoes first," he said. "Old on beach. Best behind lodges. Show fishermen and hunters gone. Maybe women and children outside. My arrow first. Fire spears. All arrows when canoes on sand. Warriors come." He added a few more details and fell silent.

Kakemook, Senequah and Tomhak looked around, imagining all Squintanasis had described. The chiefs mumbled among themselves, asked him some questions, added details, finally all agreed. I was relieved to be generally ignored in this symposium of generals, although I wondered what would happen if these preparations could be moot because we just looked up one day and there they were, in our lap.

On the way back to Tomhak's lodge I could only think about Neveah and what she had said earlier. Our child. I had not wanted to start a family – why would I in such circumstances? But now, slave or not, such an event warmed the soul. I could not have wanted her more, and I wanted our child.

When I arrived a present lay on our bed: a new conical hat woven from thin cedar strips with a colored design and a fringe of tough spruce root, tight enough to shed water and provide a shield from the sun. The chiefs and high-ranking people had hats made entirely from difficult-to-work spruce root, watertight, tough, indented crowns signifying their rank, but this hat was perfect and no one could say it exceeded anyone else's because, though it was beautiful, it was made of cedar.

I situated the hat on my head and went to find Neveah. If Howessa or Wineseek had her working I would say we had to tend the fire spears. We would walk the beach and talk about her beautiful work on the hat and about our child.

Chapter 19

After weeks of sunshine and warmth, fog came a little earlier every night and hung longer in the chilly morning. Salmon with skins a darker red than their flesh pushed far up the rivers and hid in the shade of trees dressed in hot-colored leaves. Daylight was noticeably shorter, wolves howled earlier, and the whole village hummed along in the brisk air. Any time of day men would be swimming like whales in front of the village, going under and coming up to expel a loud breath, legs kicking and arms back, going down again, being a whale. Some rolled on the rocky beach or were beaten with kelp whips to toughen themselves for the hunt. Hunters sat alone near the water, meditating, speaking with their tomanawos, preparing themselves for the dangerous challenges ahead. Kanek was one of the hunters and attacked his preparations the way he focused on anything he wanted to master. This was the winter he would throw his first harpoon at a whale, and his father would be watching.

Harpoons were honed, balanced, refitted, lines stretched and coiled, canoes completed, caulked, tested, tuned, but our canoe was not one of them. Squintanasis and the other hunters were interrupted with other tasks, such as making a supply of arrows and spears and bagging hair seals while they were nearby. They had taken enough sea lions to feed the wool dogs all winter. The bones, sinews and other parts of sea lion had many uses, but few people took the flesh, which was bitter. This was just as well, since sea lions were dangerous prey and an enraged bull could upend a whaling canoe.

One hunter showed me his one-and-a-half-fingered hand. "Sea lion take," he said.

Hunters were eager for the fur seal migration because they were regarded as the tastiest food in their varied diet. I had never tasted fur seal, but in Yerba Buena a seamen who had tried it said it was equal to venison, though richer. The fur of this migrating animal was also prized for its softness, durability and warmth. In the meantime I was quite content to gorge on salmon, with a little bear, elk or venison for variety. These land animals the natives considered secondary food so there was little competition. Steamed clams were nearly always available, as were the bumpy little potatoes, nettle stems or other greens. The previous evening three canoes came in so loaded with shooyoult and various kinds of cod they required full time bailing to make the beach. That night after the meal Sahyoul handed me two broken hooks. I replaced them from the stash Squintanasis had me keep.

After a late breakfast of salmon and apples I started for the forge. A familiar sound caused me to look up and see the most certain sign of fall's arrival, several V formations of chattering geese against a cloudy sky, heading south. Squintanasis appeared and said we must talk English words. He seemed distant, as if his mind was on other matters.

We started down the beach, then he changed his mind and we joined Kekathl at the canoe. On the way I noticed Chiefs Kakemook and Tomhak working on canoes. This was not uncommon, but to see them both helping build canoes at the same time made me wonder.

Squintanasis picked up his adze and began to draw it over the hull, smoothing the final contours. I cleaned chips out of the interior behind Kekathl's chisel, saying English phrases that Squintanasis said back to me in a forceful tone. We did not burn inside the canoe now because the interior was nearly complete and Kekathl had already drilled a few holes up near the gunwale to check thickness. The finished hardwood guard that would be attached to the top of the gunwale lay nearby.

Squintanasis produced another new whistle he'd finished a few nights before. He offered it to me and I accepted, because to do otherwise would be impolite.

"But you know I'm no good at this," I said.

"Do more. Klukwalle soon."

I was beginning to feel a little unsettled about this Klukwalle affair.

Squintanasis said after the Klukwalle they would prepare to bring their people back. Warriors from Neeah would join the war party. I must stay and protect the village with the fire spear warriors, except for Kanek and Sahyoul, who would go with them. Tomhak would also stay in Ozette, but Kakemook and Senequah would go to fight the Nittinat.

I wondered if there would be enough warriors. A volley of musket fire would certainly give good support to a surprise attack. But I did not even ask if Kanek would take his musket, and was relieved that Neveah and I would remain in the village.

The *ah-baks* (inviters) arrived two days later from Neeah, midday, four serious-looking fellows and two women in a whaling canoe. Two of the well-painted men went to lodges and threw smooth sticks that stuck upright in the ground and announced the name of each person who was to attend the Klukwalle. These formal invitations had been decided previously and the recipients came outside to acknowledge them. That evening the visitors were fed at Chief Kakemook's big house and slept in the small lodge on the slope.

Squintanasis attended the meal with the Neeah people. I was surprised when Misak appeared and sat next to me for supper at Tomhak's. He grinned and proudly showed off a raised blister on his palm where a hammer had pinched it while he was helping Neveah clean the muskets. They hadn't been fired for some time and I had suggested they be wiped down and re-oiled to avoid rust.

After the meal Misak stayed and we talked about his role as shooter and assistant caretaker of the fire spears. This job was important to him. He could never be like his father, the great harpooner Kakemook, and because of his limitations it was unlikely he would ever be a chief. I had seen him go out fishing, and he made harpoon tips and fishhooks of bone and wood that were well regarded. He was often called on to sing, and he danced in an awkward style but with total sincerity. Because of his father he would never be demeaned for his limitations, his apparent frailness, and when I looked into his dark eyes I could see this advantage saddened his warrior heart.

"Tell you something," I said in my strained Makah. "Squintanasis say I leave soon. Neveah go with me."

"Know."

"Know?"

"Spirits speak father. Squintanasis. Know spirits send you. Maybe no good slave. Maybe crazy. Come Makah show Boston Man way." He gave me an engaging grin. "Irish way maybe better."

"Who would have thought it," I said in English, maintaining the serious expression.

"Make good fish hooks," Misak continued, eyes large. "Know fire spear. Know many things. Beat Nootche. Maybe great warrior. Maybe call fur seal Ozette."

"And maybe raven change back to white," I continued in English.

He frowned and I thought it best to change the subject.

"Misak," I said, switching back to Makah, "you be in charge fire spears when Irish leave. You take this duty?"

"Know," he said.

"You best shooter. Have best eyes. Must learn all fire spear."

Misak slowly nodded. "Irish warrior teach."

The night before we were to go to Neeah the weathermen determined a big wind was coming and we should go by land. That meant walking and if you were a slave it meant a hefty load on your back. I would have attempted to plead a case of necessity at the forge, but Neveah was going too.

I asked Squintanasis how the village would be secured while we were at Neeah. He gave me a questioning look and said there would be preparations. Most of the canoes would be carried up the slope and hidden in the woods, along with food and other provisions. "Kanek, Misak have fire spear. Sayhoul know. Irish take fire spear Neeah."

Early morning our group gathered at the trailhead, paired up with backs to a brisk northwest wind. I had expected a contingent of chiefs, but there was only Senequah with one family member who brought up the rear.

Up front Squintanasis waved an arm and we got going, strung out along the trail up the slope. As predicted the wind increased, and beyond the rock islands tops were blowing off dark swells. There were forty of us including the seven initiates, children about ten to fourteen; these youngsters would join the ones at Neeah. We soon took a trail angling northeast and crossed the small river that ran from the big lake and emptied into the sea east of the village. A convenient log worn flat on top made our crossing easy and dry. There were still a few late salmon in the river, bunched in the deepest pockets, bright red from the spawn and easily seen in the clear water. On a gravelly bar I noticed a fresh salmon carcass ripped apart with entrails trailing into the water; we had disturbed a bear's breakfast.

Rain slanted at us and we all fastened our mantles. I snugged my new hat down tight against my ears.

The trail was good mostly, rugged and slippery in places, regular views of the ocean between the trees. My pack load consisted of wooden masks wrapped carefully in mats so they wouldn't be damaged, plus a musket and makings. My load appeared bulky but didn't weigh as much as what the other slaves were expected to carry, except for Neveah. Though one of the youngest slaves in the line, she had been assigned slave leader and carried only a water sack; I wondered who had arranged her assignment.

As we topped a rise I looked through an opening between the trees and abruptly stopped. The person behind bumped me but I barely noticed. About five miles offshore a ship was tacking into the northwest swell, flying plenty of sheet for the conditions.

"Boston Man cloud ship?"

I glanced at Squintanasis who had come up to my side. "Yes, I think she's American," I said. "The way she's going it's a confident captain. Maybe she'll stand in at Neeah."

"Maybe go Nootka."

Emotions coursed through me: yearning, excitement, dread. I imagined Neveah walking a Boston street, wearing a dress like my mother's favorite. I leaned back against a rock. The ship was far off but I could see she was steady in her tack, and I knew all hands were alert to her every change.

"Go," Squintanasis said.

In the afternoon we passed near a small village, Soo-ees Squintanasis called it. About twenty Makah came up to greet us on the trail and a dozen – including three initiates – fell into line to accompany us to Neeah.

The rain quit and the sun was just above the horizon by the time we reached Neeah. We filed out on the beach to a subdued wind and shouts of greeting. The village was similar to Ozette, a few more lodges, set in a bay with some protection from west and southerly winds. A carved figure stood outside what I thought must be the tyee chief's lodge here. Smoldering fires flickered on the beach in the fading light and Neeah residents gathered round to greet us, wooden drums sounded and we were hustled into lodges where food was put before us. The chief welcomed everyone, even me. "Welcome high slave," he said, and I glanced at the short-haired slaves in attendance, but no one seemed to give this distinction any notice.

We were well fed and assigned to various lodges. Neveah and I, along with Squintanasis and Kekathl, were sent to a large building next to Chief Utilla's lodge, the apparent domain of a lesser chief.

Our accommodations were less private than I was used to and we were not quite together, Neveah sleeping on a bench next to mine, our heads nearly an arm's length apart, the way most Makah couples slept. We were in a compartment with several other Ozette people, divided by chest-high boards but open to most of the lodge, so getting any closer did not seem appropriate. Especially with Squintanasis nearby filled with big thoughts, staring at the ceiling. At least Neveah and I were close and I would see this new thing they called a Klukwalle.

I was just drifting off when the first wolf howl seeped through wallboards. More howls, but these were not the wolves I had been hearing for months. Neveah had said this was a ceremony for initiates, that they must embrace the bravery and loyalty of wolf because all Makah had the heart of wolf. That seemed noble enough, but would we be allowed some sleep first? How long would the howling go on?

"Until tired," Neveah whispered back. Then in Makah, "Maybe long time. Maybe hear bird. Lynx. Thunderbird maybe, he know all."

"What does Thunderbird sound like?"

"Thunderbird thousand wings."

"How can they lay out there in the brush and make the sound of a thousand wings?"

"All Irish tribe a-whatl-tsuck?"

"I'm different."

"Go sleep," she hissed.

"Need comfort. It's the howling."

"Maybe go howl too," came a low voice from across the smoky room. "Need make noise, go be wolf," Squintanasis continued in English, "Maybe make crow talk."

The howls lessoned and I was just drifting off when there were hurried footsteps outside. I turned to see through dim light a native in black face enter the lodge. He called names.

Four boys and two girls jumped out of their beds and stood at attention in front of the man at the door. His face was completely black up to the eyes and I made out red and black designs on his chest, hemlock boughs tied in his hair and around his waist. He turned and ran out with the youngsters at his heels. There were more people out there. The sounds of many feet grew fainter.

No one else in the lodge had made a sound or even moved.

"Where are they going?" I whispered as low as I could.

"Initiates go," Neveah whispered.

"But where?"

"Go sleep. No look. No talk."

"Shut up," came the voice from across the room.

Eventually the howling began to sound like singing, and the good food and fatigue from the long day's hike caused my eyes to close. I dreamt of warriors with wolf heads and they were none too friendly.

In the morning as we sleepily picked at the food placed in front of us by women of this residence, a voice got about half the people in the lodge to step outside. It was another *ah'bak*, and he was re-inviting all qualified people of this lodge to be part of ceremonies. Neveah and

I were not qualified, nor were the other slaves, and I learned some citizens were not invited to take an active part in the Klukwalle. In reply to my whispered questions, Neveah said there was not an age limit, it was just that some people had not been initiated or were out of favor for some reason. In fact, she told me, a group of hunters were out looking for a person who had committed bad acts that required punishment. This person was trying to escape his punishment.

A growing seriousness in these proceedings caused me to reign in my curiosity. Squintanasis was absorbed in his own thoughts and Chief Utilla, as well as other high-ranking tribe members, came into the lodge and conferred with him in hushed tones. I assumed Chief Senequah was busy in a similar way.

After our meal I was sent with another male and three female slaves to gather wood for the fires that were being brought up in all the lodges. Neveah went with some women to prepare food. My group walked around the sandy beach about halfway to a point where the bay ended. Here was a large concentration of drift. We picked through tangles of debris for logs small enough to drag back to the village. How many trips would it take? How useful a horse would be, and I wondered if these people had ever seen or dreamed a horse.

I squinted up the beach and saw, above the point, a shape that looked like the remains of a structure with a small section that appeared to have been a wall of vertical logs. I did not know the people I was with and resisted the urge to go up and investigate.

As we attached lines to the longer logs, singing began in the village, *tse'ka* songs they were called, and they carried clearly over the water as we toiled. One of the women spoke sharply to a girl of about fourteen who seemed unwilling to do her share. These women seemed determined to do as much as any man and I didn't feel the need to refuse them. As we lashed kelp ropes to logs, several drums started up. The singing and drums grew in volume as we dragged our loads across sand to the village. Not everyone was singing the same song, but there was a similar cadence, the same with the different drums and now whistles and rattles, so it all blended together as variations of the same feeling.

We made two more trips for firewood and took a midday break for a meal. I only caught glimpses of Neveah and had no idea where Squintanasis was. I found it curious that there were people running around with lighter hair than mine, and I caught glimpses of skin light as mine. At the same time some residents here were darker than Kekathl, who was among the darkest in the tribe.

At twilight the singing really came up in earnest, with drum, whistle and rattle accompaniment. We took our evening meal in our assigned lodge. I wedged into a spot in a crowded circle with Ozette people as food was being served. The quiet during mealtime brought a palpable seriousness that lay like a cloak over our hunched forms. The chief of this lodge was a rugged, broad and powerful fellow who resembled our own Chief Kakemook and presided from a raised affair of inlaid benches, surrounded by family and several stout men. Neveah was one of the servers. When finished, she joined me in the circle.

"Are they dancing now?"

"Yes," she whispered back.

"But we can't go down there?"

A quick shake of the head. "No talk now."

I stole a glance around at this solemn circle of sitters and squatters, eating and listening to what was going on at the neighbor's.

A blood-curdling scream stopped my chewing. Following the scream came loud snarls. Several people in the circle began eating very fast, some even grabbed up food out of bowls and tucked it into their clothing. One man, gripping a slab of salmon, ran into a corner of the lodge and hid behind a trunk.

I looked questioningly at Neveah. "Wild man come," she whispered.

Vicious snarls outside the lodge. A muscular man leaped through the doorway wearing the most hideous mask I had ever seen: fierce, ugly, lots of white teeth but otherwise brown except for bright red eyes. Another man charged into the lodge and began stiff-legging around, roaring and snarling, causing people to cower. The second man wore a mask like the first and both were nearly naked and bleeding from numerous shallow cuts all over their bodies. Their blood made patterns in dark dirt that had been ground into their skin in swirls. They began grabbing up handfuls of loose dirt from the floor, ashes, food, loose clothing, anything they could get their hands on and slinging it around the room, over the food, people, everything, all the time screaming and snarling at the top of their voices. A sudden laugh got one of the intruder's attention. He jumped on the young man who had laughed and grabbed his face – his hand jerked – and he was up again, marching around in his crazed rhythm. The young man moaned and blood ran from the side of his mouth. The intruders pushed people, kicked them, kicked me, kicked Neveah once in the back – I resisted attacking the crazed performer – generally tore up everything in sight, although they did avoid kicking or directly harassing the chief and his family – and abruptly were gone, stiff-legging out the door.

As their screams faded into the next lodge I whispered to Neveah if she was all right. She nodded, head down. The young man who had laughed held a bloody cloth to his torn mouth.

About the time I thought it might be time to clean up the mess another scream sounded, deeper than the others, guttural to the point of gagging, and a naked man rushed through the doorway in a strange white mask that looked like a bird with teeth – not Thunderbird or Eagle. The eye sockets were sunk very deep into dark holes and a hemlock bow decorated the top of the mask. His tense body sported cuts and the streams of blood trickled over a white substance that covered him head to bare feet.

This performer wandered cat-like around the lodge making gulping and gagging sounds, stepping over people, stepping in the food, climbing up and down over trunks. Finally he grabbed up a harpoon and flung it so the point went right through the wall of the lodge. With that he rushed out.

People began to rise, including Neveah, and started cleaning up. I tried to help but she put an arm out, stopping me, and shook her head. I noticed only women and lesser slaves were doing the cleanup. I left the lodge briefly to relieve myself and wash and turned in early. Neveah was still working. I drifted off, lulled by the sound of distant singing.

I awoke when Neveah came to bed. "Do you have duties in the morning?" I asked.

"No do anything morning," she whispered back. "Cutting. Initiates come. No talk. No look. Thunderbird come. Many tomanawos." I was about to ask if anyone would mind if we had a little time together when she reached out and I took her hand. "No talk," she said. "Careful morning."

I lay back on my bunk thinking this party was certainly not as much fun as the one at Ozette.

At breakfast it was as Neveah had portended. What few words passed were in whispers. People moved in and out of the lodge carefully, as if they were being watched. The chief wasn't present but some of his family members were as downcast and silent as the rest of us. Neveah ignored me and went about her tasks of serving food and fetching whatever was needed, responding to orders in sign language. We had barely finished eating when distant drums sounded, then singing. Most of the people in our lodge filed outside and I was about to do the same when Neveah caught my eye and shook her head.

So I went to my bunk and amused myself for a time by scrubbing my teeth with a spruce-root toothbrush I'd brought along. I had shaved before we left Ozette, so used this leisure time to strip to the waist and wash with the soap we'd been issued in some water I heated and poured into a woven bucket. The sounds of drums and singing came closer.

A young boy stepped through the doorway and was followed by other mostly naked initiates, their young bodies covered with bloody cuts. Most had to be in pain, yet their expressions were serene, dreamlike. Fifteen children, including six girls, came into the lodge followed by four older initiates in their mid-teens. Two of the older ones were girls. They marched stiff-legged around the lodge as drums and singing sounded outside. No words were spoken. Completing their oblong circle, they exited with the same stiff gait.

Now people were getting up and talking in low tones to each other. I went to the center of the lodge until I caught Neveah's eye. She nodded and I went outside to stand with the other spectators. The procession of bloody initiates was entering the next lodge, escorted by a group of masked men. One was Squintanasis, unmistakable even heavily painted with a wolf mask covering his head. These older warriors had some cuts too, though not as many.

Soon the initiates came out of the lodge in that affected, stiff-legged gait and moved to the next residence. They had quite an audience now, perhaps several hundred counting children, who all stood reverently near their lodges watching. It seemed these young people were acquiring the spirit of wolf, and the cutting was a display of the brave side of this spirit. I began to understand this was the public part of initiation, their scars would be worn with pride. The rest was private and could only be attended by ranking members of the tribe, including teachers. Squintanasis was involved in all of it, and I wondered what his particular area of instruction might be.

I returned to my bunk and stretched out. I'd lived with these people for some time, been adopted, in a manner of speaking, by one of the most respected members of the tribe, yet I understood little about their ways. I was just beginning to see the great tree – the roots were still hidden, and perhaps always would be for me. There would always be doors I could not look behind.

I dozed off and was awakened by a commotion outside. I crowded out the entrance with other curious people to see someone being dragged down the beach with a line tied around his feet. A circle of ten men formed around him as he bellowed like a wounded seal. One of the men in the circle was Squintanasis. As I came closer I saw that the man groveling on the beach was Nootche. They released his bound feet and pulled him roughly up. Nootche looked around hopefully. A club cracked across his back and the real punishment commenced. He was cut and beaten by all the men in the circle. Nootche continued to scream and bellow as knives of muscle shells slashed him. Whichever way he turned he was clubbed from the side or behind, until he lay in a moaning heap with fingers vainly clawing sand.

Two men in black face stepped forward and spit on him. A few final harsh words were spoken.

The circle dispersed.

No one went to Nootche's aid. He lay there moaning, mumbling unintelligibly, and no one gave him notice. I did not know what he might have done, but guessed his ordeal had been earned over a period of time.

I walked down the row of lodges, around canoes receiving maintenance, past rows of racks holding drying clothes, fish and other flesh, and started along a well-worn trail into the trees. I had gone several hundred paces, moping along without really thinking about where I was going, and looked up to see a wildly overgrown white beard worn by a skinny white man standing in the path with an armload of wood. I was so shocked I just stood staring, as he did, until without a word he turned and hurried away.

"Wait." I went after him but he did not stop or look back. He had a severe limp and was quite tall. I caught up with him in front of a crude, weathered cabin in a small meadow, built up against a stand of spruce.

"Who are you?" I asked. "I am Aidan. From Boston. Captured by heathen Hoe and sold to Makah. Where do you hail from?"

The man stared from watery blue eyes. White hairs on his head lay like a sparse bird's nest. He walked a few slow paces and dropped his load of wood near the makeshift door of the cabin, came back to stare at me some more.

"Engliss," he said, and spit to one side.

"No. American. No Engliss. You?" I pointed at him, causing his weak eyes to flair.

He answered in a language I did not understand, then I thought I recognized it. "Russian?"

"Ah." With a parting sneer he turned and went into the cabin. The rickety door slammed shut. I heard a locking board clunk into place.

"We have things to talk about," I called. "We are not so different."

I waited, tried calling to him again through the door, but there was no response. I hurried back to the village and looked for Squintanasis, but could not find him. Finally I spotted Neveah working at a fish drying rack.

"I just saw a Russian man. He lives in a cabin near here."

She turned slightly from her task and cocked an eyebrow. "Other one die. Spaniard too. Only one now. Very old."

"But how . . . when did they come here? Why is he here?"

"Spanish from fort." Neveah pointed across the curve of the bay where I had seen the remains of a structure. "Dead now."

"That was a Spanish fort? Right over there?"

"Go maybe eight summers ago," she said, mixing English with Makah. "Go fast or Makah kill. One man die. Do bad things."

I looked across the bay at the place where the partial wall still stood, perhaps two miles away. A Spanish fort! What were they doing here? Certainly they were keen on striking a flag on any patch of ground they set foot on, but why here? Eight years Neveah said, more or less. That was about the time the big clamor started for otter, which had become scarce, and even more valuable.

"What did the Spaniard do that was bad?"

"Rape Makah not even slave."

"So Makah drove them out?"

"Makah mad," she said. "Want bad Spanish. Spanish chief no give. Makah make war drums, want Spanish chief give bad man. Spanish afraid, stay in big house. One day people go clam beach. Two canoes. Spanish make big fire spear speak. People say make fire and thunder. Canoe fly in air. Kill five people." Neveah flipped another slab of shooyoult. "Drums make real war song," she continued. "Spanish stay big house. Hide behind big fire spear. Makah watch. One day Spanish leave hurry."

"And they left someone?"

She pointed at the island across the bay. "Maybe not bad man. Some say maybe Spanish chief leave slave."

"So what happened to him?"

"Some say Makah kill. Squintanasis say Russian kill with knife. Squintanasis never say false thing."

I took a deep breath, watched her flipping halibut fillets. "He never mentioned there was another white man here."

"Russian."

"Yes, yes, but my God, we might have developed a communication. How long has he been here?"

"Suisha say twenty summers. Maybe more. No matter. Russian."

"What do you mean? So what if he's Russian?"

She stopped what she was doing and gave me a level look. "Know Russian?"

"No," I admitted.

"Russian disease. Poison blood. Kill many people."

"Well, I know what happened at Ozette was terrible – "

"Happen more," she said emphatically. "Other place. North. Maybe south, Big River. Many person die. No take Russian now. Kill Russian cloud ship. No take now."

"But there is a Russian living a double stone's throw from this village. He's been there a long time. Why? What is he doing here?"

She shrugged, continued working. "No disease. Kill Spaniard. Show things. Show how cook pig."

"What? Pig? Pigs around here? Are you talking about pigs? Oink, oink?"

She frowned at me, a kind of half-smile on her lips, and pointed toward the island at the entrance to the bay. This was not a large island, steep and wooded, about the size of Dog Island. It was quite a distance and I squinted, trying to see pigs running around. "Oh, for the taste of pork," I muttered and walked slowly away.

At the chief's lodge I paused to watch a parade of initiates down the line of lodges as they moved in a stiff dance around an outside fire. Many of them now wore masks and lines of dried blood covered their bodies like torn nets.

The midday meal was a casual affair in our lodge; women put bowls of food around the two main fires. Neveah did not join me so

I ate in silence. Several natives who sat to eat studied me. A young woman crouched near me and said, "You Irish."

"Yes." She wore a nicely decorated cedar skirt and a small bone in her nose and was somewhat attractive in a fierce sort of way.

"Squintanasis slave."

"My master and mentor." In Makah I asked, "Who you?"

"Yat-a-kula. Daughter Chief Klar-dah-shook. Chief Utilla uncle. Irish make nice coppers band for arm?"

"I did make a few, but I do not have the tools here." I bit into tasty salmon.

"Come Ozette." She put a hand on my thigh. "Make coppers arm band. Nice you."

"Um. Irish have woman."

"Slave. You high slave." Her grip tightened. "Me princess."

"I would have to check with Squintanasis," I said in English. "My master makes all my social arrangements." I threw in a couple more English words, but she was not discouraged.

"Maybe tomorrow go woods. Nice you."

"Maybe," I said with a shrug. "We must ask Squintanasis," I added in Makah. This seemed to satisfy her and she smirked at the other women who had been watching us. Yatakula brought me some berries, gave my head a little pat and left with a flourish and clatter of ankle bracelets.

After the meal a rough-looking man, painted in black face and showing fresh cuts, came into the lodge and presented me with a musket that looked much the worse for wear. He informed me that Squintanasis wanted me to take care of this weapon so we could hunt tomorrow. With that he handed me a bag of makings. I looked inside to see balls, powder and patches mixed together in one mess. The musket was not military, but a fine hunting rifle, though now it was in poor condition. When I unloaded the weapon it held at least a double load and too many patches.

I cleaned out the hammer assembly and pan, scraped the frisson, ran a little oil in pivot points. The flint wasn't too bad. I didn't think I should do more since the Charleville musket I had carried from Ozette was more familiar if Squintanasis and I were to go on a hunt. The most interesting thing about this weapon was its similarity to the caliber of the fine little rifle I had been given in Ozette. I filched a heaping handful of balls from the sack of makings and stashed them in my personal things, then set the rifle in a corner and wandered outside.

Men marched around in black face, blood lines crisscrossing their bodies. Down at a beach fire an initiate was being restrained with ropes around his wrists. He pulled against his bonds, emitting wolf howls. Several younger ones were in an equal frenzy, dashing around and over the big fire, growling and howling like wolves. All the while a group in the background sang chanting songs, *Hu-hu hu, ya-hu we, ha ya*, and so on. A young initiate grabbed up a piece of drift and began hitting the fire. Other initiates picked up firewood and began doing the same, yelling, beating on the fire, sparks flying. They kept scattering burnt wood and coals until the fire was out. When that was accomplished everyone calmed down. The boy was released from his bonds and singing resumed with a happier tune.

Pigs out there on that island. The Spanish brought pigs. I wondered if they'd brought some of their stubby cattle, but Neveah hadn't mentioned them. The Spanish seemed to bring everything except their women, which may have something to do with why they were always so hard on the locals.

In late afternoon a procession of initiates started again at the west end of the village, but now they all wore masks, a small wolf type, not the big garish ones I'd seen earlier. They were accompanied by some very active folks in strange, colorful masks. Some resembled raccoons, others dressed in yellow and black with a pointed beak. They started in our direction with a chorus of singers bringing up the rear.

As they drew nearer I heard buzzing. People close to the group uttered startled yells. Ah, the black and yellows must be bees. Neveah appeared at my side.

"It must be all right for us to watch now," I said.

"Stick you."

They were jabbing quite a few people, darting into the crowd after their prey. When they were almost upon us I pushed Neveah behind my back. She put her arms around my waist and peeked out under my arm. One of the bees jabbed at her around my hip with a sharp bone, which I deflected, but on the second try the point pierced my thigh. Neveah screamed, but I think it was mostly delight. The raccoon people were racing through the crowd causing all sorts of havoc. Through this the initiates marched stiff-legged, trance-like, blackened faces serene, gazing ahead. The group went the length of the village and back, then into the Klukwalle house.

It was a quiet, cool afternoon with clearing sky and a fire was built up on the beach in front of the Klukwalle house. When the flames flicked high, food was brought out. The Klukwalle house was crowded with tribal members, the initiates and their supporting cast. Neveah and I took our food near the big outside fire. Other slaves were there and lower tribal members, children, women. As we started to eat, Yatakula appeared and put a bowl of mixed berries in my lap. She patted my head and walked away. I felt Neveah's eyes boring into me. I shrugged, "One of the curious women I encountered today."

"Aidan take curious woman?"

"You were once curious." I met her eyes; they were large and hot. "I told her you were my woman." She kept glaring at me. "And that all social contacts had to be cleared with Squintanasis."

She turned back to her food, cheeks burning. "Squintanasis will protect me from her," I said. "I had to be nice, she's a chief's daughter."

"Yatakula want all woman's mans."

I put an arm around her shoulders. "Let's take our food somewhere and be alone. You are my woman. Don't worry."

"All man chewar (penis) like curious woman. Plenty Neeah. They like play chewar to Ozette man."

"Then let's go where you can hide mine from them."

She smiled slyly.

We slipped away with our bowls heaped with food. I threw a mat blanket over my shoulder and we took the path toward the Russian's house, but changed to another trail she knew and eventually came to a small, clear stream. As we watched a salmon made its way up a riffle, tail crest slashing the surface. I ripped up some ferns and spread them out, put the blanket over the top. We sat eating and Neveah explained what would happen the next day.

"We could take a bath here," I said.

She looked at me shyly, then gathered up the food and indicated I should follow her up a brushy trail next to the stream. Soon we came to a tiny meadow next to a waist deep pool. Small white butterflies circled our heads as we stripped off our clothes and stepped into the cool water. A salmon bumped my leg as we settled up to our necks. Neveah splashed water in my face, then squealed when I went after her.

I carried her out of the stream and lay her down on the soft cedar blanket amidst wildflowers and damp grass. We were very alone like the first night in the small lodge. I ducked my head and began at her navel, kissed inside one wet thigh, then the other, slowly moved higher. The breeze on my head and neck would have been cold, but

I couldn't be cold, any more than Neveah was. We came eagerly together and I felt her seize up almost immediately. Gradually she relaxed and we began again, slowly. She had become a very good kisser and was now teaching me.

We lay on our backs holding hands, staring through leafy branches at the patchwork of clouds surrounded by rivers of blue that seemed to move in the opposite direction as clouds slid over us. She moved her head to my shoulder, nuzzled, began running her hands over my body.

We got back to the village late in the afternoon and no one seemed to take notice. Until we got to our lodge, where Squintanasis was just coming out. He looked at both of us sternly and started to walk away.

Over a shoulder he said, "Slaves run. Make tired. Must beat." But I saw the grin.

Neveah and I ate again and decided to walk up the beach. As we neared the remnants of the Spanish fort she said this is where kautie, the bumpy little potatoes I liked, had come from. The Spanish buried things and made them grow. Some people from Ozette had watched this from hiding, and after the Spanish left the people of Neeah and Ozette ate the things the Spanish made grow. Some Ozette people took the kautie home and made holes in the ground and put cut kautie in there as the Spanish had done and now they made them grow every year. They had tried different places, until the spirits told them where the kautie wanted to grow. The Neeah people did not put kautie in the ground every year, so now they traded with the Ozette people because many Neeah people wanted them.

"Where do they grow them?"

"Some near village," she said. "Other places secret. More every year. Suisha know all place. She say, maybe trade kautie Quileute,

Hoh."

There wasn't much left of the fort: the remains of a charred wall, some scattered yellow bricks; they had been serious enough to build an oven. Neveah feared disease and wouldn't venture inside the area where the fort had been.

The compound had been big enough to comfortably accommodate about sixty people. There were the remains of outbuildings, no doubt used for livestock. Yet the scale was so different from Yerba Buena I wondered if they had a real conviction about digging in permanently. Rumbles of war between our countries and England over trading rights at Nootka had finally pressured the Spanish enough to leave that place. So they came across Fuca's Strait with a few men and squatted next to people who didn't trust them to begin with. To establish something? Or merely to keep an eye on who sailed up Fuca's Strait?

"It is strange," I said to Neveah as we walked back along the beach to the village. "Our tribes are so different. Yet there are things the same."

She hooked her arm in mine. "Chiefs want more. People want more. All want trade. Get new thing."

I thought about this for a few steps. "Chiefs want more because their people expect it. Yet it is the source of much trouble."

"You want be chief?"

"Hmm. What I want is for you and our child to be safe. For now we are known in this place, and we have some value."

"You stay, maybe Squintanasis make you citizen."

I stopped and stared at her. "What are you saying?"

"Then we marry. Now only slave marriage. You leave, take me?"

"Of course." I pulled her to me and pressed my cheek against the top of her head. "You must know I would not leave you."

"Go your tribe," she whispered. "Want woman there?"

"Stop it. You are my woman. If I go you go with me."

"Squintanasis say maybe go. Maybe not like slave too much."

I held her shoulders tightly and bent to look into her eyes. "Stop it. He does not speak for me. I will talk to him."

"High slave still slave."

"We'll damn well see about that. You are with me now and he will not change this."

She wrapped her arms around my waist and we stood for a time on the beach with the sounds of tse'ka songs and surf swirling around us. She was right of course, we were slaves, but I was involved with them now, their ambitious plans. When the time came I would use whatever advantage I had to keep us together.

The rest of the evening was spent eating too much and listening to singing. The next morning Neveah and I had few duties, and about midday we slipped away to the little stream to watch the last of the salmon struggle to get back to the place where they were born. We sat on a mat as she told me a little about her time in Neeah. When she had first been brought here everything seemed so different from her village – she stopped talking in mid-sentence and sat with her head down. I put my arm around her, but she abruptly straightened and with a determined look continued: After Chief Utilla decided to give her to Tomhak, who was in the village at the time, Suisha had come and found out *who she was*. Suisha told her husband to take her and then she had gone to Ozette. It was good luck, she said, going with Suisha. Tomhak and Suisha made a good house.

Of course I wanted to ask what had happened to her at Neeah, comfort her. Yet I held back. Perhaps it was better if I didn't know everything. I did not want to make an enemy here. She needed me, our child needed me. "You see, your father's teeth were working for you."

Neveah smiled and the cloud left her face.

In the afternoon of the fourth day of Klukwalle excitement grew in the village. To a background of tse'ka songs people came and went to various lodges and conferred with one another in hushed, eager tones. In the chief's lodge trunks were being unloaded and more masks brought out. Slaves could not be a part of this so Neveah and I took a walk along a trail she knew. We came upon several other slaves, and a few Makah citizens who were not being included in the ceremonies, out in the woods and meadows, talking among themselves or collecting weaving materials.

After the evening meal there occurred an amazing procession of masked marchers. The initiates led the parade, recognized by their carved up bodies. There were masks of every description, many wolf variations, birds, animals, even a couple of large, colorful Thunderbird masks that, as the procession drew nearer, I could see were worn by women.

By the time they came to our lodge they had already been into several others and picked up more masked marchers. The tone was not so serious now, with more laughing and teasing among the marchers and those in attendance. Neveah and I huddled together as the initiates and then the others traipsed through the lodge, the older members yelling and poking people with sticks and sharp bones. But none of it was done with malice, more a letting down of emotion. Behind the marchers came the singers, a few carrying torches. When they had toured the entire village all the masked marchers returned to the Klukwalle house and soon a big commotion arose. When I asked, Neveah said this was the time for capturing the masks. Everyone had to be "captured" and their masks taken off. Some resisted strenuously and were ganged up on by the strong men, but it was all part of the game.

Things got more and more boisterous down at the Klukwalle house until a sort of finale was reached and it grew quiet. I was very sleepy and ready to turn in, but Neveah came and cuddled up and asked if I would walk on the beach and it seemed the perfect thing to do. We took our moccasins off to feel the wet sand. A nor'wester caused waves in the bay to pound the beach and run up to swirl over our cold toes. Light rain brushed our cheeks. As we strolled more tse'ka songs began, the softest songs yet, and I asked if we could join the singing.

Neveah shook her head and spoke in Makah. "Any citizen sing any song now. No matter who own. Any citizen ask for any story, no matter who own. Slave no sing. Slave no hear story unless citizen say."

"What do you mean, own?"

"All song belong family make. All story own to family know. Family property. But Klukwalle many share. Makah *know who they are.*"

I put my arm around her shoulders, felt her chilled skin, put the soft mat I was wearing over my clothes around her and hugged her to me as we walked. "What will happen tomorrow?" I asked.

"Tomorrow klooklo. Tsu-tsu-yu'kwah. Everyone happy. Feast. Games."

"More? I will be fat and stupid by the time this party is over." I staggered with arms out and head down, as if gorged, causing her to laugh. I'd not been known for clowning, it's not the smart course when you drink with older men or get taken and made a slave. But I was once able to make my mother laugh, and now I loved to hear my girl's laugh.

Chapter 20

In the misty morning there was again much activity at the Kluk-walle house, and more wood needed for fires. Eight of us went early to the piles of drift to scavenge. A fog bank lay just offshore and ghostly wisps eddied around treetops on the island. While untangling a long limb from a pile I glanced at the island – then stared and squinted. It was low tide and there, rummaging near the water's edge, were three large pigs: one yellowish, the others with dark red markings over dull white. A slave, a native who spoke a language I did not understand, yelled something. He was shaking a fist at the pigs over on the island. I wondered if he considered them bad spirits.

We dragged our loads back to the village. A group of painted citizens were busy near the water, setting up board drums while initiates lined up for some kind of show. Spread out on the beach an audience was gathering, but there was no singing or cavorting jesters. As we took our loads to the assigned places the drumming began and the initiates, wearing all sorts of decorative masks, began a rhythmic dance; moving together and mingling, yet each alone, wolves now, showing *who they were*, coming out the other side, complete Makah. The dancers moved to the drumming against a backdrop of sea, birds, sky, and I saw something I could not define because it was not of the eye, but the heart.

I did not drop the firewood, but set it down quietly. A single dancer with a gaily colored wolf mask danced separately from the group, an older youngster, going from house to beach to another house to the beach, making swooping motions like an eagle, yet he was definitely a wolf. All this time the other initiates moved to their own rhythm.

From in front of the chief's house I watched the dancing ritual until the wildmen began to appear. They did not act as crazed as before but I had seen enough of them and went inside. Squintanasis found me checking over the Charleville musket.

"Go."

"Where?" I said.

"Get pig." He pointed at the rifle in the corner. "Fire spear get. Take Ozette." He rubbed his belly.

"Um. I did not know you were a connoisseur of pork. So you have tasted pig?"

Squintanasis looked at me a long moment. "Gifts for people," he said in English. "Teachers choose. Me choose pig." Then he switched to Makah. "Say Irish slave need. Irish slave woman need. Must have strength teach fire spear. Teach English. Make boat."

I laughed, realizing Neveah must have told him about my yearning for pork. "You said no such thing. No matter. Let's get the damn pig. But I will take the musket I brought along rather than that one."

Squintanasis became serious. He asked if anyone here had asked me to teach about fire spear. When I said no, he told me Chief Utilla had asked him to use the weapon the native had offered me to hunt the pig. It did not make fire and they wanted me to make it work.

I replied again nothing had been asked of me beyond what I had told him, and added I would come to him immediately if someone made such a request.

"Maybe Ozette people teach fire spear Neeah," he said. I took this to mean proprietary knowledge was in the same class as songs and stories, owned by the person who first acquired it. Business was business.

We boarded a canoe with me in the bow, Squintanasis as helmsman at the stern, a squat slave I did not know amidships, and paddled out to the island. As we approached I studied the steep banks and dark trees along the top. The tide was beginning to move in and I could see no animals on the beach. The shoreline was interrupted by looming dark rocks with sand and tangles of kelp and smaller rocks between. Squintanasis pointed with his paddle and we headed into a narrow slot in the lee of a large boulder.

After jumping out gripping a stout spear, Squintanasis gave an order. The slave whined a protest – the order was repeated in a stronger tone. We dragged the canoe up to compensate for the advancing tide. The native slowly walked away along the edge of the water, climbing over rocks and furtively glancing back and up at the tree line.

"Where's he going?" I said.

Without answering Squintanasis motioned to me and we fell in behind the man about thirty paces back. We made our way slowly along the beach, over boulders and drift, on the lee side of the island. Squintanasis motioned me up next to him. "Get pig," he said quietly.

At first I wasn't sure what he meant. Then I cradled the musket, re-checked the pan, cocked the hammer. We barely covered ten more paces when the slave screamed and bolted into the water. A huge pig charged out of the trees above and made for him, bounding down the steep bank. The slave ran right out until he was swimming, still screaming.

"Get!" Squintanasis commanded.

I took a bead, led the shoulder a bit, fired at the running animal and heard the ball hit. The pig went down at the edge of the water, started kicking, well hit but not done by any means. While I dropped to a knee and frantically began reloading, the pig struggled upright, swung around and came for us. From the corner of my eye I could see the mad animal coming but dared not take attention from what I was doing. Squintanasis moved forward with his spear at the ready. The pig barreled in and tried to dodge around the spear – Squintanasis thrust the point into the animal's chest. The pig flipped over with Squintanasis holding to the spear shaft and he was thrown a dozen paces into shallow water. The pig kicked sand, scrambled up, spun around and came – I fired point blank and the ball slammed in just under the chin and put him over backwards.

Squintanasis was there with his knife, but there was only the bleeding to do now.

"*For God's sake*," I said, hastily reloading lest there be others ready to attack. "You might have warned me. I didn't know the damn things were vicious!" I checked the trees, looked at him.

Squintanasis grinned, wet body covered with sand from his tumble. Some fresh cuts from the ceremonies were seeping. "You're just a mad savage," I said. He yelled with pure exuberance, as if we were merely playing, turned and yelled at the slave wading out of the cold water. This was not a happy slave.

We stuck the pig to bleed him, tied a rope around his front hooves, and all three of us hove-to and hoisted him up over a tree limb. We got the animal nearly off the ground. I guessed his weight at three hundred pounds plus. Squintanasis and the slave did a quick gutting job while I stood guard. As soon as they were done they leaned into the rope and began dragging the animal up the beach toward the canoe while I walked backward, protecting our rear. I held Squintanasis's spear in one hand and cradled the musket in my other arm and was ready to toss him the spear at first sight of another pig. It took all of us to hoist the porker over the side of the canoe.

Back at the village there was much good cheer over our pig. Once we had him hung from a tripod of poles the women took over and Neveah dove right in there to help with the skinning. They had that entire pig skinned and cut into sections in little time. A ham went to the chief, the rest bundled for our trip back to Ozette. I watched the process, mouth watering at the thought of roast pork.

In our assigned lodge I found Squintanasis. "After the harrowing experience of saving your life, I could certainly use a shot of rum."

Squintanasis gave me a look. "Irish want rum?"

"A cup if you could arrange it."

He spoke to a woman nearby and in a few minutes she came back with a medium bowl nearly full of rum. These people knew nothing of daily grog rations. I thanked her and Squintanasis and retired to my temporary bunk.

Oh my, it was relaxing. I had consumed about half the bowl when Neveah sat next to me and sniffed. "You get stupid," she said.

"Have some," I said. "The festival ends, we slew the pig beast, and when we get home I will show you how we cook it with sauce made from some of those little apples. We will use salt and wild onions and maybe some nettle stems for the hell of it, and those klooklo tubers. It will be a meal fit for my princess."

"You stupid," she said, as she took the bowl from my hands and gulped two swallows. Her eyes grew large and I quickly took the bowl away, lest she spill any. She gasped a couple times while looking a bit stark.

"You'll get used to it," I said and had another swallow.

Squintanasis came to sit with us. He took the bowl and had a good mouthful, smacked his lips. Then he indicated we should follow him. We walked along, me a little unsteady, to the Klukwalle house where wood drums and singing poured from every crack and knothole. He motioned us to follow him in. Neveah and I hesitated.

He motioned again and took Neveah's arm. Even through the rum I knew this was highly irregular. We entered the smoky atmosphere and were greeted by stares. Pungent odors filled our sinuses and watered our eyes. The singers and dancers didn't miss a beat of the several-drum rhythm. Rattles and whistles came from all sides.

Squintanasis took a place in one of the two circles and people moved to make room for Neveah and me. We sat stiffly, watching the dancers, though neither of us dared look too widely around. I made out many decorations, gay clothing, masks of all kinds worn by the performers and some in the audience. It seemed everyone had recent cuts on their arms and legs. The dancers were both initiates and older tribe members.

The songs were not tse'ka or exactly like the others we had been hearing for several days. The dancers moved as if hypnotized, shuffling out steps to a rhythm only they could fully know, *yo-yaks, tus yo ya—hu wah hu hu*, and on into a chorus. They wound their way through the circles of spectators. Baskets and utensils were moved out of their way, people edged back, and they danced all through the lodge and back again.

Squintanasis was chewing on a piece of whale meat. A great deal of food lay everywhere, and after a few minutes we were encouraged to eat. Neveah and I shared a piece of seal. When the dancers and drummers stopped Squintanasis said I should use my new whistle now. What a time to try it! I dared not refuse. I positioned it in my mouth and blew; sounds of a goose being strangled came out and this greatly amused the crowd. I put the whistle away and refused further encouragement. Soon the dancers and drummers started up again, and now the real whistlers began a sort of lead. The steps were a little different this time, slower, still trance-like and flagrantly sensuous.

During a break in the dancing we left. A west wind ruffled the water, but our little area of the bay was protected and relatively calm.

"Thank you," I said to Squintanasis.

He stopped and confronted us, put a gentle hand on Neveah's shoulder and looked down into her face. "Still want Irish?"

Her eyes were very bright. "A-hah."

We watched him walk away, thinking his own thoughts. He would always be able to surprise and impress me with the range of his considerations and understanding. What I had told Neveah about speaking to him about us would not be necessary.

We pulled off our moccasins and walked on the hard wet sand at the limit of spent waves. A finality to this night, and I felt it was the same with us. The bad feeling lurked back in my mind and I pushed it away. Tonight we were safe and together. What more could I ask?

At the end of our walk I looked beyond at the silhouetted remains of the fort wall against a darkening sky. On top of the rise from the water, an easy stone's throw from us, sat the Russian, white thatch waving in the breeze. He stared toward the horizon, a man remote, no longer a factor to anyone. The way he wanted it. Was he watching the sea for a Russian ship, or simply waiting for death?

Neveah and I turned back to the village, her hand inside mine.

Back at Ozette all the people who had not attended the Klukwalle wanted to hear about it. A meeting was called so all the attendees could tell their stories. Neveah and I were exempt from this meeting, so we slipped away and spent the rest of the afternoon gathering wild apples, onions, meaty sweet leaves, and some thin tubers

Neveah said would be good with the bumpy potatoes. The apples were nearly done, but we filled a basket from sheltered limbs in the recesses of an old gnarly tree.

The next morning I was back at the forge, making hooks and spear tips. In the afternoon I caught a whiff of roast pig. The next time I looked up most of the rifle company were there, looking friendly. Little Misak sidled up to me and said, "Custom take best shoot to meal at teacher home."

"Yes, well, perhaps I could bring you something at the door."

On my other side, Sahyoul said, "Second shoot also get food. Custom."

"Don't you have fish to catch today?"

Sahyoul straightened in his most dignified way, tattered fishermen's clothes hanging on him. "Canoe catch many fish. Joints loose. Must rest. Slave give medicine. Today fisherman need pig."

"You good warriors have a keen sense of smell, but the friendship ends with pig. The chiefs got nearly all of it anyway."

In the end four people stood at the door and they got over half our share of the pork. What was left was the most delicious meal I could remember. Neveah had done a wonderful job and cooked it Irish style, within the limitations of our makings. We ate it all. Later, with the mats down, we cuddled in our home bunk and giggled while making fun of the various noises coming from the other sleeping areas. Then we made a few noises of our own.

In the early morning dark I had a dream and when Neveah woke me I grabbed her and sat up so suddenly she was pushed against the wall. She mopped the sweat from my brow, talking quietly. Calmed, I told her it was nothing, a dream about wild pigs. She didn't really believe me, but we lay down again and soon enough she was asleep, cradled in my arm with her head on my shoulder. I stared up through food and gear hung like ornaments with strands of smoke curling past, adjusted my arm and held my woman close. And felt fear.

In the afternoon I called a fire spear practice for the following morning. This was a surprise to everyone but they all attended.

We assembled early and marched through early mist to the stream where I directed them to set up targets. I was stern, demanding. Neveah picked up my mood and became more critical than usual. Little Misak was shooting well and I used him as an example to the others, demanding they do as well as the smallest member. Finally Misak limped up and patted my hand. He just patted my hand and looked into my eyes and I knew I was being an ass. I announced it was time to eat.

Neveah put a slice of pig she had stashed in my mouth and assured me the shooters would do better in the next session. I shook my head. "They are fine now. I am not a good teacher today."

"Klooklo teacher."

"No. It is no good to make tension. A shooter must relax, have confidence. You and Misak should sing a small song."

"Sing?" she said in English. "No sing. Shoot."

"Shoot better Neveah sing," I said in Makah.

Misak was nearby and heard us. He told Neveah if it would help the shooting he would also sing. She said something to him that sounded nasty, then waved an impatient arm and said a word I did not know. Misak smiled and they sat together. Soon they began to sing a song I recognized as a good luck song used for hunting or at the beginning of any trip. Some continued chewing their dried fish or other meat, but no one talked. At the end Kanek crooked an arm around Misak's neck and hugged him, causing them to laugh with embarrassment.

The next session was better. Misak still out-shot everyone, but Sahyoul was nearly as accurate and the rest were improved. Kanek had hit three targets – the largest wood chips – and his chest was puffed like a grouse. As we walked back along the beach I had the feeling I had learned more than anyone this day. Misak helped clean the muskets and he and Neveah teased me until I had to smile.

That evening I told Squintanasis the shooters had all done well.

"What tomorrow? Fire spear? Make boat?"

"I wish to be at the forge. I want to make spearheads. Maybe arrowheads." My voice did not sound right to me, and Squintanasis's look said this was so.

"Fish hooks?"

I would not answer or look at him. After an awkward minute he said, "Make what want. Maybe talk arbie. Eat now. Be with woman."

I heard his soft footsteps and continued to stare at the sandy ground until I was sure he was gone. I had never felt so unsettled, not even waking up in the hold of that filthy ship bound for the southern continent. At least I understood in my rummy fog what had happened to me and that I was in for it, wherever the wind might take us. I didn't value my life much then, weighing my stupidity, appraising the others in the same predicament, the lot of us not worth much more than our daily grog ration. Even at home I had no direction really: part-time teacher, part-time fisherman, part-time drunk, son to a drunkard, a sister and brother no more certain who they were than me. Colonists in the New World that no longer felt new. Now it was different. I couldn't even be sure of my exact location. Except I was here. With these people. With my accidental wife.

Makahs believe in a supreme being . . . and the transmigration of souls. Respecting their religious belief the sun is the representative of the Great Spirit who resides above, and to him they make their secret prayer . . .

Chapter 21

The next day children came and asked me to make bracelets, but I just shook my head. They watched me pound iron for a time and eventually most drifted away. A fisherman I had seen with Sahyoul stopped by and asked if I had any new hooks. I showed him an iron spear tip still hot from the fire. At midday Neveah brought some food and insisted I stop to eat. We sat together, eating fresh salmon broiled the way I liked it with a little salt, wrapped in onion stems. She said soon we would only have dried salmon to eat, but during the winter I could have the klu-klu-bais and other bottom dwellers like cod that were available all year.

The rest of that day I hardly spoke to anyone.

Before the evening meal I gave Tomhak four iron spear tips and suggested in Makah to have his people put them on new spears right away. He looked at me strangely. When we all sat down in the circle I handed Squintanasis a pouch containing six new iron arrowheads. I tore into the salmon. If the fresh stuff was nearly over I wanted to eat as much as I could and get stronger. At the end of the meal Squintanasis spoke with Neveah. I went outside and wandered down the beach. Squintanasis caught up with me and said we should walk.

Fog forming offshore, great orange orb of a moon edging over the top of the slope; the wolves would salute it tonight.

We went a distance without talking. "What tomorrow?"

I wasn't used to being asked such a question. "Make spear tips."

We paused and sat on a drifted log. "Woman say Irish dream."

"When wolves do not howl."

Squintanasis picked up a white stick the sea had delivered, examined it in the twilight, running his fingers along its length as if calculating what he might make of it. "Wolf howl before dawn," he said.

"But not always in the early night. I have grown used to them. It is restful."

He tested the spring of the stick several times. "What work tomorrow?"

"Like I said, make more spear tips. Unless you say different."

He slowly bent the white stick until it snapped, startling a sleepy gull dragging an injured wing that had sidled up hoping for a handout. "First meet here."

After he left I sat staring at the curling waves, enjoying the satisfying hiss as they expended over the pebbly beach like the last sigh of ended lives. A nip in the air suggested there might be frost. The gentle nor'wester and good sky to the west meant calm water tomorrow. I would have preferred a storm. Why would I think such a thing? Was I becoming unstable? My shipmates talked of the madness that took those who went into the native world. Not made for it, they said, a civilized man can't survive. Finally you go balmy and they have to kill you. Damn few old converts out there. If the fever don't take you the madness will.

Stupid seamen talk. Ignorant fools most of them. Drunkards. I wandered further down the beach. Moonlight made shadows along the tree line. I paused at the tiny bay within the wide false bay, an alcove of water that amounted to little at low tide where the women collected clams. I sat on a patch of dry sand and watched the current eddy past.

A movement caught my eye and along the darkness of the trees, at the end of this little indentation, a shadowy form. The shadow separated from the tree line.

The wolf moved slowly down to the water. Sniffed a few feet of beach. Raised its head and turned to look at me. I did not move and could not see much more than its black form, but we stared at each other. The wolf came toward me, moving completely out of the shadow of the trees, and stopped a few feet away. I did not draw my knife, and felt no fear. He was about my size, dark, of an uncertain hue. Light shown like tiny moons in his eyes. We stayed that way for some time. I resisted an urge to reach out to him. Finally he turned and walked slowly away. Before going up in the trees he stopped and looked back at me.

I felt a rush of exhilaration.

"A wolf came to see me," I told Neveah.

She pushed back from having cuddled up in our bunk and stared at my face the way you might examine a suspect clam. Dim firelight flicked across her serious features.

"Say how wolf come."

I explained in detail. It was klooklo, I told her.

"You not right. Now wolf come."

"No, no. It was klooklo. I feel better. Really." I pulled her to me but she resisted.

"Wolf good," I said. "He came to me. I felt . . . accepted."

"Wolf know you." She buried her face in the hollow of my neck and held me.

"Please," I whispered. "We can make love. It is good now."

"Yes, yes." She pulled me over on top of her and raised her legs until the back of her knees were over my shoulders and the blanket slipped away. I grabbed it, flipped it over us. She bent up and harshly pushed me inside and it excited me so for a time I did not think about her tears.

In the morning I felt almost giddy as the food was set on the clean boards inside our circle. I wanted Neveah next to me but she had to be with Suisha and that group. Squintanasis sat beside me. It was a very good meal: cod, some left-over cold salmon, smoked bear from the one Squintanasis had slain on his trip to the lake, berries and cold spring water that Neveah had fetched that morning. She looked beautiful this morning and I kept trying to catch her eye, manners be damned. When we finished Squintanasis went over and spoke to Neveah, so I went outside and headed down the beach as he had directed me to do the night before.

From our usual log you could see the long line of crescent-shaped beach north of the village. Thick fog lay offshore, engulfed the rock islands and the far point at the north end of the false bay so only the points of dark pinnacles poked like saw teeth through the white blanket. As it moved onto the land the fog broke into wispy trails and inside the jagged point the beach was mostly clear.

I thought about the two of us taking a canoe over to fish for cod around those rocks. Maybe it would settle my turbid mind. I didn't look over when Squintanasis sat near me.

"Wolf come Irish?"

I shook my head. "A wolf came to the beach."

"Wolf never come for nothing."

"He probably had a yearning for clams. You are keeping me from my work. But I feel like a change this morning. I was thinking about us going fishing."

"Make bow Irish."

I looked at him. "What?"

"Make bow," he said in Makah, stretching casually. "Fire spear no work, shoot arrow."

"But I don't know how to shoot arrows."

Squintanasis tapped his chest. "Teach. Make learn."

"Now just a minute, I'm not a bowman. It's something you have to begin early."

He looked amused. "Fast teach."

"Oh, God . . ." I leaned back, looked up the beach . . . saw something. Something moving. Far up the beach. I stood.

Squintanasis was at my side. He stepped over the log and stared at the far figure at the edge of the surf.

Someone running. Running fast, bounding over drift – even at this distance you could see the speed. Hair trailing back. Tall. Naked. A woman.

"*Nanishum.*"

A whisper but I heard him clearly. But how? What the hell . . .

Squintanasis threw off his blanket and started running, abruptly stopped and looked back at me, expression wild.

"*Go!*" he commanded. "Say Kakemook – Nittinat. Nittinat come. Go!" He turned and ran as fast as anyone ever ran down the beach toward the runner coming toward us. For a few seconds I marveled at his form, his incredible speed on the hard sand along the edge of the waves. In the distance the runner seemed to match his pace.

I turned and ran for the village. Sand slid under my feet, holding me back, slowing my progress so in my determination I dug my feet in deeper and ran even slower as a dream when you strain to run and feel yourself going nowhere.

As I entered the village people stopped what they were doing, shouting, men running in my wake. Kakemook and Misak were with Kekathl at the new canoe. I sprawled against curved cedar, out of breath.

"Nittinat come," I managed. "Nanishum. Squintanasis. Bring. Nanishum."

Kakemook grabbed my shoulder, put his large face close to mine. "Squintnasis say?"

I nodded and pointed, chest heaving.

Kakemook reared back with a wild look. "Fire spears. *Go!*"

He ran out on the beach bellowing, "*Nittinat! Weapons! Go. Go. Go.*"

People were running everywhere, Kakemook's deep voice prodding them. As I ran I heard Senequah's baritone yelling too, feet on gravel, clatter of equipment, anxious voices of women. I rushed into the lodge to find Howessa and Neveah already pouring water into inverted sealskin bags – for warriors fighting? – how could they know already? I was terrified for her. Where were the children?

"Fire spears," I commanded.

She finished securing the top of a water bag and ran after me to Kakemook's lodge. My hands were shaking so I could hardly gather up patches and powder, which I passed to Neveah. Behind her all the fire spear squad had entered the lodge and waited for me to direct them.

Neveah and I began passing out muskets.

I spoke in Makah. "Positions. Loaders protect powder. Air wet. No powder in pan." As we came out of the lodge Neveah was repeating what I'd said in intelligible Makah and around us men were running with canoes, gear, taking equipment behind buildings out of sight. Several children stood in plain view as if awaiting instruction and I resisted the urge to grab them and usher them inside.

I got my group spread out behind the log. Neveah distributed shooting supplies.

Damn fog. The muskets were loaded but the enemy would have to be in sight before we poured flash in the pans. I wanted no misfires. Slack tide beginning, edge of the beach close to the village. Potential targets would be about the same distance we had practiced.

As I scanned the possible landing spots, Squintanasis came trotting into view holding the running woman's hand, pulling her along. She was nearly spent and stunning in her nakedness. She stumbled and he caught her, swept her up in his arms and carried her into the chief's lodge.

We turned our attention to the sea. Eyes squinting into rolling whiteness.

I thought of the plan to use warriors from Neeah. Had a runner been sent? Of course not, no time. A few men had gone down the coast looking for good drift logs that could be turned into canoes. Two canoes and several men out fishing. What did we have right now, maybe fifty able warriors? Ten boys? Less? How many would they bring? How strong would they be?

A few children played high on the beach. Three women at the fish racks.

They might not even be coming. No one could just know such a thing. *But Nanishum was here.*

Still . . .

We didn't have any of the water containers. I sent Neveah to the lodge and she hurried back with one, along with some dry cedar cloths used on babies. Speaking Makah, I told everyone to wipe the pans dry and keep them and the frissons closed, which Neveah repeated. She was all business, sweet face now fierce, making sure the flash powder pouches were covered, checking everyone's makings. She crawled up to me, patted my arm and took a position a little behind.

I noticed Squintanasis slip in back of the lodges with his bow.

Waves curled and pounded beyond the village. Gulls and terns were unusually quiet, a stray cry now and then. Along the log there was barely a movement among the shooters. Misak nearest to me, Kanek with chin calmly resting on top of his musket stock, taut arm muscles giving away his real mood, Sahyoul in all his sternness. Kanek and Sahyoul wore elk skin cuirasses on their upper bodies that tied together at the ribs on each side, a type of battle armor I didn't know they had. Misak wore his regular clothes and I was relieved he didn't plan to do any hand-to-hand combat, nor did I wish any of us to. The loaders sat with stony expressions, muskets angled over the log. Next to the shooters an assortment of conventional weapons: clubs, a short sword, a spear across Sahyoul's lap. I kept glancing down the line, taking inventory, staring into whiteness. I felt Neveah's leg against my calf.

We waited.

Out in the fog a wool dog barked. Then another.

More dogs took up the chorus and I felt sick to my stomach. I motioned everybody down. Kanek started to reach for his pan powder and I shook my head, causing Neveah to touch his arm.

A steady clamor of barking.

The form of a canoe appeared in the mist, barely two hundred paces from the beach. Another flanked it. More behind. Many wet paddles moving up and down.

"Wait," I said.

When they were one hundred paces from the beach I said, "*Pan,*" and Neveah repeated the order as I studied the approaching canoes. I made out the stick forms of three muskets being brought up to a ready position, wondered how adept the shooters might be. I scurried along my shooters and told them to aim for the people with fire spears and keep shooting until they went down.

Now the sound of their battle song erupted. Full voice they rose as one, no need for silence now, coming hard for the beach and roaring their damn song, coming to kill and take whatever wasn't destroyed.

I cocked the hammer on my musket and heard the others click

into position. Little more than a canoe length from the beach a whizzing sound passed overhead – an arrow slammed into the chest of a man standing in the nearest canoe, knocking him back and capsizing the craft in shallow water.

"Fire!"

Three rifles and my scatter load went off, hitting several targets.

Two puffs of smoke and chips flew from our protective log, two arrows socked into the wood in front of me.

"Aim true and fire," I yelled, and even before I finished I could see their shooters were down. But they had plenty of other weapons.

Arrows were in the air, then spears mixing with our musket balls. Canoes grounded on the beach and nearly naked painted warriors jumped out yelling their war cry. Some wore hide armor similar to Kanek's and Sahyoul's.

God they looked big.

Another wave of arrows and the blast of our muskets and there were already enemy bodies piling up in shallow water. A collective scream echoed off the slope as every able Makah warrior stormed the beach swinging clubs and knives, Kakemook with body armor flapping running like a naked bear in the lead, a second group led by Senequah. The harpooners in back hurled spears over the heads of those in front and the enemy was hit near the water's edge and held. I glimpsed Squintanasis back there firing arrows, moving up slowly.

"Pick your targets," I yelled in English, forgetting the Makah words. We were shooting well, nearly as fast as military fire, and our rounds were hitting the enemy, confusing them with our volleys.

It was hand-to-hand now and they fought fiercely, turning the surf red as they gained ground, hacking their way up the beach. From the corner of my eye I saw Squintanasis throw down his bow and charge forward with a short sword. I kept searching for a shot, but couldn't fire the scatter load now without hitting one of ours.

Another line of warriors came screaming at the beach – women – led by Tomhak and the naked runner Nanishum in full battle armor and paint and only half naked. The women swung knives, short swords and clubs as the men and charged into the fighting. I turned to Neveah. *"You stay. All stay."*

I jumped over the log with my musket and ran at the mayhem. When close I fired the scatter load into the painted chest of an enemy, clubbed another with the butt of the musket, picked up a short sword from a fallen warrior and charged at the nearest enemy. Three were on Squintanasis, determined to bring him down. Upper body armor gave him some protection and they were trying to cut his legs. I attacked their flank, hacked an arm.

He slashed the other two and then we were back-to-back fighting for our lives, surrounded, but it was not all enemy, Makah were in there fighting fiercely and I felt Squintanasis bump me – it gave me strength beyond what I had, skill with a sword beyond my abilities and I let the madness go, grabbing up a dropped club and using it as a foil as I thrust and chopped away. A spear came at me and I dodged, put my sword into the neck of a black-faced warrior with body armor, felt a hard bump and realized it was Squintanasis – the spear meant for me had pierced him and he sprawled against my legs. I roared and attacked two warriors in front of me, driving them back, slashing one, jumping back to stand over Squintanasis. I was screaming insanely at them to come, darting briefly ahead to jab my sword into a red painted chest, slashing out at another raised arm, moving back to stand over Squintanasis who was trying to regain his feet. I had been cut but felt nothing, knowing I must stay upright, protecting my legs, keeping my sword in front of me, constantly moving.

I don't know how long the carnage went on. Perhaps not long in actual time. In battle there is no time.

The warrior in front of me stepped back. I did not understand, but paused my attack. He was shorter than me, wider, thick shoulders and legs, heavily painted. Slowly his lips relaxed to cover his teeth and I felt mine bared. His eyes dulled and he lowered knife and club. I heard surf. Then Kakemook yelling something and marching down the line of battle. He pointed a spear at each enemy warrior until they lowered their weapon.

I heard my own breathing, turned my glare to my right where enemy were standing motionless, weapons down. I held the anger and my sword ready until I realized they were being allowed to load their dead and wounded into canoes. Bloody limp bodies, moaning, desperate sounds uttered low. Further down the beach several enemy on their knees, Makah warriors standing over them with weapons at the ready.

The man in front of me stepped back and turned, exposing his flank. He dropped his weapons in a nearby canoe and looked back at me, eyes gone dead. Defeat.

Kneeling, I got my arms under Squintanasis. Through the side gap in his armor I saw the gash in his back was severe, but perhaps it had missed his spine. My torn shirt was the only cloth handy – I ripped it off and pushed it against his wound. His expression was vaguely amused, which frightened me. Blood ran from a dozen cuts not covered by his cuirass. I held his head off the sand and looked up just as Nanishum and several other women hurried up. I tried to help lift him but Nanishum touched my shoulder and gently moved me out of the way.

"His back," I said, still pressing the cloth to the wound. "A spear went through where the skins tie." Blood welled from under his armor.

Nanishum worked her hand under mine. One side of her face bloody, cut across a shoulder, blood running down her leg. The other women showed wounds too. I sat back on the sand and watched them carry Squintanasis toward Kakemook's lodge.

I turned to see canoes disappearing into fog. The prisoners were being led away by armed Makah. War cries echoed across the water. Blearily I made out bodies, foamy red water, appendages strewn about like drift, empty canoes overturned, rolling sideways against sand. People bent over their neighbors, relatives.

I grabbed up the sword and struggled to my feet, pointed the sword at the sky, screamed, "Come back and I'll kill every one of you bastards!"

I careened around to look for Neveah. She was coming toward me. A floating apparition over the sand, bloody spear in her grip, red streaks on arms and face, slowly floating to me. I started forward. My legs felt disconnected, weightless. Dimly I saw the beach coming up to meet my face.

Chapter 22

Humming... a summer breeze rustling green leaves. Excited voices of distant children. Popping. Pop-pop. I imagined little drops of pitch boiling out of a log to meet the fire, exploding. I forced eyes open to watch good old hazy ceiling, smoke in curvy columns eddying through clutter to the escape hatch. With effort I turned my head.

Neveah rocked back and forth, humming, eyes closed, hands clasped around her necklace. I moved my hand and she grasped it, held it to her face, lips soft. She put her head against mine. Thank God. Pain in various places, not too bad. Tired. Sleep.

Smelly spoon probing my mouth. Without opening my eyes I took some of the hot, ill-tasting liquid. Several mouthfuls and I pushed the hand away.

"Aidan." A hand on my forehead. Neveah. "Aidan. Wake now. Nanishum here."

I blinked up at the tall figure standing over me. She kneeled and put her mouth close to my ear. "Squintanasis say sleep much. Say talk English words."

I started to laugh, decided that did not feel so good. "He klooklo?"

She paused, then said, "Want you come when able."

"All right –" I tried to rise and fell back. The scene overhead swirled.

"No come now." Nanishum placed her hand on my forehead, then moved it under the mat over my heart. She conferred with Neveah and they reached some kind of agreement.

Nanishum touched my forehead. I turned my head slightly and stared. She wore clean, soft deerskin and a sleeveless seal fur vest. Short hair seemed to add to her height. What had she done? How had she come home?

"We won," I said in Makah.

"Sleep," Nanishum said. As she walked away I noticed the bandage just under her shirt at her shoulder, another wrap above a knee. Tomhak, Suisha, Winaseth and Howessa stood waiting near the door. They spoke quietly and then her parents embraced her. They seemed overcome and stared at the mat after she passed through.

I reached out and Neveah took my hand, moved closer on her knees.

"I want to see your wounds." She shook her head but I insisted.

She had a wide bandage on her left thigh, a lessor slash high on her back and an angled cut on her forehead. A few nicks. Relieved, I moved over a little and she climbed in with me. Sleep came quickly.

In the night pain became intense. The old side wound had been pierced at a new angle, but it didn't seem as bad as the first time, relatively minor cuts on both legs, shoulder, a gash to my scalp – on the opposite side from what I'd suffered from the Hoh – that still oozed blood. The headache was serious, but the side wound was again most painful. I kept trying to adjust. Finally Neveah got up and came back with a small bowl. Rum. I hesitated, thinking about Squintanasis and all the others who were in pain without rum. I gulped it down.

Sleep. Eyes came at me, black, intense, ebony balls of light, shock up my arm as the blade struck muscle and bone, on to the next set of enemy eyes, blood splashing over me in waves. I came half awake sprawled at an odd angle, rid of these images, but as soon as my eyes closed they would return more vivid than before, unstoppable. Some time in the night Neveah brought more rum. When I woke the next time she was sleeping on a mat on the floor.

Two more days and I managed to stand. I took a step and called Neveah. I insisted on going to see Squintanasis. Neveah protested and enlisted Howessa, who called her father. Tomhak had been knicked up too, but was in generally good shape. He summoned two sturdy warriors who, over my protests, guided me outside, picked me up and carried me to the chief's lodge. Neveah brought up the rear. In Makah I begged them to put me down and let me walk in like a warrior. They relented as Kakemook filled the doorway, hands on hips. He looked me over.

"Come see me?" he said in Makah.

The chief smiled at my expression. He put a hand on my shoulder. "Come, Irish. Your yar-kwe-dook-uks here."

I stared at Chief Kakemook until he hacked out a short laugh and took my arm, ushering me inside his lodge. He had called Squintanasis my friend, but in his language it was not a casual term. I made my way to Squintanasis who lay on a bunk near the east end of the lodge where Kakemook and his family slept. The ranking shaman hovered over Squintanasis, shaking rattles, giving forth with a low wailing song, vaguely familiar. I didn't like the sound of it. Nanishum sat next to him weaving a small basket. *Weaving a basket.* She smiled and said something to the shaman and he faded into the shadows, wailing with less volume.

Squintanasis raised his hand and I took it. "No bad for Irish," he said in English.

"That spear was meant for me."

His mouth made an inconsequential expression. "Neveah say drink rum, chase around lodge."

I couldn't help smiling. "Nanishum says the same about you." We were speaking English so Neveah knew what we were saying but not Nanishum, although she was watching with vague amusement.

"When will you come to see me?" I asked.

After a pause he said, "Three days."

This was a great admission for a Makah – this one particularly – to accept his wounds were serious enough to keep him down for so long. He had moved his legs a little, a good sign. "Casualties?"

He broke eye contact, but held onto my hand. "Eighteen," he said. "Four women. Many wounds."

"The fire spears?"

"Some wounds." He took a careful, long breath. "One dead."

"Who?"

"Misak."

My breath caught in my throat and I sat back. "He was to stay with the others. Misak had no armor."

"Irish no armor."

"His small arm ... "

"You come, fight close. No good fire spear. Sahyoul come. All come. Fight."

Of course. I stared at the shaman, quietly muttering and shaking his rattle, working away in the shadows. I felt like hitting him.

"Kakemook son," Squintanasis said gently. "Fight like chief son."

"The others?"

"Wounds," Squintanasis said.

His pause caused me to look at him.

"Senequah dead."

Powerful, stoic Senequah. Best harpooner in the village. Then I remembered that Senequah was Nanishum's uncle. Her eyes were downcast as she gently stroked the back of Neveah's hand, as a mother comforts a child. In Makah I told her I was sorry. Nanishum nodded slightly without looking up.

"And crazy Sahyoul?"

"Sahyoul good short spear. Kill many. Few wounds."

I looked at the dressings on their wounds, lesser ones simply bare red slashes. "You two are the fastest runners I've ever seen," I said stupidly.

Nanishum looked at Squintanasis and he translated. She touched my hand, then picked up her basket and resumed weaving.

"Potlatch," Squintanasis said. "Nine days. Today next day. Listen woman. Get well. You part Potlatch."

"What is this you're talking about?" I looked at Neveah. She was faintly smiling, her eyes full of moisture. I did not ask further what any of it meant.

Food was brought. Nanishum fed Squintanasis, but he did not take much and had trouble swallowing. After each bite he wanted water. He looked so weary, an expression I had never seen. Finally he held up a hand, indicating he could eat no more. I motioned to Neveah that we should go. She helped me to my feet.

"A little rum is good for pain," I said in English to Nanishum. Neveah translated. Nanishum smiled. By her expression I knew there would be no relief with rum for either of them. They had their herbs for pain. I hoped they would not use them sparingly.

I waved off the carriers, and with my arm around Neveah's shoulders we slowly made our way along the beach and found a comfortable log. It was good to get away from the confining interior of any lodge and see my surroundings. Two boys in a canoe were headed out to feed the wool dogs and they knew, they were barking. Another canoe carried three girls on their way to the island. I thought about the wild onions there, and those licorice-smelling leaves all the children liked. Gulls screeched and sea ducks swam and hunted in the bay. Children ran and squealed along the edge of the water, the gentle waves again bluish green. Further out spray crashed up the sides of the rock islands, beautiful and comforting.

"Helluva thing to fight in your own yard," I said. "My father said this when I was a child."

"Want family?"

When I turned my head Neveah seemed intent on something up the beach. "I think about my family. It's been nearly two years. I'm sure my brother and sister have their own worries. Father, well . . . I guess they still wonder what happened to me sometimes. I wonder if any of them have taken up the fishing."

She snuggled closer and hooked an arm through mine.

"Squintanasis seems to be getting better," I said absently. Neveah didn't answer.

The next day I felt a little stronger, figured the worst was done. Neveah changed my bandages and at our morning meal I made myself eat more. Neveah walked with me. The singing of funeral songs on the beach and up on the slope was constant. Other wounded moved ponderously across the sand, some with their children or women supporting them. Several raised their hand to me and I returned the recognition. Beach fires burned out of respect for the funerals taking place. When I asked Neveah about something I'd heard Kanek say to another warrior, she told me yes, Senequah's first slave had been killed and placed next to him in the burial tree.

In front of the chief's lodges were poles twice the height of a man with heads impaled on top. Nittinat heads. The faces were smashed and bloody, flies circled, a movement. I squinted up and saw a crab tied to the top of a head. These people did not take crab, and I thought it might be because they had seen them eating human waste from the buckets emptied into tooplah, so it was a great insult to use a crab this way.

In four days, just before the evening meal, the *ah'baks* came and issued a formal invitation to Tomhak and all in his house to attend the Potlatch at the lodge of Chief Kakemook a few days hence.

White sticks were thrown into the ground.

Chapter 23

Singing continued each afternoon, mournful songs respecting the dead. Some of the voices came from lodges, others faint from the flat above the slope where the dead were placed on platforms in trees. Some of the dead were buried with their favorite belongings, but I did not know the protocol.

We seldom saw the singers, Neveah and I, but their voices penetrated our senses. We visited Squintanasis every day and although he said he was feeling stronger, he did not appear to be. He could sit up momentarily and then had to lie back down.

On the fifth day we ventured northeast of the village and found Nanishum at the place where many English lessons and conversations had taken place between Squintanasis and me. She invited us to share her log.

"Irish ready Potlatch?" she said.

"Don't even know what it is." Without thinking I had answered in English and Neveah quickly translated. I had heard the strain in Nanishum's voice and when she did not answer right away I asked how she was doing.

"Ready fight Nittinat," she said. "Irish?"

"Fight anytime."

After a pause Nanishum said, "Me with Squintanasis potlatch. Irish with Neveah. He want all together."

She held out her hand and Neveah and I took it. "Tomorrow come home," she said. "Squintanasis come father's house. Shaman say good medicine."

I glanced at Neveah and knew this was not good.

In the morning after our meal, Tomhak ordered his daughters and a slave to clean an area near his sleeping bench. The place had been cleared and cleaned the day before, but he wanted it tidied again. I expressed a need to go to the bathing place and clean up and felt strong enough to make it.

Nanishum appeared in the doorway. Howessa and Wineseth hurried to give assistance as two sturdy warriors carried Squintanasis in and took him to the bench in the cleared area. Several stuffed mats had been laid over each other and they carefully laid Squintanasis on this soft bed. Nanishum positioned his legs and covered him with a wool blanket and two mats. A man on the roof enlarged the vent so the sickness in Squintanasis could get out.

Two shaman had followed the carriers and now went to work with rattles and trailings, chanting mournfully. There was little room for us, so I motioned to Neveah and we headed for the bathing place.

"He has festering," I said, drying with a soft mat after washing.

Neveah turned so I could dry her bare back. "Know white medicine?"

"A little. Doesn't matter, we have no white medicine."

Every day Nanishum changed Squintanasis's bandages as the shaman hovered. She would allow no one else to minister him. I sat next to him several hours a day. We talked from time to time, even as the shaman wailed. Fever often took his thoughts and he could not complete what he wanted to say. His moist face caused in me a raging helplessness.

When Squintanasis spoke Nanishum would stop her weaving and focus on his every word. I did not always understand, but she did. He talked about small events in their childhood and she would remember and add details.

The morning of the Potlatch Neveah awakened me by gently stroking my forehead. She held a small bowl containing rum.

I turned away in disgust. "Woman, it is too early to tempt me with drink."

She grinned. "Eat berries? Then drink. Tomhak say drink."

After a few bites of fish and berries I did drink it down. Neveah knelt before me. "Today first day Potlatch," she said nervously. "Most important day. We marry."

I blinked, a little lightheaded from the rum. "So be it."

"Chief Kakemook marry us."

I took her face in my hands and kissed her. She took a breath and held my hands. "More people get married same time. You want?"

"Sure. Who's the lucky couple? Kanek and Winaseth?"

She shook her head. "No say. Kakemook make speech."

"He always makes speech."

I went to the other end of the lodge to see Squintanasis, but there were too many people, including Tomhak. It had turned into a group vigil. The shaman was trying to hold his place in the crowd. I put some water over the fire and Neveah and I went to the spring. It was a day for shaving and formal dress. My wedding day. Chief Kakemook would marry us. That began to sink in and I asked my bride how a couple of slaves rated a wedding conducted by the chief, especially during a festival as important as this one apparently was. She answered in Makah, saying in effect, "Never mind."

"What about Squintanasis?"

"He there. Nanishum there." She started down the trail and I asked her to please explain. "Howessa dress me," was her only reply before hurrying away.

In Tomhak's lodge everyone ran around scolding each other for being in the way or not having the correct hair decoration or some-body's dress or paint was not right. In back of Tomhak's table, oppo-site Squintanasis, singers warmed up with happy songs that mixed with excited talk close by, yelling outside and the faint howls of wool dogs.

Only partially dressed, wearing a coarse nightshirt so her festival clothes would not be soiled, Neveah painted a few small stripes on my face and neck: red and black, the serious colors, an unexpected honor. I let her do what she wanted and did not comment. When she finished I grabbed her wrist and took the stick.

"You too," I said.

Her eyes flashed wide. "No black."

"If I am to wear red and black, you will too."

She shook her head. "One red. Black forbidden to slaves."

I shook my head and stood. "Tomhak," I called, though he was nearby, being dressed in festival attire by daughters Howessa and Winaseek. He looked at me questioningly.

"Today marry my woman," I said in Makah.

A Makah shrug. "Want woman?"

I nodded. "Colors on face." I pointed at my face. "Warrior colors."

Amusement crept into his expression. "Warrior now. Fire spear. Sword."

"This woman fought at my side. She also warrior. If I wear the red and black, she will wear the red and black." I turned to Neveah's shocked expression. "You will translate what I just said in better Makah."

Neveah began haltingly. When she was finished, all eyes were on Tomhak, who was looking at his wife. I saw Suisha nod slightly. Tomhak turned his gaze on me.

"Neveah serve Makah well." He looked around at his silent audience. "No slave woman have black," he said. "Today Neveah have black. Red. Have any color."

The chief smiled. "Irish get woman ready."

"Thank you."

Howessa and Wineseth rushed forward to hug Neveah, but at length she pushed them away. "Husband paint me," she said.

Painting Neveah's face took some time because I had no experience and wanted it to be right. My efforts were not helped by her steady beaming. When I finished I went to be next to Squintanasis. Nanishum was off preparing for the festival. Squintanasis and I were able to talk a little. He seemed amused by my outburst over the paint and this encouraged me to believe he was doing better. His great strength would return and he would be a chief.

As if to confirm my confidence an early sun appeared, lighting up the village and sea as if a curtain had been drawn.

Chief Utilla and another chief arrived with what appeared to be half the sister village in more than a dozen canoes. The chiefs came ashore wearing fine otter robes trimmed with ermine, ivory ear ornaments and much white down in their hair. The women carried many baskets of food and the men unloaded stacks of prime pelts of otter and seal, booty for the potlatch. These were rich gifts and I recalled Neveah telling me the Neeah group felt badly about not being here for the surprise attack. This amounted to a debt and they had brought payment. The second chief was Klardahshook, father to my would-be suitor, Yatakula, but I did not see her in the group. Perhaps she had been told I would be marrying my slave woman.

Two outside fires were stoked high and nearly smokeless with bleached driftwood. I watched from Kakemook's lodge where we were to wait until asked to come forward. All those not part of the performance were seated between and around the big fires, a sea of faces in both directions from Chief Kakemook's lodge and nearly down to the high tide line. Children sat with their parents, low murmurs accented with babies' short squeals; Makah children seldom cried for long. Inside the lodge, Kakemook and Tomhak, both barefoot, looked magnificent in sea otter robes hanging below their knees, trimmed with lynx and ermine.

Singers assembled in front of the audience and gave forth with a song I recognized as being owned by a family in a lodge at the north end of the village. Then Kakemook's daughters, accompanied by a few women relatives, sang two of their family songs. Even I understood this would be for the benefit of the chief's entrance.

When the singing concluded there was quiet. Low talk mingled with surf and gulls. The chief's carved chair was hauled out and placed on boards supported by beach logs. Kakemook appeared, but did not go to the chair. He slowly strolled around on the boards. Near his ample waist was tied a large bandage, the gash on his right cheek uncovered. He made a motion and Tomhak joined him. The chiefs surveyed the crowd.

I understood most of what Kakemook's said and will paraphrase, which in English requires a few extra words:

"Brothers from Neeah bring us joy and respect with their presence. Chief Utilla and Klardahshook and the other good people of Neeah come to honor our dead and give tribute to a great victory our brave warriors, and our women, and our slaves too, have made on the Nittinat. These cousins from the north bring evil against us for our victory at Neeah and Tatoosh long ago. They are beaten again and driven back."

A roar from the crowd, arm waving.

"We have five of their best canoes."

Muted cheering.

"We have their weapons and four prisoners."

Yells of approval.

"Their warrior chief is dead. Many Nittinat dead. A Nittinat chief's head and three of his warriors are on poles in front of our lodges."

A few shouts and growls.

"We also suffered loss. Some of our best warriors have fallen. Chief Senequah is gone to the land of the dead."

Kakemook then named every fallen and wounded Makah warrior. The four women who had died were named. He singled out certain warriors for their exceptional fighting, including Senequah and Squintanasis. He talked about fire spears and about his son, Misak, cut down in the battle. His voice grew thick but he went on, naming each person in the musket squad, including Neveah and the slaves who had fought. Then he said Irish.

I started to step back but Neveah had a tight grip on my arm. "It's Squintanasis' doing," I whispered, but her grip only tightened and she had the beam on her face.

Kakemook pointed in my direction and paid me compliments beyond what was deserved. It was the most humbling experience of my life.

"Irish and others will come forward soon," Kakemook said. "If you have bear meat you can call him and he will come quickly."

When the laughs subsided the chief continued, "There will be a new ritual. Makah will know a new wisdom. It is what has come to us and we must understand. Now we will sing. We will sing my brother's songs. We will sing Senequah's family songs, which are also my family songs. All may join in these songs. Those that drum may drum. Those with whistles may whistle. Rattles will be heard. And when these songs are finished you will hear about the greatest woman Makah warrior. You will know how this woman gave us a great victory." Kakemook stepped to the side of the stage.

Tomhak walked to the edge of the group of entertainers. He held out his hand and Nanishum came forward to take it. Then Kanek and little Noochbe stepped forward, followed by Suisha, Howessa and Winaseek. Several more singers joined them. Tomhak quietly disappeared. They began to hum. Words began and it reminded me of church music long ago. Their swaying took me back, the way the choir moved to the rhythm.

The songs were sung sadly, but there was more to it. Some in the audience supported with low chants, a constant murmur behind the singing. The whole began to sound like naked souls. I heard confused and sharp sounds of battle, saw black dream eyes and faces and souls of the slain above the singers and it became unbearable. Neveah's arm tightened inside mine.

Finally it was over.

Kakemook intercepted Nanishum as the singers were filing off. He guided her up to sit in his chair and for all her naturally regal bearing she began to look self-conscious.

The chief addressed his audience: "My cousin, Tomhak, now your second chief and this woman's father, will explain Nanishum's ordeal at the hands of the Nittinat. We have questioned those Nittinat we captured about everything that happened to her there, and Nanishum has told us her experiences." In front of rapt expressions Kakemook moved to the side and Tomhak stepped forward.

Tomhak began to speak:

"Citizens of Ozette, you Makah, all here wear wounds of battle. You wear old scars when Nittinat came to attack women and children, when our hunters were gone to sea and mountain. Our brothers from Neeah suffered too, because they wanted to be here for both battles, as we would fight for them, as our people long ago drove the Nittinat from Neeah and Tatoosh. They have brought many fine gifts and these will be honored through potlatch. We do not have to fight Nittinat again. We will take the ones we captured and trade them for the return of our people they took from us."

Yells of agreement.

"If any Makah has been killed there, we will cut off the head of their highest ranking warrior in front of their eyes and throw the body into their lake."

More yelling, louder.

"We will bring our people home."

Yells and cheering turned into chanting, but Tomhak was able to quiet them with a raise of his hand. He slowly swung his raised hand and pointed at Nanishum sitting up there in the chief's chair.

"This chief's daughter was taken and made a slave. She was not treated like a chief's daughter. They cut her hair like any slave." Tomhak smiled slyly. "They told her she was too skinny to do the work of a good woman."

Jeers.

"They said she could not swim because her bones would make her sink."

Laughter, some yelled her name.

"Nanishum used this by eating less to make herself smaller. She was sent to the lodge of the second chief's shaman, Quanaka. A poor lodge badly kept. They made her gather clams. Pick berries. Clean piss baskets. When any women in that lodge got in a bad mood they beat her. But she could not hide her good form, and the pig of a chief's son, Coontach, who some of you have heard about, jumped on her one day when the women were digging roots. He knocked her down so her head hit a limb and at first she couldn't do anything. Then Nanishum fought him. She got his knife and stabbed him in back of the shoulder."

Tomhak reached around and showed where Coontach had been stabbed. "Nanishum got away from him, but Chief Wissinectock wanted to kill her. Coontach did not get well right away. She cut him good. Their shaman couldn't make him well, so the chief's wife sent for another shaman. They were ready to kill Nanishum in the Chief's lodge when Coontack started getting well, so the second shaman told the chief not to kill her. Nanishum heard him tell the chief, 'Sacrifice her today and Coontach's arm will be sacrificed with her. Take her back to the place where she lives to kill her, and get the wealth that was left there.'"

Threats to the Nittinat were yelled. Then they began chanting Nanishum's name. She sat very still with head raised, looking straight ahead.

"But the first shaman almost killed her." Silence fell over the audience, anticipating more. Tomhak began to pace back and forth. "He came running with spear, to put it through her throat. But chief wouldn't let him kill her, because the other shaman said she had to live until they had their great victory."

That got them on their feet. They were ready to do battle again. Tomhak let them rage for a time, then raised his hand. They quieted and those standing slowly sat down.

"Now hear what happened," he began solemnly, "They put her in the bow of a canoe and started with only one other canoe. This was to fool her, because they said they were taking her for ransom. One time Nanishum had to take the basket, and when she bent to clean it she looked back through the fog and saw more canoes back there."

Tomhak paused, watching his waiting audience. He continued: "She told them she would show the trail from the north so they could send a messenger to seek the ransom and they could wait for word. She knew they wanted to send warriors on the trail to attack from behind so the rest could land on our beach and surround us. But Nanishum," Tomhak turned to smile at her, "this weakling not good enough for a Nittinat slave –"

Yells and laughter.

"This woman took them where they wanted to go. She guided

267

them through fog to our point to the north. She brought them to tlayee (snaky) notch.

"And when it was too late to turn back, when they were into the trap, Nanishum grabbed up the anchor stone and smashed it down on the head of first paddle. The canoe went over and she dove holding the stone until she was deep enough. She swam out of her clothes and into the notch and out the other side and came up. She came out of the water and ran. She ran to warn her people. Thunderbird saw this and put the fastest runner where he could see her. And Squintanasis ran and brought her home. The stupid Nittinat thought she drowned and came anyway. But we gave them a beating they will never forget!"

Yells rose to a crescendo and underneath the chaos the chant grew louder, *Nanishum, Nanishum* . . .

Nanishum slowly stood, eyes glowing, raised her hand.

"You Makah," she said, surprising me with the new force of her voice, "I did no more than any Makah would have done. All know wolf."

Yelling and whooping, but Nanishum raised her hand again.

"Wait, wait. You do me great honor. The honor belongs to all. We have potlatch. Gifts for everyone. Songs and dancing. Weddings."

There was much cheering as Nanishum made her exit. Neveah gripped my arm, but it was no longer to support me. She stared where Nanishum had disappeared inside Kakemook's lodge.

I put my arm around her shoulders. She leaned against me and I put both arms around her and held her. After a minute she pulled away, raised her face; the red and black paint was running a little. "Go now. Must not see me until time." She hurried toward Tomhak's lodge.

Barely a breeze with sunshine sparkling along the tops of smooth swells and sea birds working the shallows. From a distance I had witnessed a wedding of citizens. The Makah way to matrimony normally required certain rituals: a procession led by the groom would approach the lodge of the intended and stack up gifts - blankets, pelts, crafted items - and, if he was of a high position, hurl a harpoon at the lodge. If he was accepted the bride would come out and there would be a day or two of preparations before the wedding, a small feast would surround the wedding vows, we would all eat klooklo while watching games of skill, and young men would run and yell and wrestle on the beach. Later, most of the gifts to the bride's family would be returned to the groom to be distributed to relatives of both families.

Today was different. I was told it was not common to have a potlatch around weddings. Neveah and I were slaves, so I was sure our wedding could only be of minimal importance. I assumed it would be Kanek and Winaseth. With Senequah gone Kanek would be hurried into a chiefly role, and marriage was part of it.

The singing was very fine with most of the audience taking part. I thought it must be strange to these people who guarded their spiritual property so rigorously to hear everyone sing their songs. But it was simply a day of good intent: a day of mending wounded, the feel of victory and its cost, plenty to eat, renewed bonds - all within an aura of redemption. After the acrobats and village clown stirred up the sand the singers returned for two songs, then Kakemook appeared carrying a bright short sword.

The chief paced slowly back and forth until the loudest sounds were the lapping of waves on the beach and the intermittent cry of gulls. "I promised you a new wisdom," the chief said. He stopped and faced his audience.

Two stout warriors carried Squintanasis out sitting in a chair and put him down behind the chief. The chief paid no attention and continued to stare at the faces before him. When I saw how pale

Squintanasis was in the light of day my heart sank.

"Makah know Russian," Kakemook said. "Spanish. King George Man. Boston Man. Know our blood. Know our enemy's blood. All blood mixed with Makah."

A murmur rose in the crowd.

"Do not say no mixing!" Kakemook yelled. "Terrible curses have come to us by poison blood. Many died. But whites keep coming. How do Makah understand this?" Kakemook paused. "Some have this mixed blood. How do we know what is poison? What do Makah do?"

Kakemook raised the sword high in the air so the sun sent bright beams off the polished sides. "Makah ask this warrior with Russian blood."

Nanishum appeared and took the sword from Kakemook. The chief stepped back and Nanishum slowly lowered the blade to Squintanasis' shoulder. He smiled weakly.

She drew the blade lightly across his shoulder muscle and blood welled. Nanishum dipped her fingers into the blood. She put it to her lips and licked it off her fingers. Kakemook stepped forward and put his fingers into the wound, sucked the blood from his fingers.

The crowd was in mild turmoil, some were standing and edging back.

Kakemook raised his bloody hand. He turned and stood next to Nanishum.

"*His blood is not poison*," Kakemook said. This was followed by a few moments of silence, then whispers among the crowd. Behind the chief, Nanishum bound the shallow wound on Squintanasis' shoulder.

Kakemook held his blood-smeared hand up until it was quiet. He rested a hand on Squintanasis's shoulder. "As your chief I say there is no greater warrior or hunter among you. Say you?"

Yells of agreement.

"And what woman should be the wife of such a warrior and hunter?"

They were onto it now and yelled, "Nanishum, Nanishum . . ."

Kakemook nodded. "As children they moved and thought as one. They obeyed our laws. Remained pure. Now we know. This warrior's blood is not poison. Who say they cannot be together?"

"NO ONE," came the chant.

Kakemook held up his hand. When it was quiet enough he said, "Squintanasis is still weak from his wounds and Nanishum will say his words." The chief faded into the background.

"Makah days," Nanishum said, waited for the chants to subside, continued: "My husband has told me to say these words to you. Honor me here at our home. Our place of battle. Behind you children play. At the water are Nittinat canoes. Those heads on poles mean no more fighting. They will not attack Makah again.

"Chief Kakemook says true things. Our spirits have been one since we were children." Nanishum came to his side and put an arm around his shoulders. Squintanasis spoke in English, though it was so low I could barely hear.

"Irish strange tribe." He smiled and continued in Makah. "Say English first so you know my studies. Many must know English. Help our people. Now you will know Irish."

Neveah pressed me forward. I was not willing. Other hands pushed and prodded until I was standing up there with friends and my girl.

"My first order as pure Makah will be to make Irish a person," Squintanasis said.

This hushed the audience. I glanced at Neveah and realized she did not know this was coming either.

"These are friends," he said. "They serve well. Fight bravely.

Teach new ways. They have earned freedom. To marry a citizen a woman must be a citizen. Today Aidan and Neveah will be married as citizens with Nanishum and me."

During several seconds of stunned silence I did not dare glance at Neveah as her fingers dug into my arm. The sea of faces began to move in the infinite rhythm of this place. Nanishum's hands on our shoulders guided Neveah and me in a circle until we faced Kakemook.

The chief said a few words I did not understand, gods were invoked, after which he touched the tip of his ceremonial spear to our shoulders and pronounced us citizens of Ozette. Two shaman came forward and chanted while dancing around us, the chief said a few more words, and we moved behind Squintanasis and Nanishum. My friend's head was leaning to one side, but Nanishum pressed against him and gradually his head straightened. Words were being said regarding their joining, but I heard only muffled voices. I looked at Neveah and she seemed as dumbstruck as I was. We had been officially married as citizens of Ozette.

After the ceremony, Nanishum hugged Neveah and me and then, as I was trying to speak to my friend, the warriors came to carry him back to Tomhak's. Nanishum followed. I wanted to go with them but a crowd surrounded us.

Neveah and I were herded to a bench and food was put in our hands. People touched us and moved away. Necklaces were slipped over our heads and straightened so they hung just so. I looked in the direction of a rough voice – Sahyoul – he pressed a knife into my hand, a knife with an iron blade, very valuable. Neveah was given dresses and beads, a good wool blanket.

They were welcoming us as citizens. We could not leave.

The potlatch continued and we were right in the middle of it. Gifts began to be dispersed and we received even more, but I was not paying attention now. Neveah spoke for me as people crowded around. It went on and on until finally I jumped up and yelled, just let out a yell. My eyes swept over startled faces. I pushed through the crowd and headed for Tomhak's lodge. By the time I reached the entrance Neveah had caught up with me. We entered quietly and sat down next to Squintanasis's bed. Nanishum acknowledged us with a smile and continued to weave. Tomorrow, I thought, he will be better tomorrow and it will be a joke.

Nanishum was making a fine conical rain hat of spruce root with a double crown, the badge of a chief. I wondered if it was for her father or husband. The rest of that day and night, the next day and night, the next day, the three of us hardly left the lodge. We seldom talked and avoided looking at each other, knowing we would see our own fear looking back. The shaman and his apprentice worked almost non-stop and drowned out Squintanasis's feverish mumblings. They cut him and sucked out blood. They shook their rattles ever louder, chanted duets, danced around the three of us as we maintained our vigil and refused to move. At one point I got up with the intention of sending both shaman packing, but a look from Nanishum stopped me.

In the last of the third night, the very still early morning time when shaman and lesser shaman sleep, when the wolves are silent before the birds announce the new day, my friend died. His fever had grown ever more intense and he made unintelligible sounds in coma. Water ran down his face but he could take no water.

Nanishum wept almost silently into his wet hair.

Later I sat near him in a stupor while everyone in the village and those from Neeah came through to pay respects. It took a long time. I wondered absently if I would be killed and buried with him, but thought probably not since I was now a citizen. Perhaps they would change their minds about that. I thought about this objectively, as

273

if I were someone else. The next day a funeral was held in the tree graveyard on the flat above the slope. The weathered platform they placed him on had been the grave of his mother. His best longbow was broken and placed next to him, some other belongings, offerings, all demolished to discourage robbers. As the mourning commenced my wife and I returned to the village. That night I lay awake listening to the wails from far up on the flat and wanted to be up there with them.

joe Wilson

Chapter 24

We walked slowly without talking. At our pace it took an hour to reach the mouth of their river that drained from the big lake to the ocean. The deciduous trees between the evergreens sported hot-colored leaves flashing in the breeze. All the colors were now deeper, vital. The river emptied into the tiny bay not far from where the wolf had come that evening, not far from where I had seen Nanishum at a distance for the first time, running to her people, Squintanasis sprinting to meet her. It was a sight etched in my memory and I could never be on this beach again without seeing the two of them closing on each other. Or perhaps any beach again.

The taste of winter filled my throat. I imagined Squintanasis here with me. We would have our lines and hooks and he would catch more fish. He would make a joke about Irish not being such a good fisherman.

"Leave funeral too soon," Neveah said. "Maybe speak Kakemook."

"I intend to speak to him. I don't know how he wants to use the fire spears."

She put her hand on my arm. "Husband no stay angry."

"It's so damn ridiculous. Senequah. Squintanasis. Our two best warriors."

She wrapped her arms around mine and pressed against me. "All must die," she said gently. "Fish go up river die. We die. Our child die. Now need you."

"Without him I would probably be dead now."

"Without you maybe me dead. Our child never born."

It was the kind of logic Squintanasis would use. Still, there was unfinished business. "You are a wise girl," I said. "But now it is time to speak with Kakemook."

I found the chief at the canoe with Kekathl and two slaves who hurried with hot rocks from the fire to place in the canoe full of water. The chief and Kekathl were placing thwarts at key points, the slaves interrupting their transference of rocks to help pull the sides wide enough so the other two could wedge them in. I waited until the thwarts were in place so Kakemook could disengage himself.

"You troubled," he said.

I answered in Makah with some English mixed in. "No troubled. Wish go with you fight Nittinat. Fire spears ready."

He saw Neveah standing a distance behind me, waved her away. We walked near the edge of the water. Kakemook paused to watch several crows harassing an eagle over the shallows.

"Fire spears train in canoes," I said. "With Nittinat muskets we six fire spears, six loaders. Irish teach more shooters."

Kakemook's raised hand interrupted me. "He say you do this." The chief stepped around in front of me. "Before you come tomana-wos say how this must be. No go against spirit. Spirit send. Spirit say go. No fight."

"That spear was meant for me!"

Kakemook's face softened. He swept his hand in an arc, taking in the village. "Makah. My flesh. Wolf spirit. Friend Irish. He say go. Tomanawos say go."

"But I must take his place for this last battle."

Kakemook shook his head. "Nittinat give our people. Know we come. *Know who we are.* No fight. You take woman."

"But where can we go?"

Kakemook looked bewildered for a moment, as I certainly was. He pointed south, "Chinook people Big River. Maybe more like you." He pointed west. "Tooplah River to calm water three days maybe. Neveah's people welcome you."

"Why her people welcome me? Maybe kill me for marrying her."

Kakemook shook his head. "Neveah granddaughter second chief. *Know who she is.*"

A swirling, cold breeze whipped sand around us. Kakemook continued, "All mourn his death. Last words say Irish and woman go. Spirit wishes. Maybe come back. Welcome here. Irish citizen Ozette. Neveah citizen Ozette."

I looked at Kakemook's sea-burnt face, crinkled around dark eyes that had seen much. I knew he was saying Squintanasis' wishes, and what he perceived to be spirit wishes. Now there was no separation.

"Decide two days," Kakemook said. He walked away like a casual bear, back to work on the canoe. I realized that I had never really talked anyone here into anything. It had all been decided in advance. My friend had protected me even more than I knew.

I found Neveah sitting with Howessa, weaving baskets from the long marsh grass that came from the lake where Squintanasis and I had crouched in the brush watching the trail. They were soaking the grass and the water was low. I went to the spring and brought back a basket full of water and poured it into their soaking basket, sat next to Neveah. In English I told her what Kakemook had said.

"Go with husband."

Husband doesn't know where to go is what I wanted to say, but I sat silently, watching them weave. I asked where Tomhak was.

"Fishing," Howessa said. "Maybe fur seal come." She shook her head. "Too soon. Maybe cod today. Maybe halibut. Maybe hair seal." She grinned. "No catch bear."

"Irish eat cod, halibut," I replied in Makah. "Eat salmon with no fire, smoke, sun."

Howessa smiled and shook her head.

I watched my wife's small hands tame marsh grass and wondered what Sis was doing at this moment on the other side of the continent. Did she and Michael give me a thought today? Perhaps Father had, though he wouldn't mention it to anyone. I thought about Neveah there, in our little enclave, weaving, later me smelling her good cooking after a day's fishing. I thought Sis might like her very much. Down the way, Morton Clandish had taken a native woman after his wife died. Father had once called him squaw man. I wondered if he would call me that. Did it matter?

Walking up the trail behind the village, thinking, I had no idea where to look for a ship or white settlement. The closest settlement I knew was Yerba Buena in the Port de San Francisco, a very long trip for two people in a canoe. And we would have to pass the Hoh village and other hostile tribes. We could travel at night, but this would be risky for one man and his pregnant wife. This was assuming I would be allowed to take a canoe, a precious canoe.

I kept on along the trail toward Sweet Water. A raven clicked his tongue at me as I walked under his perch on a tree limb. Some boys hunting with their bows at the edge of a meadow waved and I waved back. I pulled off my moccasins and kept going. A twig snapped in a thicket and I tried to guess what it might be. About halfway to the lake I left the trail for a distance and sat on a downed tree. I listened and watched for a time. Birds and small animals appeared, disappeared.

A sound in a thick stand of spruce held my attention. A bear walked into view and ambled toward me. He stopped no more than a canoe length away, swung his head back and forth, nose going, stood momentarily and stared right at me, a bare patch on his side from an old wound. I remained motionless. Finally he grunted and walked off, disappearing behind mossy trees. I smiled and looked up at a brightly fringed cloud temporarily blocking the sun. "I know you're around," I said to the cloud.

Chapter 25

The sun is now deep in the western sky. I have relived the whole story in my mind and still do not know the best course. So much has happened in such a short time, and now I must make what seems the most important decision of my life.

I walk slowly back to the village.

At the top of the slope I rest where there is a view over the trees. Beyond Dog Island the falling sun catches a dark shape: sail, another behind it, fishermen coming home. One will be Tomhak. I watch until the two canoes enter the channel on the north side of the island, then hurry down the trail, eager to help the second chief unload his catch and ask his council.

"No trust Chimakum," Tomhak said, and took another bite of shooyoult. He was hungry after a day of fishing and I had fetched some warm fish from his wife's fire. We sat on a drifted log in front of the village. I was watching a huge shark they'd towed in, more than half the length of their canoe. These sharks often drifted on the surface and the Makah used their harpoons on them. Mainly they wanted their giant livers for the oil. The fishermen who had been with Tomhak were straining to drag it higher on the beach so it could be butchered.

"They are Neveah's people," I said. "Chief Kakemook said they would welcome us."

Tomhak nodded, chewing. "Welcome anyone. Poor now. Steal

from Snohomish, Suquamish trading parties. Many tribes. Snohomish fight them." He raised a scarred brow. "Kill plenty, pretty mad. Take plenty. Take slaves."

I tried to understand what this meant. "You say not wise go Chimakum?"

Tomhak shrugged. "Maybe go Chimakum. Maybe other place."

"Like where?" I was trying to keep the impatience out of my voice.

"My cousin say Chinook? Boston Man there before. King George Man. Spanish. Want fur. Some say maybe stay winter. Many cloud ship come Big River."

"Chinook trustworthy?"

Tomhak gave me an amused look before taking another bite of fish. "Flatheads rich. Many village. Trade many tribes. Makah speak Chinook words. Chinook speak many trade words. Good trade Chinook. No trouble."

"So going to the Chinook wise choice?"

Another shrug. "Ozette get two Chinook slaves. Good slaves. Chief Comcomly want Makah wife for son."

I gritted my teeth, relaxed my jaw. "Chief Tomhak, have wife with child. We must leave. Wish her safe. Will she be safe Big River?"

Tomhak sighed, flipped a bone splinter at the lapping waves. "Too bad must leave."

"Rather stay winter."

"Spirits say leave."

"Right. How long we leave?"

"Um. Maybe six moons. Too bad. Need Irish teach."

He offered a piece of fish and I took it, chewed harshly.

"What would you do?"

We sat chewing for a time.

"Chimakum not where belong," Tomhak said, echoing

Squintanais's words. "Make troubles because no belong there. Chimakum women go with Nisqually. Go with s'Klallum. Maybe get trouble from s'Klallum. s'Klallum strong people."

"But Chimakum have no quarrel with Makah?" I said.

"Maybe raid more. Nuu-chah-nulth (Nootka), don't like them either. They fight Chimakum, we fight with Chief Maquinna."

"Maybe could stay with Nuu-chah-nulth?"

Tomhak shrugged. "Let Irish stay. Neveah . . ." he examined another piece of fish. "She Chimakum."

My choices were narrowing and I didn't even understand what they were. Yerba Buena was beginning to seem not so far away. But it sounded like there would be a good chance to get a ship at Big River headed for my home country. I wondered if I might find Kirn and Wang there, slaves to the Chinook or some nearby tribe, but had a sense it was not a proper question at this time.

Wandering barefoot on the beach south of the village, I heard running feet and turned to see Neveah. "Husband," she said, out of breath, "look many places. You not come eat. Now late. Please, must eat."

We walked up to the high water line and sat on a log. There was surf here, away from the lee of the island. I told her what Tomhak had said. She asked where we would go.

"Where do you want to go?"

"Go with husband."

"Right. How do you feel about the Chinook?" I said.

"Rich people. Many trade. Everyone want trade Flatheads."

I held my head in my hands and stared at the vast ocean.

That evening I found Kanek and we engaged Misak's young cousin, Chayooie, who had been his loader. We went to Chief Kakemook's lodge and I once more went through the routine of how to care for the fire spears. Sahyoul's loader, Weecooth, showed up too and wanted to learn, although Kanek made it clear he would be in charge after I left.

"Winaseek's young husband will have many skills," I said, causing him to swell with pride. "You will be a great chief." His look sobered, then he slowly nodded. It was his heritage to take his father's place. He had given a good account of himself in the battle with the Nittinat and had matured in the short time I'd been here.

That night I was restless and the wolves did not howl. I kept listening for them, then Neveah woke with a start and put a hand to her stomach. "Husband," she whispered, "listen."

I put my ear on her belly, which had started to swell slightly. She was very warm and I could feel her life rushing inside like fiery surf. Then I heard. Or felt. Something more. "Is that... him?" I managed.

"Yes." She rested her hands on my head. We stayed like that until I felt her relax into sleep. I gently covered her belly and lay back, her hand inside mine. Sleep for me did not come for a long time.

In the morning I ate quickly and went to work on the canoe I had labored over with Squintanasis. The thwarts were all positioned but not lashed in permanently. Kekathl was already at work fitting the stern carving. He eyed me suspiciously when I said I wanted to make the thwart lashings. Then he put down his tools and showed me how to drill the holes next to the thwarts. It took some time to get used to using the drill, a small shaft of hardwood with notches that supported carefully placed, sharp-edged muscle shells. The little drill proved surprisingly efficient in the cedar.

Smoke from the lodges signaled the evening meal was being prepared. Hunters came in chanting a hunting song, a fur seal carcass in one canoe and a hair seal in another. One of the hunters had an injured arm from the struggle with the hair seal and went to his lodge to be ministered. The fur seal was apparently the first of the season and brought an audience to admire the animal. I watched the butchering process until Neveah arrived and insisted I come and eat. After the meal I went back to the canoe to check my lashings. Tomhak came and ran his hand over the hull.

"Tomorrow sharkskin," he said. "Maybe two days burn. Two more days, chã-tic (painter) come. Six days float."

When the hull was smooth from sanding with sharkskin the last step was to singe and rub the outside with an oily mat to get rid of any "beard" so she would slide through the water without resistance. "Maybe need my help," I said.

Tomhak rested his forearms on the canoe directly across from me. The light was nearly gone and his face was in shadow. "Must decide," he said.

He knew I had already made a decision. "If go Chinook, you give something so they accept us?"

"Chinook take you," he said.

"Concerned for wife."

"Tomorrow get ready," he said. "Maybe next day go." He walked away.

When I entered Tomhak's lodge I found Neveah and Nanishum on our bed in earnest conversation. They both smiled at me and I did not know what to say. Finally Neveah said, "Where go husband?"

"Big River." I winced, thinking of her in the bow, rowing into the swell when at any moment a raiding party could intercept us.

Nanishum touched my hand. "Tomorrow get ready," she said.

"Thank you, but you don't really have to help. I don't even know how we're going to get there." I had spoken English and Neveah quickly translated.

"We go canoe," Nanishum said, and started for the door.

"What? We? What do you mean?" She did not answer, probably because I was still speaking English. The mat flopped back. I turned to Neveah. "What did she mean, we?"

"She go. Others go. Makah know Chinook. Good trade."

So as long as we were being run out of town they might as well come along and do a little trading. I wondered if I had been given the straight story about the Chimakum. "What about you? Are you sad not to be going to your people?"

"Go with husband," she said and smiled without sadness.

During the evening meal Neveah sat in her usual place and I in mine. Kanek had taken Squintanasis's place to my right. The conversations around the circle were nearly the same as they had been before the battle: fishing, when the main fur seal herds would come, who would be chief harpooner for winter whaling, how the canoes-in-progress were coming along. One of Sahyoul's fishing partners, a young man about my age, talked with pride about the baby boy his wife had delivered the day before. No one mentioned Squintanasis or Senequah. I ate little and went outside.

The sun was just slipping below the horizon. East of the village I found the bleached log with its thick branch. From my usual spot I looked across where Squintanasis would be, his brow furrowed in concentration, mouthing a word until he got it right. A gull landed and walked almost within reach. It was the one with a wing that hung slightly in repose, the one that always came hoping for a handout.

Nanishum came and sat in Squintanasis's place on the log. She wore a buckskin apron-skirt, a blanket covering her upper body. Picking up a stick the sea had delivered to the beach, she dug in the sand until she uncovered one of the course clams the Makah rejected, cracked it on the log and tossed it to the gull, startling the bird, which then attacked the vulnerable calm.

"All must eat," she said.

She reached into a pocket on her waistband and held out her closed fist. I put my hand under hers and she dropped small items into it: Two tiny bone carvings and two bear teeth with a design scrolled into them, holes for a string. They looked familiar. "Husband say give," she said. "Necklace give at potlatch make citizen. These say friend Squintanasis. Now many *know who you are.*"

"Wear always on citizen necklace," I said, staring at these objects that had been against Squintanasis's chest.

After a silence, I removed a pouch hanging from a thong around my neck and handed it to her. "These your husband own," I said. "Ask me hold." She dug in the pouch and took out a few iron hooks, copper arrowheads, spear tips, ran her fingers over several, put them back in the pouch.

"No be afraid," she said. "Woman safe Chinook. Baby safe."

I expelled a breath.

"Spirits say come back" she said. "Husband say. Makah want Irish come back."

Without thinking about it I reached and took her hand, felt her strength flow up my arm. Would she marry again? They had waited since childhood to be together and it was over in a moment. I turned her hand over and looked into the palm, looking for the ghost of Squintanasis. I met her gaze. "Believe you," I said.

Nanishum and I walked back to the village. "Klooklo weather three days," she said, casting a sideways smile at me. "Fog in morning."

"Nanishum know direction through fog," I said. "Nanishum lead Aidan out fog in mind."

"Ha," she said. "Maybe Neveah make fog come back."

The next day began as a blur of activity. They were packing a lot of whale and seal oil, as well as slabs of halibut into their canoes. It appeared five canoes would be making the trip, one of the big craft that could easily carry more than a dozen people, and all together I figured there would be about twenty of us.

The night before I was presented with a musket, a French Charleville with adequate makings. It was one of those taken from the Nittinat and in poor condition, but Neveah gave it a thorough cleaning and I told her it was serviceable. She loaded and rolled it in a protective mat. She also loaded and packed the rifle Kakemook had given me. There were balls for this I had filched at Neeah, and Neveah handed me the wrapped bundle in a casual way without a word. I decided to keep the little rifle near me, a compact and handy weapon while in a canoe.

That evening I watched from a distance as Neveah gave Suisha one of her father's teeth from the lucky ones on her necklace. They embraced, and Neveah was hugged by Howessa and Winaseek while I admired Suisha's smile in the smoky light. Suisha then approached me and put a hand on my arm. "Take care Little Princess," she said.

"Yes. Thank you for your kindness."

The next morning I was up well before daylight and went outside to listen to the last of the wolves. I hoped there would be wolves in the Chinook camp, but Tomhak said it was different country down there and Chinook people revered coyote.

At dawn as we were preparing to leave, Tomhak strode down the beach, Nanishum at his side. I stood next to a canoe taken from the Nittinat that Neveah and I, and three other people, would be paddling.

"Follow daughter and me," Tomhak said. "Second canoe. Like your canoe?"

"This our canoe? For Neveah and Irish? Is big enough for whaling canoe."

"Is whaling canoe. How Makah present citizen to rich Chinook?"

I looked into Nanishum's dark, smiling eyes. Beyond I saw Suisha watching from the shadow of her lodge. I looked at my wife and beyond at the brightening sky. A fog bank offshore, but good visibility for a half-mile out and soon the sun would push it back. The swell rolled in smooth and there was little wind.

287

"We are wasting good conditions," I said.

We were loading the last of the provisions when a group of children came running down the beach. I recognized Wikibowkwitch and Kishkani, and many of the children who had been my audience at the forge. They gathered around yelling, waving their arms, copper bracelets reflecting points of light. Finally Tomhak announced play was over and we must get going. All I could do was nod and smile until Neveah pushed me into the canoe. I had removed my moccasins and slipped them under a mat to stay dry. I snugged down the hat Neveah had woven for me.

As we paddled for the rocks and the narrow south exit past the island, the wool dogs began to howl a greeting. I knew I would miss them, and other things. The children were still yelling and I resisted looking back. Neveah paused her paddling and turned with a reassuring smile. Her brown arms glistened with the oil she had applied.

"Rest," I said. "Your condition."

She grinned. "Baby say go now." Her paddle dug into the blue-green water.

Printed in the United States
215803BV00001B/2/P

9 781427 636065